Books by the author:

THE KINGDOM CARVER

THE TWELFTH MILE

THE TWELFTH MILE

THE

DOUBLEDAY CANADA LIMITED, TORONTO, ONTARIO

DOUBLEDAY & COMPANY, INC., GARDEN CITY,

NEW YORK, 1972

E. G. PERRAULT

TWELFTH MILE

All characters, with the exception
of well-known historical personages, are fictitious,
and any resemblance to actual persons,
living or dead, is coincidental.

"to Audrey . . . and to the old ocean now becoming the new frontier and possibly a final battleground."

1 . . .

The tug shouldered its way through Active Pass, its bow wave splashing through a flat ribbon of mist that spread from Galiano to Mayne Island. Behind it, riding light and empty on the end of a 1500-foot cable, the 12,000-ton limestone barge slid solidly through the light chop of the slack tide.

The big government ferry had passed by minutes before, its rail lined with clusters of early autumn tourists, more than one of them focusing a camera on the unfamiliar sight of a barge larger than a football field making its way behind a tug less than one quarter its size. With the ferry passed, no other major obstruction remained in the narrow channel.

Westholme retained his grip on the wheel with his right hand while he leaned over to take one last reassuring glance at the radar screen. Except for a scattering of blips along the Galiano side of the passage where trollers were trying for cohoe and spring salmon, there was nothing to worry about. Ten minutes and they'd be out of the pass and into the broad sweep of the Strait of Georgia. He could take a break now.

The mate, long familiar with Westholme's method of doing things, appeared at the wheelhouse door almost as though he had been summoned. Christy Westholme glanced over his shoulder and made a brief beckoning gesture. "How'd you like to take over here, Larry?"

The mate advanced to the wheel. He had a full cup of coffee in his hand which he passed to Westholme. All of this was a familiar ritual; these two worked well together. In fact Westholme got along well with most of the company crew members; which is not to say that they all liked him, or that any of them counted him as a close personal friend. But four war years on Canadian corvettes, mostly in the North Atlantic, and twenty-five years on tugs graduating to the big, ocean-going salvage jobs had made him a good man to crew under. On this coast with its 14-knot tide rips, its sudden gales and hurricanes tearing in from Japan, its murderous outcroppings of hidden reefs, and the ever-present danger of shipping lanes shrouded in fog; on this far Pacific edge of Canada, tugboat crews picked a good skipper over a good friend every time.

Christy Westholme had the unquestioning confidence of this crew or any other crew he was likely to be assigned. At the same time none of the five men aboard the tug would ever share a game of cards with him in his comfortable living room, or sit down to one of Lee's great roast-beef dinners.

The dispatcher's voice filled the wheelhouse with a clatter of sound. "*Trident,* we've got you coming out of Active Pass. Confirm your position."

Westholme leaned into the microphone and pressed the button. "*Trident* here. Three minutes and we're into the

2

Strait. ETA to port . . ." He glanced at the wheelhouse chronometer. "1745, give a little, take a little. Give my wife a call will you, Alex?" He turned inquiringly to the mate and received his nod. "Larry's wife too."

"I'll take care of it," the metallic voice promised, and then the sound and its surrounding static were gone, replaced again by the powerful throb of the tug's engines pushing its way through three layers of plate decking and insulation.

Westholme was feeling pretty good about things. Right through the summer everything had gone right for him. The limestone run had been a break from a tough six-month stint on salvage operations and transoceanic tows fighting bad weather and dangerous towing situations most of the way. The limestone run was pure routine; three days down the coast to the mouth of the Columbia with a loaded barge, then pick up an empty barge for a two-day return to the British Columbia port of Vancouver. Five days at sea gave him better than seven days ashore—which was a far cry from the rough days of towboating when the Guild couldn't make anything stick. Equipment was better now too. *Trident* was less than a year old with all the latest Department of Transport improvements. Her 3800-horsepower could handle the floating mountain of limestone with something to spare.

"You going to break down and take your shore leave this time?" the mate asked as he squinted against the sun bouncing off the surface of the Strait. "You must have almost a month coming."

"I'd better take it if I want to stay in good with Lee," Westholme said, and he meant it.

She was beginning to show the wear-and-tear of too much solitude, he knew that. With both boys now away on their own at McGill, time hung on her hands. She lived for his homecomings—and they didn't happen often enough. Nowadays, when he did come home after a week or two at sea, there would be little arguments, little differences of opinion, small things said or alluded to. It was time, Westholme decided, for the company to pull him in to a desk job.

"I took a chance on building up thirty days," he told Larry. "It'll give me the opportunity to spend some real time with the wife. Maybe take a trip to Vegas; get to know one another again."

"That's good thinking," Larry said. "In this business the best girl in the world can turn a little strange after a while."

There were other reasons for Westholme's thirty days, of course. "I can't get much done around here a week at a time," he had told Lee. "A fence in the backyard is way overdue, and I'd like to work a few days fishing in at Wendigo, just to change the pace." As an afterthought, he said: "That'll be after you and I get back from Vegas."

"We don't have to go to Vegas if you can't spare the time," she said.

There would be little enough time, that was true; house trim to be painted, leaves to be raked. On the pleasure side of things, there was the pool table he was going to build.

"You play any pool at all, Larry?" he asked the mate.

"I haven't shot a game in years. You play much?"

"I'm putting together a pool table this time ashore," he said. "Maybe we can have a game sometime." It was a token invitation neither expected would be fulfilled.

They withdrew into a relaxed silence, each absorbed in the anticipation of their shore leave. On deck the deckhands hustled to stow gear and get the tug shipshape for arrival. In the galley the cook, having arranged the perishables in the freezer and stacked the plates and cups in their storm-proof racks, proceeded to his cabin to change into his city clothes.

Trident dropped the barge at anchor shortly after 1700 hours. At 1741 Westholme brought the tug alongside the company wharf and left it with the mate to secure. Fifteen minutes later he was in his car proceeding at an easy sixty along the freeway toward home.

4

2 . . .

Lee must have been gone for a few hours. Twilight had crept into the house along with the chill of a September evening, and Westholme felt a sudden irritation. The dispatcher had phoned Lee. She knew he was on his way in, and she knew what he liked to find when he got home; the lights on, the coffee hot, wood crackling in the fireplace if it was raining or snowing. Those things weren't too much to ask after a week, two or three weeks at sea.

He slipped out of his duffel coat and stowed his suitcase in the bedroom closet, then returned to the living room where he turned up the thermostat to put some warmth back in the house. To further make his point he proceeded to arrange paper and kindling in the fireplace. Crouched above the small flame beginning to lick the paper he heard the key turn in the front door, the dry sound of the door swinging on its hinges. Deliberately he remained crouched away from her, waiting until his silence had become significant. Then he stood up and turned around.

"Alex said he phoned you. He told you I was coming in."

"That's right, he did," she said flatly. He had remained unsmiling and she made no effort to warm him.

"Run out of food or something?" He wanted the impasse to be broken now. The point had been made; she knew he was displeased and disappointed.

"No I didn't," she said. She removed her heavy cardigan and shook her thick, dark hair down around her shoulders in a gesture that was almost defiant. For all her thirty-eight years Lee was a spectacular kind of woman, her face and frame modeled slightly larger than life; like one of those old Irish goddesses, Westholme thought. She had Irish in her all right, and a bit of Scots and more than a smattering of some Scandinavian race. She had inherited the best qualities of all those races in his opinion.

5

Westholme was not opposed to looking at other women. On a few occasions—two or three times in Tokyo and the same in Hawaii, mostly after long and tough voyages—he had yielded with virtually no twinge of conscience to a night or two with an amenable girl. But this had nothing to do with the way he felt about Lee. There was no one like her; it was as simple as that. He liked being with her. He was proud to be seen in her company. Her companionship, her understanding of his needs and desires were so right that he had never had any real need for close friends. Her love was important, but her friendship went deeper and further than that. His marriage with Lee was a comfortable, unshakable way of life.

It had been that way with his mother and father, which explained why Westholme was neither surprised nor impressed with his good fortune. To have a woman waiting for him when he came home from sea was his natural right. To have Lee for his wife, Lee whose face and manner grew finer with the years, whose attention to him never flagged, was a subject for occasional contemplation during those long nights at sea.

"Something troubling you, Merilee?" he asked, grinning now to break the tension. He used her full name, which in itself was an obvious attempt to relax the situation. She detested the name and he used it only when he was teasing her or when the occasion was lighthearted.

Her face was expressionless, cold. "I'll put some supper on," she said in a voice that rejected his grin, and turned away from him toward the kitchen.

Westholme watched her go and felt worry growing in him. There had only been one other time like this in their nineteen years of marriage, and that had been when the little girl was stillborn while he was working a tandem tow of rail cars down to Seattle. He didn't have to take that job, but they needed the money at the time and it didn't seem likely that Lee would have the baby for a good week or more. When he came to her in the hospital she was cold as she was cold now, as though a switch inside her had been turned off and darkness had fallen on all the things she was. The doctor told him not to worry, that the experience of childbirth did strange things to a woman, that depression was a normal thing to expect . . . and in time she had become the old Lee again.

He went through a deliberate ritual of arranging wood on the fire, letting it thump against the grate to establish his presence in the house. His pride was hurting. He didn't deserve to be treated like this. Finally he went into the kitchen.

She was whipping eggs into a plastic bowl. Bacon was sizzling in the electric frying pan but the kitchen was cheerless. The centerpiece of flowers, chrysanthemums at this time of the year, was missing from the table where they took most of their meals. She had failed to turn on the lights, a warm arrangement of hanging fixtures with bamboo shades he had brought back from Japan. The only light came from the rapidly dimming kitchen windows and the small working lamp built into the kitchen range.

He came up behind her and put his arms around her waist. "Have I done something, Lee?" he asked.

"Nothing, Chris. Nothing at all." Like a flat, bitter reproach.

"I'd like to get to the bottom of this."

She began to transfer the bacon to a pan lined with tissue to absorb the hot grease. He took the fork from her hands and completed the job himself, his eyes concentrating hard on what he was doing.

"Every criminal gets a chance to read the charges," he said. "It's not like you to keep from leveling with me."

She poured the omelet into the hot pan slicked with bacon grease.

"I love you, Lee," he said.

"I don't know what you mean by that. I don't think you do either."

"I mean you're the only woman I've ever wanted. You're the only one I'll ever want."

She turned and placed the empty bowl on the table and confronted him squarely. "Christy, something has happened . . . I don't feel anything where you're concerned. Nothing.

I don't feel love. It might come back again, but I wouldn't know how to bring it alive. I just don't know . . ."

Anger flashed through him. She was being totally unreasonable, unfair. "What the hell is this, Lee? You're not giving me any kind of a break at all. Is there someone else coming around? Any kind of a clue would . . ."

"Someone else coming around would be an easy answer. Maybe that's the trouble with you, Chris. You have an easy answer to everything. This isn't easy . . . and there's no one else coming around."

"Okay! Let's eat. Let's let the whole thing drop for the time being!" He could feel real anger boiling in him now and he didn't want it to break loose. "There must be something to drink in this place somewhere." He went to the accustomed cupboard and found half a bottle of rye tucked in the corner. "Have one before supper, Lee?"

"No thanks."

He poured a heavy shot of rye into a glass, added ice and water and swallowed hard. "All right, Lee, we've got thirty days together and we'll sort this thing out, but I'd like to sort it out now, not later. We've got time to spend together and I'd like it to be as usual."

"As usual!" She flared. "You mean you want me to jump through the usual hoops for the next thirty days, pack your bags and kiss you back onto the boat. I can't do that, Chris. Not any more."

"What in Christ's name is wrong with you, Lee? I've never seen you behave . . . never heard talk like this before."

"You asked me if you'd done something, and I said, 'no, nothing!' That's the truth of it, Chris. I haven't; neither one of us has done anything. Here I am approaching thirty-nine. You're almost fifty, and we haven't really done anything of any importance. We've raised . . . two kids. We've paid off a mortgage. We visit around and take in a movie or two. What else?"

"The boys are out on their own now," he told her. "You've got no one to take care of. You're bored out of your mind,

Lee. That's all that's happening here; you think your usefulness is over."

She turned her head away from him stubbornly.

"Lee, I count on you for so many things. On the street, walking with you, I want to wave my arms and say, 'Look what I've got—the greatest wife in the world. Come on over and take a look!'"

"Come on over and take a look at my prize pointer bitch; at my prize housekeeper; at my prize baby sitter!"

Westholme stopped reasoning: "You've been reading all that garbage about women's rights. You've got nothing better to do than read crap, Lee. You're poisoned!"

"I'm going to bed. I'm not hungry . . ."

"Stay here and talk this thing out," he commanded harshly. "You're running away from it!"

"If you say so. I'm tired." She turned and left him, walking out of the kitchen as though she were walking out of his life. Westholme's feeling was one of desolation and mindless anger. How could she write off all those great years together? She was sick! She was brainwashed by editorial crap, by the local gossip of frustrated women. She was—to hell with it!

He got halfway through his bacon and eggs, every mouthful tasting like sawdust, and then pushed the plate back, went to the hall closet, put on a coat and left the house.

The cold September air with its faint smell of burning leaves did not soothe him. He felt what Lee felt, the loss of something beyond recall. The feeling of hopelessness was overwhelming, and yet it couldn't be hopeless. It was ridiculous to believe that all these years and good times could be written off in one evening. Oh, she had brooded about it, spent time thinking about it, built up a good case in her own mind, and her mood had rubbed off on him. That's what was happening. He was allowing himself to panic when all that was needed was to bring the thing into the perspective it deserved.

A half an hour later, considerably calmer, he returned to the house, took a shower and slipped into clean pajamas. The door to the bedroom was closed and he opened it, letting the bolt click audibly in the darkness, knowing she was not asleep, but wanting to justify her pretense to awaken.

He slipped under the covers beside her and moved in close, his hand reaching out to touch her as he was accustomed to touch her. But he stopped. She was awake; he knew that. She was lying on her back, flat and unresponsive, her entire body rejecting him. He could feel it. He knew her eyes were open and staring at the dark ceiling, that she was waiting for him to touch her, giving her the opportunity to turn away from him and reject him completely. He did not touch her.

He lay there as rigid and as tortured as she, and in the end he rose and went into the living room. This mustn't get out of control. Give him a crisis with a tug, or a crew, or a barge gone berserk in a high wind and a following sea and he would know what to do. This was a different kind of crisis. It was stabbing him in the most vulnerable part of his being. He had a feeling that his heart and his brain had been delivered physical blows.

He went over to the fireplace and poked up the fire; and at that moment the telephone rang. He moved over to it quickly, welcoming the opportunity to turn his mind to other things. At the other end the night dispatcher spoke apologetically.

"I shouldn't be calling you, Christy, but Hargreaves has gone into the hospital with a rupture or something. Playing football with his kids. He was supposed to take *Haida Noble* out tonight. The drill rig job. You can say 'no' if you want."

Westholme didn't hesitate. It was a straw to grasp at, a chance to sort things out. "What's the departure time?"

"0100 hours."

"Who's the mate?"

"Lindstrom."

"Okay, I'll be there half an hour ahead of time. What does the weather look like?"

"Nothing to worry about on the inside of the Island. There's a gale warning on the outside. Nothing to write home about."

"I'll take her," Westholme said, and hung up.

He put on trousers, shirt, and jacket in the hallway; then

entered the bedroom and pulled his suitcase out of the closet. In the darkness he turned to her.

"Lee, I'm going out on a run. West coast of the Island and back in about five days. When I get back . . . maybe things will be a little better."

She said nothing.

"I love you, Lee. You may not know what I mean by that. But I know, and there's nothing more important to me."

She remained silent and he left, walking out of the bedroom and down the hall to the front door.

3 . . .

Westholme had never been fond of midnight departures. It went back to the days on corvettes. Sailing out of Halifax and the other eastern seaboard ports; sailing out of Murmansk and the English and Scottish ports, the midnight hours were synonymous with icy rain, snow, peasoup fogs, or gusting winds. As often as not a combination of those conditions prevailed.

Between midnight and the first gray light of dawn disaster was more likely to happen. The sub packs worked best in those hours. Wounded or sick men who had rallied in daylight lost their vitality and died in the dark hours before dawn. That was wartime, but the feeling had carried over.

He was at the company wharf at five minutes to midnight. By twelve fifteen he had checked in with the dispatcher and picked up his orders. They were clear enough. In any event he was familiar with the job. He had skippered *Haida Noble* when the giant drill rig was first towed to a starting position outside Clayoquot Sound; and he had gone out six weeks later to move the rig to its next drilling position.

The dispatcher continued to be apologetic:

"I'm really sorry about this, Christy. I suppose I could have called Bill Lindsay or one of the others, but you've made the run before . . ."

"Forget it," Westholme said as he checked over the crew roster.

"A few minutes ago I looked at your time sheet. You've got thirty days built up. The front office doesn't like people overdoing it that way."

"Are the provisions on?"

"They went aboard with the cook half an hour ago. He should have the galley in shape by now. You take a good holiday after this one, Christy. Treat the wife to Vegas or something."

"Any more on the weather?"

The dispatcher shook his head. "I heard a forecast a while back. They're expecting a new five-day report from the U.S. side sometime tonight. The local scene hasn't changed."

Westholme picked up his bag and left the office. Outside, he squinted into the fog beginning to roll in off the inlet. Above him was the big painted arch with the company's name and symbol on it. Angled spotlights made it readable in the swirling gray:

OCEANLINK PACIFIC LIMITED

He liked the company. With 83 tugs in the fleet it was probably the largest of its kind in the world—but not too big to lose the personal touch Westholme regarded as important. Forty-five years ago it had been a small, one-owner company with a strong family feeling. In some way the feeling of family had been preserved. Generally speaking, Oceanlink's masters, crews, and shore staff got along well. Pride of company had much to do with it: employees, no matter how junior, identified with an organization that had pulled itself up by its own bootstraps over some difficult years. Oceanlink had made some world headlines in its time. When people talked about towing and salvage operations in the Pacific, particularly the North Pacific, Oceanlink was the name that came to mind.

Christy Westholme was quietly convinced that Oceanlink's success was wrapped up in one boat, one superlatively designed and equipped tug with more ocean rescues and more towing "firsts" to its record than anything else afloat. Oceanlink was a front office for *Haida Noble* . . . and there she was ahead of him, deck lights ablaze, her bow sharp as a chisel, unlike the conventional tug design, angling almost thirty feet up into the wall of fog.

Midway along the foredeck, disappearing into the blackness beyond the circle of the deck lights was the thick trunk of the forward mast with the spars of two 20-ton booms rigged close to it. High above, at the invisible tip of the mast, riding lights shone like ghostly planets. Light streaming from the windows of the bridge cut luminous panels in the fog.

Even before he took command of her, *Haida Noble* had become something of a legend in the Pacific. Her 4000-mile salvage of the stricken *Hellas* in 1962 had earned her the first headlines. A fire on the freighter to be extinguished at the height of a gale; auxiliary pumps to be transferred aboard and put to work while the job of underwater hull repair went ahead; then the long tow back to drydock. For thirty-seven days she towed *Hellas* through worsening weather, the last seventeen through a parade of gales that focused the attention of the world press on her.

The line parted on three occasions under the terrific pressure of the sea and the helpless ship astern. Three times new lines were secured and the tow went ahead. On the thirty-seventh day *Haida Noble* came through the Lions' Gate with the listing *Hellas* on shortened line astern. The city of Vancouver stood on the beaches and cheered. A two-hundred-piece band, the mayor, and an impressive collection of federal and provincial officials waited at the company wharf to greet the returning tug.

The skipper, Harold Bradbourne, a friend of Westholme's now dead and in an ocean grave, had received the citations and been lionized for a short interval; but Westholme knew, and Bradbourne had admitted readily, that the ship as much as anything had made the rescue possible.

The *Hellas* incident had been difficult and dramatic. *Haida*

Noble went on to perform assignments even more difficult but with less drama attached in terms of life and death. An aircraft carrier and a Liberty towed in line from San Francisco to Tokyo Bay, taking the edge of two summer hurricanes in her stride. Westholme had been skipper on that one, and on the recovery of the drifting drill rig 300 miles north of Hawaii.

He had shown Lee over *Haida Noble* on a night like this, a night when illuminated mist and sea sounds emerging from the far darkness had invested the great tug with a quality of myth. Westholme's dedication to a good ship was simple and absolute, bordering on a personal fundamental religion, and Lee made good fun of it. Halfway through the tour of *Haida Noble*, she turned to him in exasperation and said: "It's great, Christy. It's absolutely great! But it's not a cathedral. I have a feeling you'll genuflect every time you walk onto the bridge."

Westholme knew she wasn't serious, but she was a woman with a woman's attitude to things, and she couldn't be expected to be impressed with *Haida Noble*'s twin GM EMD diesels, 20 cylinders each, turning out a total of 10,000 horsepower. *Haida Noble* had a top speed of 18 knots. Lee's little Japanese convertible could beat ninety on the freeway when the police weren't looking.

She thought the galley and the adjoining messroom were nice, and that was to be expected. The storage cabinets and the walk-in refrigerator with a six-week supply of food in the racks impressed her.

"It's a tough life you lead," she said, lifting a cellophane-wrapped package of inch-thick New York steaks. "It's a wonder to me you ever come home at all, Christy. Where do you keep the dancing girls?"

He didn't bother to show her the salvage equipment lockers, or the wire room, or the machine shop where practically any broken ship's part could be repaired or duplicated. And he didn't think the diving gear or the underwater repair equipment would mean too much to her, although he did show her the recompression chamber on the top deck. She squinted through the thick, circular window in the heavy door and sized up the single bunk dominating the interior. "I've got a wonderful idea for a second honeymoon, darling," she said; and it was at that point that he took her ashore.

It was on a night like this that he had first shown her *Haida Noble;* six years ago in mid-August, with thousands of miles logged since then, millions of tons of cargo hauled, scores of ships towed to safety, and all of it done in large part because of her, because thinking of her made it easier to do the job, because he liked to come back home and hear her say:

"Honey, you had your name in the paper again. Should I ask you for your autograph?"

Because a man didn't do things for himself in isolation. He did them for someone, and the someone wasn't the company, or the newspapers, or his crews.

"Goddamn it to hell!" he said, and went aboard.

There were a couple of crew members at the top of the gangplank as he went up. One of them he hadn't worked with before, a man in his late twenties, heavyset, heavy sideburns, dark hair spilling onto the collar of his wetback. The crews wore their hair all ways and Westholme no longer measured a man by that. He sized up this one squarely:

"My name's Westholme, Chris Westholme. I'm taking her out tonight. Have you ever worked *Haida Noble* before?"

"Twice this summer; second engineer. Both times out to the rig. Name's Read . . . Stan."

The other was a deckhand Westholme knew and was pleased to see.

"Galbraith, you should be ashore. I thought the plan was to get another year of university?"

Galbraith grinned. "Two reasons: one, I spent all my money this summer; two, if I had money I wouldn't spend it on education this year. I never paid to go on a picket line yet."

"The way I see it," Westholme said, "the teachers should be picketing the students."

Galbraith shrugged, one of his light blue eyes closed tightly in a broad, freckled face. "Me, I'm on the fence. I'm watching."

"Try saving some money for a change," Westholme said, and proceeded up to the bridge.

Lindstrom was there tinkering with the radar. He was a good mate with a deep water master's ticket to his credit. He had worked with Westholme on several of the *Haida Noble* assignments. Tall, painfully thin, he was the antithesis of the thin man. To begin with, his voice had the deep resonance of a man twice his girth. He had the sense of humor of the proverbial fat man, and in his thin, skeletal arms was the strength to put down the arm of any man who cared to engage in a game of Indian wrestling. Lindstrom had made a small fortune Indian wrestling. Out of pity strong men allowed him to lock arms with them. Lindstrom had little pity when he took away their dollars.

"You're too early, Christy," he complained. "I wanted to have a bunch of flowers tied to the binnacle."

Westholme was used to the patter. He didn't acknowledge it. "Who's aboard?"

"The cook's aboard. That's all that matters."

"Come on!" Westholme complained.

"First officer; that's me," Lindstrom said. "Second officer is down trying the cook's coffee."

"Fenton?"

Lindstrom nodded. "Chief engineer is aboard and he's a good one."

"Thomson?"

"You've checked the crew list. Yes sir, the Scotsman is with us, complete with list of complaints. Second engineer is on."

"We've got twenty minutes," Westholme said.

"Number three deckhand is missing."

"Time enough. Bunkers?"

"We're full. I've checked all that stuff. What's the plan? We're not moving BUTCO to another drill location at this time of year?"

"We're moving her out," Westholme said. "The trick is to get her into shelter before the first of the big storms."

"Where is she?"

"Eight miles southwest of Amphitrite Point. We've got to take her into Ucluelet for winter layover."

"That's no trick," Lindstrom said. "We shouldn't take pay for a job like that."

"I'm not proud," Westholme said. He pulled out two charts from the slot under the navigation desk and tacked them into place one beneath the other.

"I don't know about your wife," Lindstrom said, "but my wife is ready to climb my frame. I promised her two weeks on the beach. The dispatcher told me you had thirty days coming."

"Why don't you go down and check the others on board," Westholme said. "Tell them to shake their asses. I want to catch that tide."

Lindstrom departed, brandishing his thin arms like an emaciated ape about to mete out punishment. A little too much of a clown, Westholme thought sourly. He surveyed the bridge carefully. It was a great set-up and the company kept it in top shape. Two of everything spread across the full 33-foot width of the bridge:

Two engine room telegraphs, plus a remote control system, two gyro and magnetic compasses, two radar systems, two independent intercom systems, all of this backed up by the latest in echo sounders, rudder angle indicators, automatic pilots and other navigational stuff. A new trick had been installed since last he commanded; closed circuit television which gave the bridge an immediate view of the vessel's main quarters, as well as fore and aft maneuvering positions. He didn't try the equipment; it was too much like spying.

Beside the nearest radar scope was the ship-to-shore telephone, an installation long familiar to him on that bridge. At this moment its importance grew to immense proportions. In the distance he could hear Lindstrom scolding the last of the crew members on board. Foghorns were sounding out in the inlet, each with its own tone of warning. He had thirty days coming to him; thirty days to tear down the wall Lee had erected in her own lonely mind. He could walk off the *Haida Noble* right now. He could telephone her and tell her he was coming home. It would take something like that to put things right.

Lindstrom spidered into view, filling the doorway. "They're all aboard, Chris. What's your pleasure?"

Westholme looked at his watch. Three minutes off 0100 hours. "Prepare to cast off," he said.

4 . . .

The chairman of the Committee on the Peaceful Uses of the Sea Bed and the Ocean Floor worked late that night. Many of the committee chairmen were putting in longer hours these days, as the United Nations year moved into its final months. His committee in particular had its work cut out for it and no one was more aware of this than the chairman. The frustrations that prevailed in the General Assembly were no less apparent here; the need to proceed diplomatically, to observe protocol and the niceties of debate, to sift from the carefully contrived statements of the committee members the true intent and purpose of the nations they represented was desperately time-consuming. And time for the Sea Bed Committee, in common with many other UNGA projects, was in danger of running out.

How far had they come in all these years? Not far, not nearly far enough. He had gone back several years to the file of reports on the Twenty-fourth Session. Tomorrow he would present excerpts to the full committee in an effort to impress on them their desperately slow progress. Words! He was a career diplomat and words were his tools and his weapons, but he had a feeling approaching disgust as he thumbed through the pages in that old file. All this time to promulgate those opinions and proposals! If fifty percent of them were to culminate in action tomorrow it might still take a decade to observe any useful result. He wondered if mankind progressed because of words, or in spite of them:

Mr. Amerasinghe, *Ceylon*

"I should now like to refer to the most important aspects of this question, as we of the delegation of Ceylon see them. We are in favor of the sea bed and its resources being treated as a common heritage of mankind. If the area and its resources are to be saved from competitive exploitation —restricted necessarily to those with financial resources and the technological power to exploit them—it is necessary for us to abandon those traditional concepts and evolve a new concept . . ."

Mr. Phillips, *United States*

". . . Another item of work for the Sea Bed Committee of great importance will be the reaching of an agreement on a set of principles governing the exploration and the exploitation of the deep sea bed.

". . . We regret that, owing to a shortage of time, the Sea Bed Committee was unable to deal adequately at its sessions this year with questions of exploration, research, and pollution. These are subjects to which the Committee plans to return when it resumes its work next March . . ."

Mr. Badawi, *United Arab Republic*

"We all recall the lengthy discussions in the Ad Hoc Committee, and later in the Standing Committee, on a question which undoubtedly falls beyond the jurisdiction of the Sea Bed Committee, and I refer in particular to the question of the definition of the boundary between that area of the sea bed and ocean floor lying beyond the limits of national jurisdiction and the area which falls under national jurisdiction . . ."

Mr. Rossides, *Cyprus*

". . . Anarchy and a scramble for possession and exploitation can bring no good to any nation. It will be the cause of conflict and friction and will create new problems further threatening our precarious peace. On the other hand, if we decide to proceed to an orderly exploitation of the wealth of the sea bed for the benefit of mankind, we will be providing the solution to many threatening world problems . . ."

Mr. Schram, *Iceland*

". . . In the view of my delegation, outer space is still far beyond the reach of most nations and access to it and its exploitation is severely limited even for the few nations that possess the necessary technical capabilities.

"The situation is radically different as regards the sea beds. There the race for their hidden riches is already on and every new step constitutes an extension of the sovereignty of some State over what was hitherto an unclaimed area. If that conquest, by gradual acquisition, under the cloak of the highly imperfect Geneva Convention on the continental shelf, is not checked in time we will find the area, so nobly declared the common heritage of mankind, being reduced to valueless, deep oceanic creeks and ravines . . ."

Mr. Mendelevich, *USSR*

". . . Who would gain from this delay? Would the Socialist States stand to gain from this? No; the Socialist States—and let nobody have any doubt on this score—are not at all interested in seeing the sea bed remain for a long time the object of rivalry and competition among States and an arena for the rapacious exploitation of capitalist monopolies. The Soviet Union is firmly in favor of developing international co-operation in this important field, not for arbitrary activities or marine exploitation in the bad sense. Could it be that further delays before an agreement is reached on legal principles of the sea bed would be in the interests of the developing countries of Asia, Africa, and Latin America? It is highly debatable that they would have anything to gain from such a turn of events. Delay in an agreement on the legal principles of the sea bed, no matter what pretexts are used to explain it, such as it must be complete, comprehensive, and so on can only play into the hands of those who are interested in a juridical vacuum, the exploiters, the capitalist monopolies . . .

"The Soviet Union, which has a large research navy—over one hundred ships from 400 tons to 6000 tons—is spending tens of millions of rubles and, together with other socialist countries, is engaged in tremendous work for the exploitation of the sea bed and ocean floor which will be widely used in the interests of the whole of mankind . . ."

Mr. Kaplan, *Canada*

". . . If I may quote again from Mr. Sharp's statement:

" 'In the Disarmament Committee, Canada advanced a group of interrelated suggestions for the disarmament of the sea bed. In summary, these suggestions involve (1) the prohibition not only of nuclear weapons and weapons of mass destruction, but also of conventional weapons and military installations which could be used for offensive purposes, without, however, banning installations required for self-defense; (2) the establishment beyond the 12-mile coastal band, of a 200-mile security zone to which the proposed arms prohibitions would apply in full but where the coastal state could undertake defensive activities; (3) the elaboration of effective verification and inspection procedures to assure compliance with the terms of the treaty, together with an international arrangement making such verification possible for countries with a less developed underwater technology. With the exception of the prohibition of the emplacement of nuclear weapons and weapons of mass destruction, these Canadian suggestions are not reflected in the draft treaty put forward by the USA and the USSR . . .

" 'In summary, the U.S.-Soviet draft treaty is unfortunately silent on a number of important questions.' "

Mr. Zelleke, *Ethiopia*

"I should like to make a suggestion, if possible. It seems to me that some of the suggestions and amendments and draft resolutions are at cross purposes. I think it would be good if the authors of these were to get together and work out a document that would be acceptable to all. I don't think there is any very, very serious difference on most of them."

The chairman chuckled humorlessly. Mr. Zelleke's observation had been one of the choicest misstatements of the entire Twenty-fourth Session, coming as it did in the final moments of the final day. Some of the differences he alluded to were bridged by the most fragile of threads. How to make a cable out of those tenuous bonds capable of drawing differences together into common accord?

He pencil-marked the passages he required from the files and coded them for insertion into the statement he had prepared earlier for tomorrow's meeting of the Sea Bed Committee. Shortly after 2330 he shuffled the last of his draft into order and telephoned the night stenographic pool for a messenger.

Rain began to slant across the broad glass of his office window and he walked over to stare vacantly at the wet glow and shimmer in the New York streets. He was physically tired and mentally depressed. More depression than tiredness, he decided. In this business tiredness was quite often a state of mind.

The Sea Bed Committee was dealing with the world's last and greatest source of food and raw materials—or with the last of the battlefields—a battlefield where navies would stalk one another in the deeps and where fortresses and rocket emplacements would lie concealed in a hundred fathoms or more.

"We're not moving fast enough," he told his reflection in the rain-dappled window. "There's never enough time these days."

Behind him he heard a brief rap on the door. The messenger entered, received and signed for the draft, and departed silently.

The chairman watched him go, then sat on the edge of his desk and dialed the apartment:

In his own language he said, "I'm through here, Ingrid. You should see me in half an hour."

The voice at the other end was sleepy but soft and welcoming. Deliberately he let the world close in to a manageable size, until it contained no more than the thought of his wife waiting in a Manhattan apartment.

5 . . .

Normally, Westholme would have gone to bed as soon as the tug was under way. Lindstrom tried to persuade him of it.

"The fog is bound to clear as soon as we get into the open," he said. "I can do this leg with my eyes shut."

Westholme danced a pair of dividers over the face of the Canadian Hydrographic Service chart. It was an aimless, preoccupied gesture. "Don't feel much like sleeping. I'll hang around for a while . . . unless I make you nervous."

Lindstorm laughed. "You've got me in a cold sweat." The big windows, port and starboard on the bridge, were half open to let in the sounds of the Narrows. The music of the fog bellowed and rang around them; foghorns and bell buoys marking the passage of *Haida Noble;* first Brockton Point, then the giant buttresses of the Lions' Gate Bridge arching invisibly above them; then the towering cliffs of Prospect Point, each with its own hoarse or clanging warning, all of it as familiar to them as a popular tune. From time to time Lindstrom checked the radar, but the fog had slowed traffic down to a shuffle and they cleared the port of Vancouver without having to alter course.

Far to port they heard the bray of the Point Gray horn, answered by the warning from Point Atkinson equally far to starboard. The powerful Point Atkinson light was still lost in fog, but Westholme's eyes registered interest as a sudden, fresh breeze whipped gray mist through the wheelhouse.

"Wind coming up. We should lose the fog in a few minutes."

"Like I told you," Lindstrom said. "Why don't you turn in? Eight o'clock's not far away."

Westholme didn't answer him. He rummaged through a drawer beside the chart table, sorting through a collection of outdated magazines, mostly skin publications. The banner across an ancient issue of a *Reader's Digest* caught his eye and held it: *Twenty Ways to Make Your Marriage Work.* He buried the magazine among the others, looked farther and then hunted out the *Digest* again. It would be crap, he knew that. All the *Digest* stuff promised one-page answers to the problems of the universe. He sprawled back in the bolted-down chair and tried to read.

The wind continued to freshen, a brisk southerly tearing the thick fog to shreds. Midway across the Strait of Georgia visibility was good enough to increase speed to 10 knots. Westholme watched as Lindstrom made a scrawled entry in the logbook. The chronometer showed 0237 hours. On the corner of the chart table the *Digest* lay rejected. He had stopped in disgust at Magic Formula Number Three: "Tell her she's the only girl in the world, first thing in the morning, last thing at night."

"Damn!" Lindstrom said in sudden irritation. "I meant to tell Bunny to take the car in for a brake reline."

"Get on to Alex," Westholme said. "He'll be glad to hear a voice this time of night."

Lindstrom lifted the ship-to-shore telephone from its bracket and put the call through to the dispatcher on the company line.

Westholme listened to him giving the instructions on the brake job. Here was a chance to leave a message for Lee—something casual—to let her know he wasn't bothered by what had happened tonight.

"Anything you want to say, Christy?" Lindstrom asked.

"What's he got on the weather?" It was small talk, a running away from the thing he wanted to say.

"Chris thinks you know something about the weather the Bureau boys don't know."

"You should have it," the dispatcher's tinny voice told him. "There's some kind of a system moving up from the southwest —gale force winds—but the betting is it'll dissipate."

"Tell the Met boys it dissipates or we don't do business with them any more," Lindstrom commanded. "Anything else?"

"That's it. What's your position?"

"Active Pass in sight."

"Right. You can expect more fog in Swanson Channel and beyond."

"Great!" Lindstrom said in disgust. "How far beyond?"

"Don't give me a bad time, Lindy," the dispatcher said. "I'm not the weather man. Say, have you got a camera on board?"

"Somewhere."

"U. S. Coast Guard reports a fleet of thirty to forty Russian fishing boats moving north along the Twelve Mile. They should be in your neighborhood tomorrow."

"What do you want . . . a snapshot of a bucket of borscht?"

"They say some of the big trawlers have girls in the crew. Bring me back a pin-up."

"You disgust me," Lindstrom said, and hung up.

"More fog," he repeated to Westholme.

"I heard. September's the time for it." He turned the wheel back to Lindstrom and went back to sprawl in the navigator's chair. "Bunny's worn out the brakes again," he said casually. "You and the wife having trouble?"

Lindstrom grinned into the darkness beyond. "You know what I mean. She doesn't like the way I comb my hair; I don't like the run in her stocking. It gives us something to talk about. Bunny and I make out pretty good together, generally speaking. I think the truth is we like to fight a lot. Something would be wrong if we stopped."

"Glad to hear it's nothing serious," Westholme said.

"I'm not saying we have what you and your wife have," Lindstrom said. "The way I make it out, you've got something pretty good going for you there."

"I think I'll turn in," Westholme said getting up. "If there's fog in Swanson Channel we'll be back to half speed or less. Better plan to make contact with the rig around dark tomorrow."

"First fog," Lindstrom said, "and with the way things are going the gale will show up twelve hours early. I think I'll send a signal to Bunny. Tell her to find herself another man."

"Make sure they shake me loose for the 0800 watch," Westholme said. He went down the gangway to his quarters, hearing as he went the far-distant bellow of a foghorn penetrating the muffled throb of the engine room.

In his cabin he turned on his desk lamp and lowered himself onto his bunk. He kept his clothes on. Lying there in the dim light, with his arms up behind his head, he waited for his watch to come around. There was no way he could turn his mind off.

6 . . .

One hundred and thirty navigational miles from *Haida Noble*, eight-point-seven miles almost due west and slightly south of Amphitrite Point, the monster straddled an infinity of whitecaps dappling the early morning darkness. In that luminous predawn it looked like a gigantic crab mutation, its three armored legs supporting a carapace of steel 130 feet above the surface of the sea. Bright eyes glittered along the edges and top surfaces of the carapace, some of them illuminating the antennae-like tracery of cranes and the drill mast itself, rearing another 140 feet above the shell of the beast.

BUTCO 17 was the biggest semi-submersible drill rig in existence. British United Traction had fourteen drill rigs of various types working the continental shelves of the world; all of them were huge, but BUTCO 17, the newest and most advanced of them all, had benefited in her design from the success and failures of her predecessors. BUTCO 15, in fact, deserved the credit for much of 17's design. In 1968, BUTCO 15, then the largest semi-submersible oil drilling vessel afloat, was in the process of punching her third successful hole of the season in a promising area of shelf in the South China Sea, when she was set upon by a typhoon. The rig was designed to take one-hundred-mile-an-hour winds in her stride, but the forces working on her that afternoon were far out of her class. She broke up and foundered with all hands, and British United's designers went back to the drawing boards.

BUTCO 17 was a floating equilateral triangle with each side 400 feet long. The triangular island was supported on three massive caissons 155 feet in height. These in turn rested on pontoons, one to each caisson, with the total capability of floating the 12,000-ton mass of steel and drill equipment.

She had been working on a drilling program on the west coast of Vancouver Island since March of that year, and had already weathered a spring hurricane with wind gusts measured at better than 100 miles an hour. This time British United had done the engineering job properly, and it would appear that the investment was close to paying off. Six drill holes put down that spring and summer had led her with increasingly promising core samples and gas traces toward the Amphitrite shelf. Each time she moved, *Haida Noble* took charge of the operation, towing her at a steady 6 knots to the next drill site.

She waited now for *Haida Noble*, her caissons pumped almost clear of water ballast so that she floated high, her great island blotting out the pattern of stars and scudding clouds passing swiftly above. Early that afternoon the last of the drill pipe had been pulled up after the hole had been capped. She rode on three massive anchors, one planted beneath each point of the triangle. The continental shelf lay slightly more than twenty fathoms below, with the drill rig's anchors biting deep into the sand and silt.

It was an unaccustomed position for BUTCO 17. She liked deeper water, and was designed to work with a draft of 147 feet on the bottom, or 90 feet in an effective floating position. Either way she would hold virtually rock-steady while the drill steel went down foot after foot to a maximum depth of 25,000 feet. She could work her drill in water up to 900 feet deep, and this she could do in gales or with a heavy sea running.

BUTCO 17 wasn't the last of the technological behemoths to exploit the resources lying below the continental shelf; she was merely the biggest and the best to date. At that she was a precursor, an early forerunner of greater, more startling things to come.

Michael Volkoff was in an excellent position to know what was yet to come. He had trained for it, worked toward it, lived and breathed it for the past sixteen years.

He came awake in the small hours of the morning, feeling the slight movement of the rig, alert to changing sea conditions. The hours surrounding the repositioning of BUTCO 17 were always critical. Her wave transparency design offered the least possible resistance to pounding seas, but she became more vulnerable in relatively shallow water, riding light on nearly empty caissons.

Volkoff climbed into cork-soled boots, trousers, and insulated windbreaker. Dark-complexioned, he reminded those who met him of the stereotype of the handsome Spaniard, rather than of his Russian ancestry; he was tall, just edging six feet with smooth musculature arranged on an athletic frame. He had the build of a swimmer, and swimming, which had begun as his favorite sport, had served him well in his university years.

He had entered UCLA on a swimming scholarship, and there had never been a doubt in his mind from that first year onward that oceanography would be his elected field.

"What is it?" his father complained. "What can you do with a thing like that? Go fishing? Sell seawater?"

The senior Volkoff understood mining and very little else. In the course of earning a living, the family had grown in rented houses in virtually every major mining community in Colorado. Mike didn't take him too seriously. The old man was secretly proud of a son who could come home with straight A's all through high school and make the state swimming and track teams at the same time. Still, mining was a sure living; this oceanography wasn't much more than a word he had trouble pronouncing.

"You take it from me, Mike. Get a degree in mining engineering and you can name your own ticket anywhere. I'd be working for you. How do you like that—a chance to fire the old man!"

Mike Volkoff couldn't remember when the ocean got in his blood. Perhaps it wasn't so much that the ocean obsessed him, as it was that the mines, and the mining towns, the slag heaps, the tailings ponds and the smoke spreading out across sunbaked landscapes repelled him and turned him away. All he knew was that, at the age of ten, on a rare family visit with an uncle in Santa Barbara, he had first seen the ocean and had known in that instant, as clearly as he knew he was alive, that the sea would become his life.

He made one significant concession to his father and elected to make mining engineering his option when he entered the School of Oceanography. After that things simply fell into place. His presence on BUTCO 17 was part of a natural progression. On more than one occasion Volkoff had stopped to consider how smoothly the whole thing had gone. He was one of these few, fortunate people who have always known what they have wanted to do in life, and have always been able to do it.

There were the three great summers with the Scripps Institute, the year with Smithsonian after he emerged with his doctorate. There was the International Oceanographic Congress in Moscow in 1966, followed by three weeks in Paris, when his family-learned Russian and his college-learned French served him well both professionally and socially.

And then the job with British United was the real breakthrough. Both the Navy Department and British United had acquired his papers on the handling and storage of deep water oil well production. The Navy made the first bid for his services and, in fact, put him through the complete screening process. But British United made it no contest. He was flown to New Orleans on a Sunday afternoon, following a long distance telephone call that same morning. Monday morning was spent with the vice-president in charge of engineering. The entire afternoon was taken up with senior members of the research and development staff; and that evening, following an excellent dinner, a persuasive executive vice-president made the offer.

It was no more complicated than that. British United had done its homework well. When Volkoff had a chance to see their dossier on him some months later, he realized the weeks of preliminary investigation that had preceded their simple, straightforward offer.

"It amounts to a roving commission," British United's man said. "You'll be our idea man in the field. Whenever we put a rig into action, or lease one to a client, you'll go with it for as long as you feel necessary. Watch the machinery in action. Watch how the rig works. Be critical. Keep your eyes open for new and better ways. We don't want to hear the good things about these rigs; we want to hear the bad things. We want you to come up with your own ideas in the field and we want you to supervise the application of our own research and development ideas." He leaned ahead and lowered his voice slightly. "There is one other thing we want you to do. I won't go into it now, but you'll meet with me and some government people tomorrow afternoon. We'll have to have your acceptance of our offer before we can hold that meeting."

"Any idea what it's about?" Volkoff asked.

"I'm briefed, but all I can tell you is this, the assignment is not demanding and it shouldn't involve you in any difficulties. It calls for more watching—a specialized kind of watching. We like to work along with the federal people for obvious reasons. You'd be helping our position."

Minutes later Volkoff signed the agreement, scrawling his signature quickly by candlelight, in the midst of the dinner dishes. That was the way British United worked. As for the meeting the following afternoon; it concerned him at the time, but no longer bothered him. The federal agency was the CIA . . . and their people required him to file a report, whenever the occasion arose, on a number of specific subjects.

That was about it. He stopped off at home on the way back to the West Coast. His father met him at the door in his stocking feet, still dressed in his dusty mining clothes. He had just come off shift.

"By God, Mike!" he said. "What are you selling, fresh fish?"

It was good to sit at the dinner table with them again, after months of being away. He outlined the job for them broadly, told them of the opportunity to travel. They could sense his enthusiasm.

"Never could see you making much money out of seawater," his father said. "Looks as though I was wrong."

His mother limited her observations to the only thing that really concerned her. "It's nice you got a good job, Mike," she said, the Russian sounds rolling richly from her tongue. "But all this traveling, like a rolling stone. Thirty-one years and no sign of a wife and family."

"Time enough for that," he assured her. "You make great chocolate pie, Momma."

That reunion had been not much more than a year ago. Time could be running out, Volkoff thought to himself as he slipped up the hood of his windbreaker. In twelve months he had spent two off the coast of New Guinea, three off the coast of Labrador, four on a jinxed rig in the Caribbean, and the rest on BUTCO 17, with a few weeks off here and there for head office briefings and holiday time. In the past few weeks he had begun to feel the grind. He needed time off, bright lights, good food, entertainment, and girls. Not girls, he decided. One girl would be fine if she was the right combination of things, and there seemed to be a future.

It was the end of the season for BUTCO 17. The time was ideal for a four-week leave. He decided to put in for it, as he pushed the door open into the face of the southwesterly.

The wind wasn't doing more than twenty, but there hadn't been any wind at all when he turned in at midnight. The wind didn't concern him as much as the sea; it was pushing a heavy swell against the rig from the same southwesterly direction. He squinted into a slanting curtain of cold rain and headed for the communications shack, passing the recreation-mess building where some of the graveyard shift were sipping coffee and watching a movie on closed circuit TV. The blue-gray flicker of the tube played across the insulated window glass like cold fire.

Voices carried to him by the wind drew his attention to the helicopter pad where several roughnecks were tying down the helicopter against the possibility of increasing wind. It was a six-passenger, Sikorsky S 55. Tomorrow morning it would begin the job of ferrying BUTCO's crew to Ucluelet on the first leg of their journey back to the mainland. It was an easy, 9- or 10-mile hop from the rig to the small fishing town.

He went over to the rig and watched the action for a moment. "Expecting trouble?" he called up to the pilot.

"That you, Mike?" The pilot knocked drops of rainwater off his nose. "The only trouble I worry about is the company, if I get a dent in this bloody contraption. Nicked a blade tip coming in tonight. I want to steady things up for a repair job tomorrow morning."

"Serious?"

The pilot shook his head. "They can fix it with a Band-Aid."

Volkoff turned away and finished his walk to the communications shack, feeling the shifting of the massive deck beneath his feet. Thank God the drill steel was up and out of the way.

There was quite a collection inside the room. The graveyard foreman was there with the rig supervising engineer and the night-shift first-aid man. The radio operator had passed coffee around and they were all sitting back enjoying a bull session.

The radio operator inclined his head toward the coffeepot. "Draw yourself a cup, Mike."

Volkoff poured a mug, and sugared it. "Nice to have some peace and quiet around here Charlie," he said. "After a couple of months you get the notion the drill hole's going through your head."

"Son, you don't know music when you hear it." The rig's head man was a square-set Texan with thirteen years of roughnecking behind him before he went to floating drill rigs. "When I don't hear drill steel turning I get a mournful feeling."

"You're up late, Charlie," Volkoff said.

The rig engineer nodded. "So are you. Something we ate?" His Texas inflection was so broad it sounded deliberate.

"We're getting more movement than I expected. That's quite a swell shaping up."

"Coast Guard weather report says we don't have to worry too much," Charlie said. "They caught a system a thousand miles or so west of Sacramento. Gale force winds pushing this way. They think it'll wear itself out before it gets here."

"It's here now," Volkoff said. "That swell had to start somewhere. How old is the report?"

"It came in at 0215," the radio operator told him. "Say an hour for the weather plane to file an accurate position report, and another hour or two to build it into a five-day forecast. It's probably three or four hours old. No one seems to be worried about it. It's just part of a routine forecast."

"Stick around, Mike," the first-aid man invited. "We're waiting for the late, late television special." He indicated the bank of radar screens at the radio operator's eye level.

The rig engineer drained his coffee cup and went over to the pot to draw another. "U. S. Coast Guard says there's thirty or forty Russian boats coming north along the Twelve Mile line. They should be showing on the screen any time."

Volkoff's eyes became alert and interested. "That's a lot of boats in one flotilla. Are they sure of their count?"

"Stick around," Charlie said. "You can count them for yourself."

Volkoff stared closely at the only one of the four radar screens functioning. The conformation of land mass and islets revealed by the sweeping green band of light was familiar to him: Amphitrite Point with its adjoining islands to the right of the screen. The jagged edge of Vancouver Island filling the right-hand portion of the screen top to bottom. On the left-hand side of the screen the nothingness of the open sea disturbed only by three small blips almost dead center.

"Gillnetters," the operator told him. "They've got to be Canadian. They're working half a mile inside the Twelve Mile, and that's where they're going to stay until that fleet passes by."

Volkoff didn't feel inclined to join the general laughter. Canadian fishermen had taken a beating that summer, one of the worst summers yet for harassment by the big Russian trawlers, even though the Russians were now permitted to fish inside the Twelve Mile on the west coast of the Charlottes. Canadian fishing waters extended twelve miles out from the farthest point of Canadian land. Only Canadian fishermen could work inside that limit. Outside the limit any nation could put down its nets, including the Canadians.

While the Canadian fishing vessels seldom fished in groups of more than two or three—more often by themselves—the Russians fished as a team: seiners, trawlers, a cannery ship, and quite often a tanker all moving together, following the migration of the fish. God help the Canadian fishermen with gear down in the path of a big Russian trawler. In those international waters the trawlers moved inexorably, holding their course, no matter what lay ahead. The massive, bottom-scraping nets fanned out to tear and wreck the light gear of the Canadians.

On more than one occasion, moving their vessels precisely along the edge of the Twelve Mile mark, the Russian seines and trawler set-ups had reached out to destroy Canadian nets working inside the Twelve Mile limit.

How much of it was deliberate . . . how much of it was bad seamanship or accidental were questions the Canadian Department of Fisheries and the Department for External Affairs were laboring to determine before Canadian fishermen took the law into their own hands and began to use the rifles all of them carried in their wheelhouses to keep off the blackfish and seals.

"Do you think they know the Russian fleet is moving up?" Volkoff asked.

"They know it all right. We watched them hustle inside the Twelve Mile over an hour ago, just after the message came through."

Volkoff turned back to other problems. "Charlie, it's your ball game, but what's the plot if that wind reaches us before the tug does . . . or if we're on the line behind the tug?"

"Give me a choice and I'd like to see that wind before we go on the line. The last two rigs to get into trouble caught it while they were at the end of tow lines. I'd rather put the legs down to the bottom and sit it out."

"We should have gone into shelter two weeks ago," Volkoff said. "Don't they read our reports?"

"This last hole was important to them," Charlie said. He didn't develop the thought farther. Only he, Volkoff, and the rig geologist knew what the final cores from the last hole had revealed. BUTCO 17 would come back there next spring. In three days they'd be through into oil.

"Quite a poker game," Volkoff said. "In the meantime we've got *Haida Noble* heading this way, with the outside chance that the sea will be so rough she won't be able to put a line on us."

"That's what it is," Charlie said. "An outside chance. I wouldn't worry. This baby can take a lot of punishment."

The radio operator leaned over and stared hard at the radar screen, reaching across to fine-tune it. "I think the show is starting," he said.

At first Volkoff saw nothing, just a little blur of light, an interference pattern on the bottom left edge of the screen, and then the first blip appeared and disappeared as the beam swept by; appeared again along with another. They gathered in close to watch as the flotilla paraded onto the screen in long line. Big and little stabs of light, luminous teardrops weeping across the radar field.

The first blip appeared at 0349. By 0517 the men in the communications shack had counted thirty-seven vessels, several of larger than normal size. At 0517 Volkoff said, "They've stopped. We've got company."

"By Christ, you're right," Charlie said. He pressed into the radar screen as though willing them to move on. "No more than three miles off."

"Don't waste time on the radar," Volkoff said. "In half an hour there'll be enough light to see them from the deck."

7 . . .

Far north and west of *Haida Noble,* on the Pacific's very northern edge, the chemistry of a cataclysm moved to its final conclusion. Secret, deeply confined in a vast retort of basalt and granite, its ingredients bubbled and fumed, building up a mountain-smashing pressure. When that bomb exploded the entire Pacific would feel its impact.

At 0630 hours on September 28, the duty seismologist at the Klyuchi Vulcanological Station on the Kamchatka Peninsula made a routine check of the station's seismograph tapes. The familiar inked patterns greeted his eye. Nothing out of the ordinary, if you could call this electrocardiogram-like tracing of the earth's inner agony an ordinary phenomenon. Mount Klyuchevskoi's giant bulk was sending forth its usual intricate pattern of tremors. Over the years, the station scientists had memorized the tremor patterns of every square acre of the massive Kamchatka volcano. Klyuchevskoi was a king attended by a retinue of physicians, each a specialist on some aspect of his rocky interior.

It is therefore interesting that it was a Klyuchi seismologist who had first noticed renewed action in the region of Bogoslof Island. Possibly the fact that he was a junior, recently appointed from Moscow University accounted for his perception and his attention to events beyond the kingdom of Mount Klyuchevskoi.

While conducting the noon reading on August 13th, he had spotted an abrupt splinter of red going well beyond five on the Richter Scale. It could have been Klyuchevskoi relieving himself of a little gas far underground, but this was not likely to be the case. The junior, with the condescending approval of the Station Director, had wirelessed his findings and his inquiry to Tokyo and Washington. In due course he received confirmation of the tremor, together with the information he required to work out his own triangulation. It was not far from that established by the United States Coast and Geodetic Survey. After more than forty years Bogoslof Island appeared to be making noises again. The chemistry of the bomb had been triggered.

Bogoslof Island was a juvenile delinquent in the Aleutian Island rogues' gallery of volcanic trouble spots. Most of the big volcanoes on the Aleutian Chain had million-year histories. Bogoslof hadn't exploded into sight until 1796, in time for a few Russian sea otter hunters to confirm its fiery birth for the outside world.

In a matter of days a complete island emerged from the sea; a low-contoured, flame-belching cone with white hot lava oozing like treacle into the cold water. The steam and the multitude of explosions were prodigious.

Because it was a relatively smooth birth, the earth tremors ranged only a short distance along the Aleutian Chain. Where these were felt the Aleuts gathered together in their underground dwelling places, their eyes glistening with fear in the light of the fish oil lamps. Their shamans chanted and rattled the sealskin tambourines—and in due course their gods subdued the infant island of Bogoslof. It ceased to grow, and it became silent.

In 1883 the sealskin tambourines rattled again, though this time there were fewer of them, and the remaining Aleuts had come to know that there were scourges worse than erupting, volcanic islands. The men who had followed Vitus Bering into that land possessed Cossack mentalities. The Russian fur hunters—the *promyshlenniki*—hunted the Aleuts the way they did the seal and the otter. Twenty-five thousand natives were reduced to a few thousand, sped on their way in the final years by American and Canadian sealers as callous as their Russian predecessors. But those Aleuts who remained within sight and earshot of Bogoslof Island in 1883 trembled and prayed as their ancestors had done.

In 1906 a further eruption occurred, this time for the interest and edification of vulcanologists. The same thing happened in 1910, 1923, and 1927. Bogoslof Island, in the lexicon of volcanoes, had established itself as troublesome but not really significant.

Still, when the junior seismologist at Klyuchi drew attention to the island's new mutterings, the United States Coast and Geodetic Survey considered it important enough to check out. A group was sent from the Adak Station to look and listen. They flew twenty-two miles north of the major island of Unmak and touched down in the one, sheltered bay indenting the grass-topped patch of volcanic rock that was Bogoslof. They took three days to give the island a thorough medical, although they could have done it in one. During that time the geologist on the team bagged a trophy, a large sea lion bull, and spent one day meticulously removing its cape and tusks.

They pressed their instruments, like stethoscopes, to the island's twisted chest. They probed its scant acreage for signs of fissures or other stress. They found nothing and they heard nothing. Their report, eight pages double-spaced, reduced itself to a simple but expert observation. There was no sign of volcanic resurrection on Bogoslof Island . . . and they were absolutely right.

At 0647 hours on September 28, the duty seismologist at Klyuchi completed his entries in the seismograph report and proceeded to leave the instrument room. Hot tea was waiting in the staff room. It was pure chance that caused him to look down at the tape as he passed. There, again unmistakably, was the red spear of ink projecting well beyond the line of five on the Richter Scale. It had inscribed itself at 0642.2.

Either Mount Klyuchevskoi was playing a jealous trick, or something of importance was happening somewhere. Being a seasoned scientist, with caution born of considerable years, he did not behave in the impetuous manner of the junior. He decided to think about it, to wait until some other station made a move.

As was to be expected, the United States Coast and Geodetic Survey had picked up the tremor at several of its stations, as had a number of seismographs in Japan and elsewhere. Routine triangulations were carried out and the location was Bogoslof Island, give or take a few miles. More than one seismologist began to suspect that the troublesome amateur was showing professional muscle. Bogoslof was going to bear watching.

8 . . .

Westholme endured it until 0730 hours. He kept looking at his watch as the hands moved around. Right on the minute he slid from the bunk, stripped off his shirt and underwear top and went into the lavatory he shared with the first officer. There he turned on the cold water and filled the basin with it, staring at his image in the mirror. The face was alien to him; the blue-gray eyes paler than they should be; the harsh light picking out gray in the rumpled, black thatch of hair; the heavy musculature of jawline, neck and chest appearing to have lost its tone. He rejected his image, just as Lee had done earlier that night.

He wanted the cold to snap him out of it, to numb the hot, wild, incredible thoughts that raced through his mind. Lee had never loved him from the beginning. Lee waited for him to go to sea. Lee let someone in the back door when he went out the front. She was going to destroy those years he placed so much value on. She didn't value those years. She didn't value anything he believed in! She was a bitch! A true bitch!

None of that was true! Feeling that way she couldn't have stuck it out the way she had. He was letting his mind get the better of him. Lee was the best woman he would ever know, the best person he would ever know. She had gone farther, waited longer, endured more, given more love . . .

Westholme plunged his head into the numbing coldness of the water and willed it to put out the fire. He came up spluttering, his scalp soaked inches back into the hairline. His groping hand found the towel and he dried himself, abrading the skin until he felt that he must have drawn blood.

He narrowly missed striking his head against the top of the undersized doorframe as he returned to his cabin. His preoccupation made him clumsy as he slipped into his underwear and shirt—and then *Haida Noble* regained possession. As he lifted his jacket from the wall hook, the tug rolled sharply to starboard and his mind was torn from the woman and returned to the sea.

His inclination for the past hour had been to go to the bridge, get the weather report, check the situation, but the move would have been a bad one. A man was entitled to his watch, and Westholme placed considerable importance on that in any circumstance. Sleep with one eye open and one ear listening, but don't interfere with a man's watch unless he invites you to, or the situation calls for it.

In this case he had no cause for worry. Lindstrom was as solid as they make them; so was Fenton when his turn came. He stepped outside and made for the companionway to the main deck. The wind was building all right, a good southwesterly, and they weren't out in the open yet. When they cleared the dubious shelter of Cape Flattery they'd be into the worst of it.

"Never got a straight forecast from a Met man in my life," he said audibly, and then realized that he was talking to himself—a habit he deplored in anyone else. Suddenly he was genuinely angry with his own performance in the past few hours. It had been years since he had allowed anything to shake him in this way. He was standing outside himself now, looking at himself as though he were a green, clumsy deckhand.

"Don't be goddam ridiculous!" he said—and realized once again that he had said it out loud. He shook his head in disgust and entered the galley-cafeteria.

There were two deckhands seated across from each other at one of the six bench-table arrangements. Bibaud he knew should be going off watch in thirty minutes. He shouldn't have been sitting there dealing blackjack past a half-empty coffee cup; but Bibaud was a good man, a seasoned man, and Westholme didn't give it more than a passing thought.

The other deckhand he didn't know. Young, wearing glasses with silver wire rims, thick, blond hair uncut for too long, wiry forearms poking from rolled-up shirt sleeves.

Bibaud looked up briefly as Westholme entered, used his head to make the introductions, moving it back and forth as he shuffled the cards.

"This here is George Tait. George, this is Mister Westholme, the skipper on this thing."

Tait inclined his head and picked up the first of his cards.

"Too late to deal me in?" Westholme asked.

Bibaud grinned at him expansively, his flinty black eyes reflecting the mischief he was famous for. "You want to deal in before you check the cards?" His accent was elaborately thick, loaded with the cadence of French Canadian patois. Most of the crew members he worked with knew he could speak almost flawless English when he wanted to.

"Come on, Ernie," Westholme said. "If you've got it stacked I'll find out. What's the game?"

"Ten cents to get in. Ten cents to raise. You got that kind of money?"

"Will you take a check?" Westholme said. He threw a dime on the table and felt, as he did so, a perceptible lurch of *Haida Noble* to starboard.

"Have you crewed on *Haida Noble* before?" he asked Tait.

"A couple of times this summer."

Westholme looked at the two cards Bibaud had flicked his way. "Hit me," he said. Bibaud dealt him another card. "Hit me again." He added the new card to his hand, shrugged and tossed the hand in. "Maybe I should have looked at that deck after all."

Bibaud chuckled happily and turned his attention to Tait. The new deckhand stood pat. Bibaud dealt himself a card and raised ten cents. Tait met it and raised again. Bibaud threw his hand in.

"Okay, you got blackjack. Lemme see."

"Too late," Tait informed him. "You've got to pay to see my hands."

"You bum, you!" Bibaud said in a good imitation of anger. "I pick you out nice winning cards and you treat me like a dog." He turned to Westholme. "How do you like that!"

From the chrome and hardwood island of the galley the cook called across to Westholme. "What can I fix you, Captain? I've got some real good steaks this trip."

"Something simple," Westholme said. "Coffee, a couple of eggs, bacon." He looked at his watch. "I'll need it in a hurry."

To Tait he said: "Been with the company long?"

"Short of a year. I came over from Oceanic last July."

Oceanic was where they had had the labor trouble, Westholme recalled. "Working on papers?"

Tait nodded and sipped his coffee. "I've got my deep water mate's ticket."

"Good," Westholme said. He might have known the company would crew *Haida Noble* with the best. Tait, with a deep water mate's ticket, was just a deckhand on this run. A year or two from now, with more tug experience to his credit, he'd probably sit for his deep water master's and qualify for his own tug.

Both his first and second officers held deep water master's tickets. Even Bibaud was working toward his towboat master's 350-ton ticket.

"I thought you were supposed to write your towboat master's exam last shore leave," he reminded the stocky deckhand.

Bibaud scowled at him fiercely. "I was a little bit late getting there. An hour, maybe an hour and a half—no more. I was sick, you know. The night before puking all over the place."

"Still going with the same girl?" Westholme inquired pointedly.

Bibaud's face brightened momentarily. "You know JoAnn, hey? Isn't she a woman? That woman deserves to get married to a nice guy . . ." He returned to the subject. "There I am sick like a dog, knocking on the door just a little bit late. The examiner comes to the door and says: 'You can't come in. Come back in three months.' Captain Ogilvie! You know him? Limey bastard!"

"Hard luck," Westholme said, without a trace of sympathy.

"If I was English. If I had one of those names like Smith, or Jones, or"—he looked at the other deckhand—"Tait, he'd let me in that door and I'd have my master's ticket right now. One of these days, you guys . . ."

"The Quebeckers are going to cut themselves loose from Canada and float down the Saint Lawrence to the sea. You better get your master's papers quick, Ernie. You can be captain." Tait rose to his feet and started to slide into his jacket and slicker, lurching heavily against the bolted-down table as *Haida Noble* shrugged off a big sea.

Behind them they heard the crash of crockery and metal, and the soft cursing of the cook. "It's all here, Captain," he said, surveying the jumbled contents of the tray, "but you got a little coffee in with your eggs."

"Sounds good," Westholme said. "I'll try it."

The cook shambled over to the table on wide spread legs and set the plate and cup down in their receptacles. Bibaud had joined Tait in jacket and slicker.

"You gonna need help checking that deck gear," he said. "Man oh man, that's a good sea piling up."

Westholme tried a forkful of bacon, drained his coffee cup and headed for the bridge. "Maybe you can hustle me some kind of a sandwich in an hour or two," he called over his shoulder to the cook. "Keep it clear of the coffee."

"I'll take it up to the bridge myself," the cook assured him. "D'you think there's a storm shaping, Captain?"

"The weather folks didn't tell us there would be a storm," Westholme said cynically, "so there won't be a storm."

Up on the bridge, Lindstrom was making his final entry in the log before going off watch. Galbraith was taking a turn at the wheel, gripping it with a wide stance as the sea continued to attack from the southwest abeam. Westholme acknowledged their brief nods and crossed to the barometer, leaning in close to check the calibrations.

"Twenty-nine eighty," Lindstrom said, turning away from the log. "She hasn't changed a degree all night."

"Just a dirty little squall," Westholme said. He glanced at the chronometer. It was seconds away from 0800. "Might as well get the weather report." He reached over and switched the receiver to 1630 and almost instantly the voice of the Canadian Weather Bureau burst through the background of static:

". . . West Coast cloudy with sunny periods. Winds southwesterly at five to ten knots, seas moderate . . ."

Westholme turned the switch in mid sentence.

"Who makes up that guy's patter," Lindstrom said indignantly, "a junior Boy Scout with a wet finger? I figure the wind at twenty to twenty-five."

Westholme nodded. "And the sea's bigger than that. We'll keep a close eye on it. See you later." He took the wheel from Galbraith. "Get some shuteye, and see if you can round up Tait on your way down. I'll need him on the wheel for an hour or so."

Lindstrom and Galbraith went below, moving with the peculiar stiffness that comes from bracing against the force of a shifting deck. Alone, Westholme scanned the oceanscape in front of him, sweeping to either side. In the early morning light he could see the dark outline of Cape Flattery slightly ahead of him and ten miles to port. Flattery had seen some massive storms and a long parade of doomed ships. Beating in from the open sea, sailing vessels for two centuries had given Cape Flattery a wide berth as they headed for the entrance to Juan de Fuca Strait. Then, with a dropping wind and their sails no longer ballooning, the unfortunate ones found themselves caught in the strong current and tidal forces that moved northward across the mouth of the Strait. When that happened nothing could save them. They ended up on the reefs and beaches of Barkley Sound, their crews drowned and pulverized, their timbers pounded to slivers in a matter of days, set upon by the sledgehammers of the surf.

The surf was rolling in pretty good, Westholme noted. He could see the unbroken white line of it ribboning the foreshore of San Juan Point directly to starboard. The sea was marching, dark and chunky, past the bow of *Haida Noble,* to mount its endless assault on San Juan Point, and Carmanah beyond that, and Pachena still farther beyond—all those points and prominences upon which doomed ships had foundered and would continue to founder even in these days of automatic beacons and warning horns.

He noted that the rain was abating, the wind streaking it like diamond slashes across the glass of the navigation bridge. There were startling tunnels of brilliant blue sky in the tattered cloud cover moving overhead. "Cloudy with sunny periods . . ." the man had said. Maybe so . . . He felt rather than saw Tait standing at his shoulder, and turned to give him the wheel.

"Can you take her for a while, George? She's Kort nozzle-equipped. You'll find she responds without too much fuss."

"I've done a turn at the wheel before now," Tait reminded him expressionlessly. "She handles pretty good." He positioned himself squarely in front of the wheel and almost immediately was called upon to compensate for a larger than usual wave piling in on the port bow. Westholme was satisfied with the deckhand's almost cold assurance.

He went over to the navigation desk and sized up chart 3001, using his eyes like calipers on the familiar configurations of the tortured west coast. Perhaps sixty miles to go. *Haida Noble* was making 8 knots now for comfort's sake. As long as the sea continued to build, he wanted to keep her at that speed. Eight hours to reach the drill rig. They'd have two hours of good light left to put the line on the rig for towing. If the wind died down they could start the tow to Ucluelet Inlet that night. Better to wait until tomorrow morning, he decided. With the rig moving at an easy four knots they could have it secured in the shelter of the inlet by early afternoon.

He crossed over to the VHF radio set and switched to BUTCO 17's private frequency; at a sixty-mile distance the rig was probably out of range, but it was worth a try:

"*Haida Noble* calling BUTCO 17. *Haida Noble* calling

BUTCO 17. Come in please." He switched to receive and was greeted with humming silence from the speaker.

"Out of range," Tait told him rather than questioned.

Westholme tried again, and this time had luck. "Hello, *Haida Noble*. What can we do for you?" inquired a cheerful voice.

"Captain Westholme here. Can I have words with the rig super?"

The new voice introduced itself in a relaxed Texas drawl: "Charlie Knight here, Captain. Whereabouts y'all located?"

"Mid-channel, Juan de Fuca Strait. San Juan Point to starboard. We've got something like sixty miles to go. How are you riding?"

"Tolerably well, Captain, but it would be real nice to be under tow and heading for Ucluelet. We got a wind building up out here."

"That's our problem too," Westholme said. "Keep smiling. We'll have a line on you by four o'clock, all being well."

"1600 hours. We're going to hold you to that, Captain, and I'm not funning. All being well or not, if this wind keeps on we're going to put the legs down starting at 1600 hours on the button. There's no way I'm going to drift this rig onto the beach."

"Nothing to worry about," Westholme assured him. "Get yourself cleaned up for company in eight hours."

"Captain," the Texan said in a flat voice, "we got all the company we can handle right now. Thirty-seven Russkie fish boats three or four miles west of us, sitting there like they were going to spend the winter."

"Sit tight," Westholme said. "We'll keep this frequency open from now on."

"You do that, Captain," the rig superintendant said, and signed off.

9 . . .

Volkoff tried first of all to use the helicopter to scout the fleet, but the repair to the rotor blade was not completed and was, in fact, turning out to be more difficult than expected.

"I can take you up in three—more like four hours," the pilot offered, "but she's not going anywhere right now."

Finally Volkoff settled for a ride in the drill tower elevator up to the 100-foot level. There, with the gusty southwesterly driving rain fragments into his eyes, he tried to train his binoculars on the Russian flotilla. It was a frustrating exercise. The not-uncomfortable movement of the drill rig at deck level was magnified 100 feet up into a sickening oscillation in slow motion. His high-powered glasses brought the fishing boats close—when he was able to fix them in his field of vision —but the five-mile interval of moving water compressed and disturbed the scene. The boats heaved one way and the drill tower swung another until Volkoff began to feel the first uneasiness of motion sickness.

The fleet was strung out along an irregular four-mile course, ranging back another three or four miles. It was impossible to count them, let alone fix his lenses on an individual boat for any length of time. He had to content himself with a general review of the types of vessels and their apparent activity. Principally they were trawlers and seiners, not one of them less than 150 feet in length, and most of them well over 200 feet, with deck gear capable of handling formidable nets.

Not one of the boats he was able to study for any length of time was without signs of wear and tear. This group had been at sea for some months. On the far edge of the group, like a buttress between the smaller vessels and the open sea, a rusty-hulled tanker sat and watched.

Closer in, two cannery ships in the 10,000-ton class, spurted feathers of steam whipped away by the wind. Obviously they were processing a catch. At the stern of each, port and starboard, in spite of the running sea, fishing vessels were discharging their cargo. He couldn't identify the species, and regretted it. A preponderance of salmon would have been further evidence to support the claim of the Canadian fishermen that the salmon resource was being intercepted and depleted on the high sea.

He tried desperately to train his binoculars on further details, feeling the thick, upswelling spasm in his throat as the swaying movement of the tower continued to work on his balance mechanism. What was that? His glasses found it and lost it again, fully half of its hull concealed by the larger bulk of one of the cannery ships. He swallowed hard to keep his stomach down and tried to find the vessel again. Finding it, he tried to compensate for the movement of the tower. There it was, and there could be no doubt in his mind this time. The conformation of the bow and superstructure, the unusual arrangement of equipment on the foredeck were completely familiar to him. He had seen the prototype of this vessel in Baltic waters adjacent to Kaliningrad during the International Oceanographic Conference in 1966. Perhaps it was the same vessel, *Nikolai Zubov*. If not it was one of her class built in Poland in 1964, designed and equipped for oceanographic research. There had been quite a stir at the Conference when the Russians refused delegates a tour of the impressive new vessel.

A strong gust of wind threw him off balance and the ship disappeared from his field of vision, replaced by an expanse of whitecapped water. The motion sickness had gotten to him now. He stumbled over to the elevator cage and pressed the button, willing himself to keep the contents of his stomach in place.

Knight was waiting for him when he stepped out of the cage onto the drill deck. He grinned at the pallid, tight expression. "What's the matter, Mike? You don't like the view from the top?"

Volkoff was feeling immeasureably better already. "The view is great . . . well worth the trip."

"Let's get out of this goddam wind," Knight said. He led the way to the communications shack, scowling up at the moving pattern of cloud and blue sky. "The helicopter can't start ferrying the crew until two o'clock at the earliest. Fifty men and their gear to Ucluelet before dark! We don't stand the chance of a snowball in hell." He opened the door and ushered Volkoff in, and watched him as he moved to the radar screen to study the pattern.

"Look here, Charlie," Volkoff said. "We've got some interesting people in the neighborhood." He poked his finger at a cluster of blips and waited for the band of light to come around again. "This big one is a cannery ship, a ten-thousand tonner."

"Imagine that," Knight said drily.

Volkoff ignored him. "And this one here, tucked in behind, maybe two ship's lengths away, is a *Nikolai Zubov* class oceanographic research vessel. Maybe it's *Nikolai Zubov* herself . . . Twenty-six hundred tons displacement, two hundred and ninety-five feet long. Tremendous lab facilities and accomodation for seventy scientists . . ."

Knight cut in, interested now. "You sure about that? What's a ship like that doing, keeping company with a bunch of rusty trawlers?"

"Anybody's guess," Volkoff said, "but I'd know her anywhere. She was the envy of most of the delegates at the Moscow Conference. The United States didn't have anything to compare with her . . . and as far as I can remember there are eleven of them in her class. We've got to send a signal to the office right now, Charlie."

"What for? She's entitled to snoop around. Those are international waters."

"Because she's carrying new stuff on her deck and masts up forward. I made out a fair-sized golf ball mounted above the navigation bridge. God knows what she's got mounted astern. The cannery ship was blocking the view."

"What the hell's a golf ball?"

"A protector globe for electronic stuff, powerful antenna, that sort of thing. She's got some impressive-looking direction finders and troposcattering sensors up on the foremast. We ought to let the office know, Charlie."

Knight wasn't inclined to be excited. "Go ahead if you want to, but my betting is they know all about it. The U. S. Coast Guard planes have been scouting that fleet all the way north. The Canadians will be on to it by now. You can't keep a boat like that a secret."

"The point is," Volkoff said patiently, "that a first class, superlatively equipped oceanographic research vessel is sitting five miles west of BUTCO 17. It's not a coincidence, Charlie—and we don't know what that ship's capabilities are. This drill rig is a little bit more than a tourist attraction. You and I know it. How long will it take for them to know it?"

"We're inside the Twelve Mile," Knight reminded him. "If they come over for a look they'll find themselves in Canadian custody. I say live and let live, Mike. We'll be out of here in twelve hours." He looked at his watch. "The next weather report should be coming through in twenty minutes."

The telephone rang and the radio operator picked it up, listened for a few moments, spoke a brief word into the receiver and hung up.

"That was Amos over in the lab," he said. "He thought you'd want to know the barometer has dropped from twenty-nine eighty to twenty-nine sixty in the past half hour."

Outside, the wind pummeled the wall of the shack with new vigor. The light coming through the uncurtained window seemed to have lost its morning brilliance. It possessed clarity, a startling clarity, but it was devoid of warmth, as though it had filtered in from the distant horizon and had been chilled by the sea.

Knight pulled up his coat collar and headed for the door. "I'm going to put the goose to those mechanics. That helicopter should be up and flying by now."

10 . . .

Neither weather station ship *Union* nor weather station ship *Nectar* could be faulted for paying small attention to the minor system that passed them by two days previously. Spawned northwest of the Hawaiian Islands, the hurricane infant crawled past them blindly and mindlessly in the night, its muscles strengthening, its rage beginning to show in fitful squalls and darkened patches of troubled water on the face of the moderate sea. Thirty hours later a United States Coast Guard weather plane found it grown to a full gale, relatively localized and butting its quarrelsome head against a formidable cold front reaching north to the Arctic. The position was one thousand miles due west of Sacramento. The direction of the system was northeast moving at 15 to 20 knots. The time was 1600 hours and the crew of the weather plane had little doubt that the marauding wind would beat itself to death against the south-ranging front in the hours of darkness.

What happened in those next hours will never be known. The ways of hurricanes are not fully understood. Unpredictable, refusing to conform to a pattern, they long ago inspired some female-soured weatherman to bestow upon them women's names. This one, in three days' time would be officially accorded the name of Faith.

Faith! A totally inappropriate name for the incredible hag that grew to maturity that night, going into her whirling dance, her shroud of wind and cloud spinning out from her in a deadly pirouette almost three hundred miles in diameter. When finally a portrait was taken of her and relayed back by weather satellite, it revealed what could have been the top of a monstrous head, the hair unkempt and wild, twisted in a counterclockwise spiral across Faith's inexorably moving skull.

The winds in her spiral attained velocities of 100 knots as she plunged erratically north and east. By dawn she was screaming ahead at 30 knots, pushing giant seas ahead of her, their surfaces marbled with foam, their crests torn to shredded spindrift. Miles ahead in inlets and coastal shallows as yet untouched by her wind, a tide mounted out of phase with the lunar tides, unnerving to those who read its meaning. Above, the sky was streaked with high, far-reaching clouds, their line of travel northeast and moving fast. Rain began to fall, driven by a fitful, 25 knot wind skimming the white foam off the building sea.

Mindless and vicious—nature in a paranoid rage—Faith raked the ocean with her claws and goaded it into destruction matching her own.

If any shipping lay in her path, it issued no warning. It was not until 1000 hours of the following day that the first signal was received, rechecked, processed, and then incorporated into a special weather report. A lonely NOMAD, a moored weather buoy, bobbing three hundred miles west of Portland, Oregon, caught the right edge of Faith as she passed over. NOMAD's instruments recorded the data faithfully and accurately. Her transmitter continued to function for twenty-two minutes after the full force of the hurricane struck. In that time she relayed running information that caused the duty officer at the U. S. Weather Bureau station to doubt the facts. He waited the full twenty-two minutes, until the transmitter failed, before he proceeded with a final deciphering of the information. Air pressure had dropped twenty-one millibars in three hours; wind velocity had ranged from 62 to 103 knots; position, 45 degrees north, 130 degrees west; direction from the southwest. Exact direction and rate of movement would call for more refined measurements.

He was on the telephone filing his report with Weather Information within minutes. Behind him another duty man was issuing instructions to the standby captain of the weather plane. Hurricane Faith had attracted attention, the attention she deserved. She had her audience. Soon she would have her victims.

11 . . .

At 1100 hours Westholme had no doubt they were heading into trouble. The wind velocity exceeded 45 knots, wailing through the standing rigging of the masts, driving rain in a straight line across the port side windows. He tapped the barometer again and turned to Tait:

"We've got ourselves some kind of a record. She's down to twenty-nine inches on the nose."

On the port beam a gray mountain of water heaved itself up. It was as though the entire ocean had placed its shoulder below that wave and pushed upward. The wind chewed white fringes on its curling edge. *Haida Noble* dipped her bow momentarily and then climbed up on the gray-green mass, angling through it and plummeting down the other side to bury her foredeck under water.

"That sea is bigger than the wind," Westholme observed. "The real stuff hasn't reached us yet. Ever worked through a hurricane?"

Tait shook his head and braced himself for the next wave. "I've been through tougher than this, though. You think we've got a real blow coming?"

"All the signs are up. We've had an increasing sea running for the past four hours, even when the wind was moderate. Barometer's dropping as though it was going to lose its bottom. The wind has doubled in the past hour. There's something big southwest of us, that's certain. I think we'd better have a talk with BUTCO."

He reached for the switch on the VHF set:

"BUTCO 17. *Haida Noble* here. Are you receiving? Over."

Instantly the voice came through, brisk and cheerful as ever. "Nice to hear your voice. Mr. Knight was about to call you . . ."

Knight's voice cut in abruptly. "We're getting strong winds

up here now, Captain. The waves are piling up real good. What kind of speed you making?"

"No better than before," Westholme said. "I think we'd better brace ourselves for a good blow, Mr. Knight. That's what I called about. We can't tow you in this stuff—and it's going to get worse. We can put a line on you and hold you, but we can't tow you."

"Look here, Captain, this rig'll turn into a sailboat real soon now. The wind will blow it from here to hell and back. How far are y'all away from us?"

"Six hours," Westholme said. "A good six hours."

"All right, Captain, we can't wait six hours. I'm not taking a chance on those anchors dragging or an anchor chain snapping. I can't put the legs down after we start to drift."

"That's my point," Westholme persisted. "Put the legs down now. Get her rock solid, and lower your wind resistance."

"If that's all you called about," Knight said, "we're wasting one another's time. I was going to put the legs down anyhow."

"Crusty bastard," Westholme heard Tait say behind him.

"Good," Westholme said. "We're both thinkers. We'll be with you in six hours, put a line on board, and ride this thing out together."

"That's real sociable," Knight said. "Shake a leg."

"Russians still hanging around?"

The humorless chuckle came through clearly. "That's the one little bit of joy we're getting. Those Russkies are tossing around out there like corks in a cauldron."

"So are we," Westholme told him. "I'm not laughing."

"Shake a leg," Knight told him, and signed off.

Westholme crossed over to stand beside Tait, reaching up to tune in the transmitter-receiver. He selected a frequency and turned the volume up. The recorded voice boomed in halfway through a sentence:

". . . warning. Hurricane force winds reported approaching west coast in north easterly direction. Established position, 0800, 45 degrees north, 130 degrees west; system moving between 25 and 30 knots; winds peaking to 120 knots, approximate diameter of system, 300 miles. All shipping take warning. Hurricane force winds . . ."

Westholme turned the volume down and returned to the chart table. "That would put the trouble about three hundred miles from us at 0800." He looked at Tait. "Two more hours and we could be in the middle of it. With the local prevailing winds helping out, the strongest winds are going to be on the right hand side of the system—the landward side. So-o . . ." He scratched his head and stared out at the seas piling past *Haida Noble*'s bow, as though looking for an answer in the driving rain and spindrift. "What we'd better do is give this beauty a better margin of safety. Bring her around to port, George. Two-ninety should do it. We'll hold her on that course for as long as we can. I want to get more water between us and the rocks."

Tait looked dubious, but he swung the wheel over to put *Haida Noble* on a compass course of 290. The tug was taking the full brunt of the seas on her port side now, causing her to roll alarmingly close to a broaching position.

"She can take it," Westholme said. "I want to run on this course as long as we can. Then, when the big stuff comes we can decide whether to go with the wind or to turn and face it." He returned to Tait, bracing himself on the sharply tilting deck. "I'd like you to go below and raise Brad Fenton for me."

Tait lifted an inquiring brow.

"Fenton—the second officer." He reached over and took the wheel from the deckhand. There was a certain lack of enthusiasm in this man. He couldn't put his finger on it. He was cool. He knew his business, but there was no joy in him. "I'd like you to get him up here in a hurry," he said, his voice just a little more brittle. Then he leaned ahead and squinted through the rain pattern on the glass, aiming *Haida Noble*'s handsome bow down the green trough of the troubled sea.

This was going to be interesting. By now the office types would know about the weather situation. It was their option to call him back—call *Haida Noble* back, because that would be the main concern, to remove the flagship from possible danger. On the other occasions they had had no option: that time, four hundred miles from Yokohama, with two rusting Liberties on the line, holding tight while the wind built to 80, 90 knots and swung the old derelicts like waterlogged kites. The company couldn't do anything about that one, and *Haida Noble* had come through with flying colors. Westholme had received a bonus and a dinner in the Terminal City Club when he returned from the assignment. There should have been some way to reward *Haida Noble*.

The salvage of the *Hellas?* Well that was in a class by itself. All those days, storm after storm, winding up with the tail end of Hurricane Farida . . . and all those people lined along the beaches cheering as they came in through Lions' Gate. They were cheering *Haida Noble*.

Beside him the ship-to-shore buzzed sharply. He picked up the receiver, anticipating the voice. It was Harmon, Jake to his friends, putting the full authority of his 200-pound frame into his voice. He was a good administrator, with maybe a shade too much push.

"Chris?"

"Speaking. Is that you, Jake?"

"Right. Christy, I suppose you've heard the weather report?"

"Heard it! Jake, we're in the middle of it. It's shaping up to be a good one."

"What's it really look like, Chris? I mean . . ."

There was no way Westholme could hold both the receiver and the wheel. "Look, Jake . . ."

At that moment he felt Fenton's hand reach under his armpit and take control. He slid away from the wheel and concentrated on the ship-to-shore. "I think there's going to be a lot of wind, Jake. I've talked to the rig . . ."

"I know, I know. They're putting down the legs."

"You call the shot, Jake. There's still time for me to turn around and take her back."

"I'm not sure there's any advantage," Harmon said. "That goddam wind has got a three-hundred-mile spread. It'll take in the Gulf of Georgia. You'd be pounded by it all the way home. How much time do you think you have?"

"Hard to tell. An hour and a half maybe. I could duck into Port Renfrew . . ."

"What I am trying to say," Harmon cut in quickly, "is that we've got a good contract with BUTCO. If you think *Haida Noble* can take it I think you should get up there and stand by. Show them we're trying. You know what I mean?"

"I'm with you, Jake," Westholme said. "I promised them I'd be in the vicinity around 1600 hours. I think they're counting on us."

"What about you and the others? This could be pretty dirty . . ."

"No problem, Jake, most of us have been through worse."

"Good enough! Look, I'll give your wife a call. Tell her I've been talking to you. Tell her everything's fine. Can I give her a message for you, Chris?"

"The way you put it was pretty good," Westholme said. "Tell her everything is fine."

"We'll keep in touch," Harmon assured him. "I'll be here until 1500 hours and then Andy will take over. Any kind of decision you want to make, we'll back you up."

"Thanks," Westholme said. "I'd better go about my business now."

"Good luck, Christy."

Westholme placed the receiver back on its hook.

Without removing his eyes from the heaving trough along which *Haida Noble* plunged, Fenton said, "The VP?"

Westholme nodded. "My hunch was he'd want us to run for shelter. He's asking us to stand by BUTCO 17."

Fenton shrugged. "It's his tug. What do you think of this stuff?"

"You were with me on that Yokohama run. It started like this. There's always a chance the cold front will force it out to sea."

"That's true," Fenton said. He thrust chest and belly against the wheel as *Haida Noble* plunged into a steep roll to starboard. Westholme wedged himself against one of the radar housings and watched a needle move on a dial on the instrument panel.

"Forty-seven degrees of roll that time," he said. "If we wait too long it could be embarrassing."

Tait and Fenton remained silent. Both of them knew the tug's low center of gravity would give it a critical angle of roll approaching 55 degrees. No real danger yet. The waves were increasing in size, but they remained uniform both in interval and impact. At the moment the sea was dangerous but predictable, well within the capabilities of *Haida Noble*. What could destroy her in this vulnerable position was the unpredictable—the first enormous wave erected by the hurricane, 20 or 30 feet in height, slamming the hull far over, pressing down upon it and pinning it for the finishing assault of other great waves following behind.

12 . . .

The tug rose on a crest and Westholme took a sharp look port and starboard, squinting through the spray-fouled glass. "We're well clear of Flattery, but I'd like to put more water between us and Pachena Point." The dangerous point lay fifteen miles to starboard, close enough with the prevailing current and the sea running at it together.

"Pick a number, Brad," he said to Fenton. "Fifty. Let's make it fifty. The first time the angle of roll reaches fifty we'll quit this and set a straight course for BUTCO 17. Right now I want all the water we can grab before things get tough."

"We're going to have ourselves one hell of a following sea when we change course for the rig," Fenton observed.

"Have to tough it out. If things get really bad we'll come about and ride into the stuff." He made it sound easy—and definite.

"The cook's having a hemorrhage," Tait reported drily. "The galley looks like elephants ran through it."

"He should know better," Westholme said sharply. "Everything should be stowed for heavy weather. That's what I called you for, Brad. I know everything's O.K., but I think you'd better look things over. Go along with him, Tait, and lend a hand. Start with the wire room and the salvage gear lockers. I don't want one of those spare anchors running wild and punching holes in us when the going gets rough."

"Bibaud and me checked out the deck gear a while back," Tait reminded him. "Things looked tight enough there."

"I'll need you back here as soon as you're finished," he told Tait. "Brad, you can cool your heels until your watch. But keep your shoes on."

Brad grinned at him. "Here we go again," he said. "I hear tell you have thirty days shore time coming. Any guy who'll take a hurricane over thirty days with a woman like Lee . . ." He shook his head in elaborate disbelief and departed with Tait following behind.

Almost guiltily Westholme turned his mind back to Lee. For the past two hours she had been out of his mind, crowded into a dark recess while the business of the sea took over. Just a few days, he had told her, just a routine trip out to the West Coast and back. This storm would change all that—add a day, three days, quite possibly a week. By then whatever she felt now would have had a chance to eat deeper into her being. He should have stayed ashore while there was still a possibility of killing the worm that was destroying her—destroying both of them. He wondered what she was doing now. Almost noon; three minutes short of 1200 hours. Getting ready for a solitary lunch, he guessed. Grilling a cheese sandwich to go with a cup of coffee. Turning up the radio for the twelve o'clock news. Listening for the weather and realizing bitterly that news of the storm was bad news for her, delaying his return indefinitely.

He glanced at the chronometer and turned up the volume on the radio receiver. The weather report would be coming through on 1630 frequency. The corner of his eye caught and assessed the approach of a new wave. Instinctively he knew it was a rogue, higher, broader, more aggressive than anything preceding it. Seventy-five yards away it rose up and wiped out the distant outline of Cape Flattery, and without hesitation he swung the wheel hard to starboard and reached over to ram the throttles on the remote control to full speed ahead. Almost immediately he felt the great tug respond. Ten thousand horsepower, its thrust augmented by the Kort nozzle steering system, spun the tug to starboard in the blue-green trough. *Haida Noble*'s bow sideswiped the trailing edge of the last passing wave. The turn was almost completed when the rogue wave struck, mounting the stern and rising just short of bridge deck level before it parted and passed by. He felt the stern of *Haida Noble* thrust down by the force of tons of water. Then, as the foaming mountain passed, the vessel hung suspended on the trailing edge of the wave, bow pointed at the gray, streaked sky before it slid back, tobogganing stern first into the trough. From below, penetrating thinly through the sounds of the wind and sea, Westholme heard the sounds of metal and wood colliding.

Near his left ear the recorded voice continued with the weather report. ". . . hurricane force winds. Storm center at 1130 hours, 47 degrees north, 120 degrees 50 minutes west; bearing north northeast at approximately 30 knots; wind velocities right semicircle gusting to 110 knots; wind velocities left semicircle gusting to 93 knots; estimated diameter 300 plus miles. Warning to all shipping . . ."

"Nice to have plenty of warning," Tait shouted laconically behind him. He was dragging himself toward the security of a stanchion, working hard against the tilting deck.

"What was all the commotion down below?"

"A rack of welding tanks broke loose in the machine shop. Galbraith and Bibaud are lashing it down. I thought I'd better hustle back here."

There was no feeling of forward movement in the following sea, although both wind and current were working with the tug's engines now. *Haida Noble* seemed to slide back on the slope of each passing wave, none of which were breaking higher than the afterdeck.

"You didn't waste time changing course," Tait said.

"What does the barometer read?" Westholme demanded.

"28.90 . . ." For the first time Tait's voice carried a trace of inflection. "I've never seen a barometer drop that way—in three hours."

"The way I see it," Westholme said, "we don't have much of a choice. The wind hasn't changed direction one way or another, which means the eye of this thing, if it has an eye, is going to pass close. There's a twenty-knot difference in wind left to right so there's not much point in trying to run for the easy side. There isn't any easy side to this one. We'll stay on this course and try and get as close to the drill rig as we can before . . ."

As though responding to a cue the voice of BUTCO's operator penetrated the sea noises:

"*Haida Noble. Haida Noble.* Are you receiving us? Over."

Westholme turned the wheel over to Tait and let the sharply sloping deck propel him to the set. "*Haida Noble* here. Westholme."

It was the Texan's voice now. Exasperated, querulous. "Captain, what the hell kind of weather you throwing at us?"

"We're in for a blow, Knight. You're getting the reports. Are you standing on bottom yet?"

"We'll have the legs bedded in another ten minutes. Man, we've got waves coming at us like there was no tomorrow. Where *are* you guys anyway!"

"Just about level with Pachena Point. We've got the wind and tide with us now. We'll make better time."

"Well, shake a leg, goddam it!"

"Listen," Westholme said flatly, "we need to get there more than you need us right now. You're the only breakwater on this whole stretch of coast, so stop your bitching."

"Nothing personal, Captain," the Texan said. "It's been a tough day, that's all."

"I hate to spoil the rest of it," Westholme said, "but it's going to get tougher."

13 . . .

It rained all night in New York. It was still raining when the Sea Bed Committee reconvened at two o'clock the following afternoon. The tall windows dominating one entire side of the conference room were streaked and running with a gray sheet of water symbolizing, it seemed to the chairman, the atmosphere of the meeting.

When, three hours later, tempers began to wear thin, the rain obligingly began to fall harder, driving in big drops against the window wall until the impacts became faintly audible in the dramatic pauses employed by the hotly debating Committee members.

"I commend the chairman for his masterful summing up of the business of this Committee undertaken in the Twenty-fourth Session . . . history!" The representative from Pakistan struck his desk lightly with a rolled bundle of notes, which was in itself a dramatic departure from his usually controlled manner. "I regret, however, that he was obliged to take the time to do this, and I believe the chairman shares my regret that such a reminder should be necessary.

"His message is eminently clear. We have wasted time. We are wasting time at this very moment. While I and my delegation were prepared, in the beginning years of this Committee, to share with everyone here the principle of caution—the principle of laying proper groundwork for the ultimate administration of international seas for the common benefit of all nations, I am now inclined to believe that what we accept as caution is, in fact, a delaying action imposed, perhaps not deliberately, by certain of the major nations . . . nations determined to chart the resources of the international seas and lay claim to them before an international body of law can be framed to either limit their activities or share these resources among all nations . . ." He was obliged to stop for breath, and in the interval, Yugoslavia stepped in:

"Mr. Chairman, I must rise on behalf of my delegation, to protest the strong innuendo delivered by the representative from Pakistan. There can be no doubt he alludes to the extensive oceanographic research program being conducted by the USSR in many of the world's international waters. His implication is that this is an act of exploitation on the part of the USSR, the benefits of which will be withheld from all other nations. The Socialist States propose to share these benefits with established and emerging nations. This intention is enunciated in the records of this Committee.

"On the other hand, if the delegation for Pakistan is directing its allegations against the exploitive actions of the capitalist monopolies in the international seas, then we agree readily that there is cause for alarm. Traditionally these monopolies have worked from the premise that possession is nine tenths of the law. Having entrenched themselves in international waters, they will not be easily moved, nor is there any reason to believe, on the basis of past performance, that they will share the vast profits extracted from the oceans with anyone other than their shareholders."

The head of the United States delegation cut in sharply. "Mr. Chairman, I suggest that we are achieving nothing by descending to unfounded allegations . . ."

"Is it not true," Yugoslavia called across the room, "that a United States consortium is, at this moment, preparing to ocean-mine rich deposits of manganese nodules from an extensive area three hundred miles north of Hawaii?"

"And that the USSR is deep-dredging gold in the Sea of Japan?" the United States retorted.

The chairman called sharply for order. "As the representative for the United States suggests, this meeting is in danger of deteriorating into something totally unconstructive. I recognize the representative from Canada."

The Canadian chose to speak from a standing position. "Mr. Chairman, I can only concur with your own preamble this afternoon, in which you demonstrate how little we appear to have achieved in the years since the formation of this Committee.

"We have heard reference to international oceans this afternoon, but we do not yet have a clear definition of what international waters are, or what they will be in the event that legislation, not yet formulated or agreed to, delineates them.

"We have not yet come to grips in an effective way with the critical problem of the disarmament of the sea bed. While the USA and the USSR appear to agree in principle that the sea bed should not be used as a battleground or a base of attack, there is no clear evidence that the sea bed is being disarmed. On the contrary there is evidence that its armament continues in a multiplicity of ways.

"While delays on the part of this Committee and at the level of the General Assembly itself may not be deliberate, they do give nations with the technology and the economic capability time to stake claims, so-to-speak, and to consolidate positions in what are now regarded as international waters.

"The danger is that once these positions are consolidated, international legislation will have to proceed, not in spite of them, but to accommodate them.

"I submit, Mr. Chairman, that tensions could quite easily build over the issues of the international oceans. At this moment we are not equipped, even in a rudimentary form, to confront these issues with unanimity. Presented with a crisis of whatever magnitude, I doubt seriously that we have established either the authority or the accord to provide a solution."

The Russian delegate was standing. "My delegation interprets that statement as defeatist in the extreme—the opinion of a nation expert in the giving of advice, but without the means or strength to accept the realities of responsibility.

"The Soviet States have not wasted time theorizing. We have not and we will not stand by while capitalist monopolistic forces establish claim to the open oceans—the common heritage of all nations. We will not stand by and watch rape in the name of . . ."

The chairman rapped his gavel repeatedly, overcoming the words of the speaker. He pushed his lectern aside and pulled his papers together in front of him as he addressed the Committee.

"It is now five o'clock, gentlemen. It would appear that we have spent the better part of this afternoon agreeing that we do not agree in certain important areas, and I see no indication that further discussion would be of value today. I call this meeting adjourned and request you to reconvene here tomorrow at the same time."

To his left the tall glass windows streamed with water against the deep black of the evening sky. Far in the depths a plane swam by searching for La Guardia, its navigation lights blinking feebly like phosphor beads on a lost sea creature. The low cloud engulfed and extinguished them. The illusion was very much as though the sea creature had drowned.

14 . . .

Volkoff stood huddled in the entrance to the recreation room-dining hall on the deck of BUTCO 17. Minutes before, the massive pumps and hydraulic systems on the rig had completed the flooding and lowering of the legs. With the gigantic tripod firmly planted on the gently shelving continental shelf in 130 feet of water, she stood as steady as a piece of the mainland, in spite of the mounting waves battering through the maze of tubular bracings in her understructure.

He noted with considerable satisfaction that all perceptible deck movement had ceased although loose tarpaulins and lashings on various parts of the metal island were flying horizontally in the 70-mile-an-hour wind. Many of the approaching waves were cresting at 25 and 30 feet now, but with the deck of the rig riding 50 feet above the surface of the sea, the margin of safety was ample.

Butting their heads against the slashing rain, the roughnecks struggled to secure fuel drums and other potentially dangerous objects capable of being hurled into action either by the wind or an inordinately high sea. Three of them were completing the stringing of one-inch nylon rope between the various buildings and shelter areas on the deck. If the wind attained the predicted velocity of 100 knots it would be foolhardy to venture anywhere in the open without a safety line—which would serve as well as a guide line, because with winds of that force filling the air with spray and debris, men became blind.

An empty grease bucket tumbled past him, was kicked into the air by a vicious gust and disappeared from sight beyond the far edge of the deck. Not long now, Volkoff decided. The sounds of the wind were louder, more urgent, as they shredded themselves against taut guy lines, and the intricate latticework of girders and structural steel. Beyond the wind was the incredible, encircling roar of the ocean, made resonant by the hollow members of the drill rig's underpinnings. The waves approached in an endless procession, each the duplicate of the one preceding it, each bulling ahead at the same speed and interval as every other, each attacking, curling around, climbing the squat caissons in an effort to reach the deck, then raging over and through the tubular supports and crossmembers that gave the island its strength. The identity of each wave was destroyed as it passed through the rig's enormous supporting grid. On the trailing edge of the rig each emerged as a broad wall of froth and spindrift 400 feet wide. Five hundred yards beyond the steel island its shape began to reveal itself again. A thousand yards out and it was up and running, its blue-green neck arched like a charging bull's, indestructible, galloping to the distant reefs of Amphitrite.

Volkoff marveled at the enormity and the chaos of the sound, all of it contained in the unbroken cadence of the oncoming waves. Ahead of him he could see the helicopter

66

tugging at its moorings. The main blades had been lashed down but the wind was keening around the airfoil edges and the blades seemed to lift in the struggle with their ropes. The helicopter had not been repaired until the wind velocity was too great to risk a flight. So all of the crew remained on the rig—fifty-three roughnecks and technicians.

What a hell of a mess! He was frankly and bitterly disappointed. Having built up the expectation of a four-week leave and come within a few hours of achieving it, he felt something approaching a personal grudge against the storm. The rig could be pinned down by this weather for a week or more. There was the outside chance that trouble could develop. He would feel considerably better with BUTCO 17 in deeper water. He would feel considerably better if he was the hell off this rig, getting ready for a night out in San Francisco.

The door swung open behind him and the assistant geologist stood beside him for a moment, bracing himself for the dash to the lab.

"Isn't this great!" he exulted. "I've never seen anything like this in my life. Never!"

"Once is enough," Volkoff shouted in his ear. "Where you heading?"

"Over to the lab to wrap up the core samples. Wouldn't want to get them scrambled. Isn't this a three-ring circus though." He hurled a long wolf call into the wind, grabbed the safety line and plunged out into the eerie, two o'clock twilight, his coat and trousers flapping around him like the scales and wings of a giant bug.

Volkoff watched his stumbling course until he reached the lab door and ducked inside, then turned and entered the recreation hall. Half the crew were inside, playing cards, shooting the breeze; a few were huddled around the closed circuit TV set watching a dated movie they had all seen earlier in the week: *Five Easy Pieces;* Jack Nicholson playing the part of a drill rig roughneck. The crew was leaning in critically to pick out mistakes in the detail, and Volkoff chose to see the irony rather than the humor in it.

He cast his eyes around for Knight and found him in the far corner crouched over a cup of coffee, making an argumentative point with the geologist. He picked up a chair, carried it over and sat down, aware as he did so, that the crazy sounds of the storm were filling the room, circling it, coming at him from every wall, from the ceiling and floor.

"Steve bumped into me on the way over to the lab. He seems to have the idea the company sent us this weather as a bonus. Either that or he's on grass."

"We should get a bonus for this," Knight stated flatly. "The company should have had us out of here two weeks ago."

"That's what I said last night," Volkoff reminded him.

"Not that I recall," Knight said belligerently. He was in a bad mood, dragging viciously on his cigarette.

"Where do we stand in relation to that wind?" the geologist asked. "Are we going to get the worst of it, the edge of it? What are you guessing?"

"I've been watching it for the past half hour," Volkoff said. "If we were on either side of it there should be a wind deviation one way or another. There isn't a deviation so we must be close to its central line of approach."

"That's bad," Knight grumbled. "Couldn't be worse."

Volkoff shook his head. "Not necessarily. With luck we'll miss the worst of it."

"What's to choose between 93 knots and 110 knots?" Knight demanded. "The company is going to hear about this, if it means my job."

"If the thing has got an eye," Volkoff continued, "we could get a breather when the center reaches us; an hour or two to clean up before the tail end of it gets here."

"Great!" Knight said savagely. "You got me feeling better already." He pushed his chair back and stood up. "I'm going over to the radio shack and get the latest bad news. You coming?"

"Think I'll get some bunk time," Volkoff decided. "Things could get interesting in the next hour or two."

"We've got it a lot easier than those Russian boats out there," the geologist called after Knight's retreating back. He winked at Volkoff. "We ought to be counting our blessings, Charlie."

"He's got a lot on his mind," Volkoff said. "I feel for him."

He took off his windbreaker, slung it over his arm, and made his way back to his room, using the short cut through the kitchen into the service corridor. Volkoff had no desire to step into the teeth of the wind until the need was absolutely imperative.

In his room he stretched his frame out on the comfortable bunk and pulled a blanket up over him. He wasn't cold. The room temperature stood at seventy, but the many voices of the storm, the awareness of it pushing against the insulated walls of his quarters, the knowledge of the rain now falling in horizontal sheets and thundering on the roof above him instilled a coldness in him. Volkoff had seen many of nature's violent faces. He thought he knew the sea at its worst. But this thing surpassed his experience.

He didn't expect to sleep. He knew he wouldn't. Lying there he tried to focus his ears on one individual sound—one sound familiar to him—something he could befriend: rain driving against the window pane, the rattle of a loose aerial wire on the roof, the whipping of a tarpaulin; but he could distinguish nothing. The rage of the thing outside had drawn every sound together into one concerted roar, all of it contained somehow in the unwavering metronome of the oncoming waves. Not by one second did the impact of those seas vary. He listened intently, trying to detect or sense one break in the cadence of the waves. No break . . . unchanging. He slept.

15 . . .

When he wakened again it was to the sound of a splintering crash and a sudden gust of wind and wetness across his face. The room was in darkness and he groped frantically for the light switch before he found it and turned it on. Outside, all hell had broken loose. There were no lows in the wind sounds now. The exterior darkness was filled with a hoarse, falsetto scream. Impaled in his doorframe was the remains of an empty nail keg hurled like a cannonball from the muzzle of the hurricane. Rainwater rifled through the jagged hole and trickled down the opposite wall.

He rolled out of his bunk and charged at the door, trailing his blanket behind him. The wreckage of the keg was wedged in tight, but he managed to pull it clear, the loose staves spinning into the room on the dripping shaft of wind. The blanket was totally useless; balled up it didn't come close to plugging the ragged hole. He tossed it onto the back of a chair and scrambled around the room picking up shoes, and getting his personal gear out of the path of the water beginning to move across the floor.

He looked at his watch . . . 7:40! He had been asleep five hours in the middle of this. In his closet he located the rubberized pants and jacket he used for foul weather on the rig. He climbed into them, working in a violence of sound that had a physical dimension to it. Rubber bush boots completed his preparations. He decided to leave his quarters the way he came, along the service corridor, through the kitchen and the recreation-dining room.

In the dining area a group of exhausted, drenched roughnecks were trying to draw some comfort from hot coffee and cigarettes. "Any idea where Charlie Knight is?" Volkoff called to them.

One of the men tossed a thumb in a vague direction. "Somebody seen him at the radio shack."

Volkoff pulled the jacket hood over his head and laced it tightly under his chin before he went to the door. Two of the roughnecks got up and followed him. "You're going to need help with that door," one of them said. Standing ten feet from Volkoff, he had to shout to make himself heard. Volkoff turned the handle and pushed out, exerting his full strength. The door yielded a few inches, fighting him all the way, and then the thing on the other side overcame him and the door slammed shut again. He glanced over his shoulder into the grinning faces of the roughnecks. "I get your meaning."

"Some good advice," one of them said. "There's a safety rope on the left-hand side of the door as you go out. When we open up, grab it and don't let go."

Volkoff nodded and the three of them put their shoulders to the heavy panel, easing it open. The wind and the solid sheet of rain were there waiting for them, savaging past them, tearing at their ears and eyelids, pressing the heavy rubber clothing against them as though it was made of silk. Half-blinded, Volkoff groped for the rope, found it and secured it with both hands pulling himself clear of the door. He saw his grotesque, wavering shadow in the panel of light from the room behind him, and then the light was gone and he was alone in a drenched and howling darkness.

He knew exactly where the radio shack was. Under other circumstances he would have taken bets that he could walk to it with his eyes shut. But now, even with the rope in his hands, he wasn't sure of his bearings. The hurricane voice seemed to have destroyed direction. He made the mistake of turning his head into the wind as he looked through slitted lids for the familiar lights on the drill tower. Arrows of rain stabbed his eyeballs. Fingers tried to spread his lids apart. He turned away in real pain and then began to pull himself along the rope, his feet reaching through inches of driven rainwater to find a grip on the steel deck, his body tilted and held at a 45-degree angle by the force of the wind.

Two hundred feet. No more than 200 feet, and it took him ten minutes to get there. He reached a junction in the rope at one point and had to remember which turn to take. One line led to the life rafts and the escape stations. He turned right. With his body now assaulted from behind, he found the rope impossible to grip in this position, and turned to back the last 50 feet to the shack, jackknifed by the force of the hurricane, his jacket hood ballooning with wind and water.

Ultimately he butted up hard against the door of the shack, turned and pounded for entrance, one hand holding the rope so tightly he had the feeling he was clutching cold space. The interval was far too long! He pounded on the door again and it eased open a meager foot or two. He released his grip on the rope and dove for the yellow oblong of light. A hand reached out and steadied him as he came through, and behind him the door slammed shut as though it had been hit with a pile driver.

By contrast with the chaos of sound outside, the interior of the radio shack seemed silent. He stood there dripping and speechless, his eyes burning from the punishment they had taken.

"Don't just stand there, for God sake," Knight said. "Get out of that stuff and draw yourself a coffee."

Volkoff looked around him as he slipped out of the wet gear. There were Knight and the geologist, one of the drill bosses, and three roughnecks who had stopped for a breather on the way back to quarters.

The radio operator was huddled over his equipment, playing with knobs and switches. There was a certain worried tension in his movements.

"Where've you been?" Knight demanded. "Somebody said you were in the sack."

Knight's manner irritated Volkoff. He was taking out his grudge against the storm on everyone else. "I was building a kite," he said. "Somebody told me there might be a breeze coming up."

One of the roughnecks laughed thinly.

Knight glared at him and turned back to the operator. "Well, what do you think, Ron? Is the trouble at this end, the other end, or somewhere in between? Christ, you should have some idea by now."

"It's got to be atmospherics, Charlie," the operator said defensively. "Everything checks out here just fine. So far the antennae are holding out."

"I want a weather report," Knight said to no one in particular.

"What for?" the geologist demanded. "We've got the weather report all around us. We've got ourselves a fact of life, Charlie. This is a hurricane. The barometer was standing at 28.90 when I came over here. The anemometer was spinning so fast you could run a generator off it. I saw it clock one gust of 112 knots. The wave pressure gauges on the caissons were averaging 4300 pounds to the square foot. Average wave height 27.4 feet, and it's not going to get any better." He turned to Volkoff. "Maybe you can tell him," he said.

"It's pretty much what we expected, isn't it, Charlie? All we have to do is tough it out. The rig is built to take it."

Knight made a frustrated gesture. "All right, but one thing is for damn sure, the company is going to hear from me on this. Letting us sit here into the winter storms, grabbing for that last thousand feet of hole. If we could make radio contact I'd tell them now. Ah-h!" He brushed the whole problem away with the flat of his hand. "Who's got a deck of cards?"

"Right under the radar panel," the operator obliged. "Middle drawer. There's chips there, too." His eagerness to get Knight off his back was too obvious.

Volkoff looked at the blank radar screens and was reminded of the Russians. "What's happening to the fishing fleet?"

"They started to scatter to hell-and-gone a couple of hours ago," Knight said. "Last time we looked there was one cannery ship still in position, the research ship and a couple of trawlers. Turn on the set, Ron."

The operator reached over and manipulated dials. The first screen in the bank of four came alive in the semi-darkened room. The beam of light began scouring the cathode ray tube, leaving a wake of jumbled images. "It should clear up," the operator said hopefully. "We didn't have any trouble an hour ago." Volkoff felt sorry for him. He was young—not more than twenty-two or -three. Probably his first good job. Knight was riding him hard.

They watched the scanning beam go around again . . . once more, and then the operator said, "We're getting blips. That'll be the cannery ship—the big one." There were five ghostly lights on the screen, where there had been thirty-seven before. Of the five, three were scattered on the periphery of the screen. Two—the cannery ship and one other—occupied a central position in the left-hand segment of the field.

"My guess is the smaller of those two is the spy ship," Knight said.

"Research vessel," Volkoff corrected him.

"Come on," Knight scoffed. "Direction finders, hydrophones, sonar domes, troposcattering sensors! What's the difference between her and the *Pueblo?*"

"She's not Navy for one thing," Volkoff said.

"You speak any Russian, Mike?" the geologist asked. "With a name like that . . ."

"I speak a little," Volkoff said. "What about the game of cards?"

"Spy ship's moving off," the operator cut in.

Volkoff didn't think so, and then it became apparent that the gap between the two blips was widening. The research vessel was moving slowly astern, her engines apparently providing steerage, but with the wind and the waves pushing her back until she was a full four ship's lengths from the cannery ship.

"Afraid of an accident," Volkoff said. "She wants more room between her and the floating cannery."

"No, sir!" Knight said excitedly. "She's coming about. What's that bastard up to?"

They crowded in to watch as the vessel made her slow, dangerous way in the trough of the sea toward them. She held that course for several minutes, moving closer to the center of the screen.

"She's pushing it," Knight said as though he were trying to warn her away. "She's pushing it!" He nudged the operator roughly. "She must be damn near on top of the Twelve Mile?"

"She's across it," the operator said. "That piece of tape on the edge of the screen marks the Twelve Mile."

"Hold it," Volkoff cautioned. "He's discovered his error. He's changing course."

The ship was, indeed, changing course, making a 90-degree

turn to port and running north with the hurricane riding her tail.

"That's more like it," Knight said. "Get herself back into international water where she belongs."

But she did not go back across the Canadian boundary. Instead she proceeded north for one mile, made a 90-degree turn to starboard and rode the trough straight across to the vertical center line of the radar screen. There she appeared to halt for a moment before she turned hard starboard again and came straight down the screen toward BUTCO 17.

"She's breaking the law, by God!" Knight exclaimed. "We've got her, cold turkey!"

No one spoke. The approach of the yellow-green blob of light mesmerized all of them. There was a dreamlike quality to it—the substance of a nightmare. Out there in the dark, riding south toward them into the teeth of one of the worst West Coast hurricanes in years, was a ship—a foreign ship, a Russian ship trespassing in Canadian waters.

"She must be in trouble," Volkoff said. "She wouldn't try a thing like this otherwise."

"Where are the rockets?" Knight demanded. "She'd be firing rockets. Try that bloody radio of yours again," he told the operator. "We're going to let the Defense Department know. Maybe the Department of Fisheries."

The operator returned to the radio panel and began riding the frequencies again, while the others continued their watch. In the overcrowded, overheated room dominated by the penetrating scream of Hurricane Faith and the answering roar of the ocean, they watched the blip approach dead center and then fade from sight, riding under the probe of the radar antenna.

"She's arrived," Volkoff announced. "What kind of a skipper would take a ship this close to a lee shore, on a night like this?"

"Why not? A good chance to look and listen," Knight said.

"In this weather!" said Volkoff. "He's riding behind us in the lee of the wind. The poor bastard has picked the rig as a breakwater."

"He can't do that," Knight protested. "He's breaking every goddam law in the book."

"He's doing it," Volkoff said, "And there's not a navy or a coast guard that can stop him tonight."

16 . . .

At 2000 hours Westholme didn't bother listening to the weather report. He was too busy. There was no need to rouse all hands; none of them could have remained comfortable in their quarters while *Haida Noble* ran in those seas. In the engine room, both first and second engineer were dividing their time between the main engines and the repair of two auxiliaries whose sumps had lost their oil in the heavy rollng action just before the tug came about into the sea.

There was a certain amount of damage throughout the vessel, in spite of the fact that great time and effort had gone into securing *Haida Noble* for heavy weather running. The galley was a shambles, mainly the fault of the cook who had failed to take any precautions whatever until he was lying on a deck tilted at a 45-degree angle with his pots and pans descending on him. Even the freezer door had been left unlatched and had swung open during Westholme's sudden change of course to avoid the first of the hurricane's big waves. Frozen vegetables and packaged meats had tumbled from their shelves and spilled out of the gaping door to mix with scalding coffee from the one-gallon percolator the cook had moved from its bracket for his own convenience.

Lindstrom gave him no sympathy as he treated a forearm badly scalded by the coffee. "It's the last time you ship on *Haida Noble*," he promised. "What the hell did you think this was going to be—a bloody Mediterranean cruise? Clean up this mess and start building sandwiches, baskets of sandwiches!"

The automatic washing machine in the laundry room adjacent to the galley had broken its fastenings and pounded in the side of the dryer. Galbraith and Bibaud had stopped the destruction with considerable difficulty, relying finally on use of a spare mattress and several two-by-fours to trip it and wedge it against a wall. The square chunk of enameled metal charged and fought them like a living thing, flailing its hoses and pipes murderously as the action of the sea gave it motion; but in the end they subdued it and lashed it down.

The welding tanks running amok in the machine shop had smashed a cabinet full of cutting tools and broached a gallon can of drilling lubricant, leaving the razor-sharp instruments skidding in a slick of oil.

In the wire room where the gigantic drums of steel cable and the salvage anchors were stored, all was reasonably well —except that this was the one place in the tug where fire broke out. Gasoline spilling from a tipped auxiliary pump was ignited in some fashion, probably by a spark created by metal striking metal. Galbraith in a companionway smelled the heat and went to investigate with a fire extinguisher. By the time Westholme had been alerted by the fire warning system on the bridge, and sounded the alarm, Galbraith had the thing under control. He walked out of the wire room, his face smudged and the color of raw beef, grinning reassuringly. Fenton started to make a wisecrack, and caught him as he collapsed. A whiff of oxygen followed by half an hour of deep breathing by an open port seemed to put him right again.

Up on the bridge, Westholme was pleased to let Fenton have the wheel once more. *Haida Noble*'s controls were the best; the Kort nozzles gave the tug something approaching fingertip steering, but in this sea nothing was easy. The waves climbing the tug's stern were uniformly gigantic, and Westholme had never been partial to a following sea of any kind. A following sea was a stalking sea. It crept up on you, delivered its sledgehammer blow, and then raced on. You had neither the time nor the opportunity to measure it or pre-

pare for it. Westholme liked an oncoming sea. It was dangerous but honest.

Tait, with his face glued to the radar mask, said in a
muffled voice: "I'm getting three or four blips off to port."

Westholme braced his legs against the sharply tilting deck
and made it to the second radar screen. He counted five blips
in all; definitely vessels, but none of them anywhere close
to BUTCO 17. *Haida Noble* had to be at least 20 miles from
the rig. So far the radar hadn't picked her up.

"Some of the Russian boats, I'd say. They're well outside
the Twelve Mile. Poor bastards!" He meant it. Anything the
Haida Noble was enduring those trawlers were suffering in
spades.

This was a hurricane all right—as good as anything he had
ever been through. As big, quite possibly bigger than the
one he would always remember on the approach to Yokohama. He felt a perverse pride in the fact that the West
Coast could give birth to a hurricane as impressive as anything in the eastern seas. The thought was ridiculous. The
main thing was the job, and it would always be the job,
that was why tugs went to sea. BUTCO 17 was waiting for
Haida Noble; it had contracted for her services.

He decided to try head office again. Jake had said that
Alward would be standing by after 1500. It was a tradition
with the company to have the president stand by when the
flagship was in a critical situation. He picked up the ship-to-
shore and dialed through on the company's private line.
Almost immediately the dispatcher answered:

"Christy? We've been waiting for you to ring through. Mr.
Alward didn't want to bother you if you were busy."

"Is he there?" Westholme knew Alward was there, otherwise the dispatcher wouldn't have called him "mister." In
the big man's absence his pseudonym was "the Brass."

"He's right here, Christy. Here and waiting."

"Hello, Chris." It was Alward, sure enough. "We've been
waiting to hear from you." There was a veiled reprimand
built into the hearty voice.

"I'm sorry about that, Andrew. We've been pretty busy."

"Can you speak up, Christy? The line's bloody awful."

Westholme raised his voice, knowing it would be useless. The wind and the sea were competing with him for the mouthpiece. "We've got our work cut out for us, Andrew. This is a big wind."

"We know that, Chris. It's the worst one in years. How's she standing it?"

"Fine, just fine. You're going to have a million-dollar cleaning bill."

"Don't you worry yourself about that. You're keeping in touch with BUTCO 17?"

"The VHF isn't making it for some reason, Andrew. They've tried to get through to us a half-dozen times, but it's mostly static. I don't think they're picking us up at all."

Alward's voice took on a board room persuasiveness. "This is an important one, Chris. I guess you're aware of that. I mean to say the contract with BUTCO is just the beginning of larger things. I want you to do the best you know how . . . don't endanger lives, mind you. These are—uh—your decisions."

"I know that, Andrew. Stop worrying."

"I'd like to say this, Christy. You're not to concern yourself if you have to run a little risk. There's a lot at stake here. We want you to do your level best."

Suddenly Alward's message was coming through. Westholme couldn't mistake it. Neither could he believe it. "I understand, Andrew. We'll do the necessary. Look, I've got to go now. Things are beginning to hot up."

"Absolutely, Chris. I—uh—there's not another captain in the fleet who could manage this."

Westholme didn't reply.

"Christy? You hear me? Take care now."

Westholme didn't answer. At the other end he heard Alward cough and direct a comment to the dispatcher: "The weather must be bloody awful out there. The—uh—line has gone dead."

Very carefully Westholme hung up.

The sea was incredibly bad. There wasn't a man on board

who wasn't holding onto a stanchion or a bulkhead. The high scream of the hurricane penetrated to every corner of the ship, plugging the eardrums with sound. At intervals Fenton activated the big spotlights mounted port and starboard on the bridge roof and halfway up the forward mast. The purpose was psychological, to signal the drill rig that they were approaching. The big arcs could be seen for miles under normal conditions. All they did tonight was illuminate the conditions surrounding *Haida Noble;* immediately ahead, the shoulder of a vast wave as high as the bridge itself, its entire surface leprous with wind-driven foam; above it, reaching as far as the light would go, the fragmented tatters of ocean driven through the slanting lines of rain. The world was an agony of water.

Alward's message was that *Haida Noble* was expendable. What a sweet contract that must be when you could write off four million dollars' worth of tugboat and still make a profit! *Haida Noble* was the whole goddam company and still Alward could write her off. Behind him he felt the next wave descend on *Haida Noble's* stern, its curling top slamming on the deck with a thousand-ton impact; its waist sliding along and under the hull to lift it high, surging along the keel to drive the bow skyward into the wind—then releasing it to let the tug slide backward into the deep valley of the sea.

"To hell with it," Westholme decided. The contest was uneven. *Haida Noble* deserved better than this. Twenty miles ahead the drill rig was sitting solid as a rock, its whole design and structure intended to take this kind of punishment. Alward said "do your best." Get up there and do something to make the BUTCO people feel they're getting their money's worth. "Do your best!" Put *Haida Noble* on the block—and a tug crew, too, when it came right down to it!

Westholme eased around the magnetic compass housing and reached for the wheel. "I'll spell you off, Brad," he said. "Go find yourself a coffee or something."

"You just gave me the wheel," Fenton protested. "What's eating you?"

Westholme slid in behind the wheel and felt the surge of the passing wave. He waited until the *Haida Noble* was tipped skyward, the spotlights highlighting the chains of spindrift streaming from her bow. Just as she began to slide back, he reached over and pushed the throttle levers on the remote control to full speed and started the wheel swinging hard to starboard. The engines responded as he went into the full 180-degree turn. By the time the next wave was in position the bow of *Haida Noble* was facing it, engines throttled back to one quarter speed.

Fenton stared at him incredulously.

"Nothing we can do tonight," Westholme said. "We're going to let this sweetheart fight back for a while."

17 . . .

In the aftermath, days later, they would say that it was long overdue, that all the signs and warnings were there, if only a little more time and concern had been taken to pinpoint the activity down to the last mile. Small blame could be attached considering that the Aleutian Chain is largely uncharted oceanographically—in spite of the fact that it is one of the most seismic areas of the earth.

The line of volcanic islands extends in a perfect arc, like a red-hot pendant, from the equally seismic Russian peninsula of Kamchatka all the way to the Alaskan mainland, proceeding inland almost to Cook Inlet. The chain of dead, active, and latent volcanoes sits precisely on the edge of one of the earth's great rifts. The south side of this wall of mountains plummets 25,000 feet into the depths of the Aleutian Trench. The north edge of the barrier contains the relatively shallow waters of the Bering Sea. And up from the earth's deep layers, for countless centuries, the magmas—the molten oozes—have crept along this rift, seeking freedom. They have surfaced along this North Pacific arc like a line of boils and scar tissue on a wound that refuses to heal. The surface wound is called the Aleutian Chain.

Bogoslof Island is one of the boils, a recurring irritation in the curved incision. If anyone or anything could be blamed for what happened that night, it would have to be Bogoslof Island for drawing attention away from the real site of the catastrophe.

The United States Coast and Geodetic Survey station at Adak was probably the first to pick up the tremor. But the Alaskan stations at College and Sitka were only seconds behind, and both Tokyo and Victoria, British Columbia, were remarkably alert, considering their distance from the apparent epicenter.

It wasn't a significant tremor. Adak registered it 3 on the Richter Scale. Other stations, in the process of the terrible post-mortem that followed, agreed that it was no more than scale 3. Nevertheless it was duly triangulated and discovered to be Bogoslof Island clamoring for attention. The time of the tremor was 2300 hours, 15 minutes, 7 seconds plus or minus .2 seconds, Pacific Standard Time.

Approximately forty minutes later Bogoslof Island demonstrated again, not much more dramatically than before—between 3 and 4 on the Richter Scale. The seismographic stations were uniformly unimpressed, although the station at College was credited with the observation later on that the triangulation did not fall precisely on Bogoslof Island, but some seven miles west and south. A close examination of other triangulations conducted previously that month by a score of stations revealed that none of them had fallen on Bogoslof Island. One was a good nine miles west and south. Several were six to seven miles in the same direction.

The focal point was a small, unnamed island not far from Unmak Pass; a few acres of spiky grass dappled with ragwort, fireweed, and lupin. There was a rudimentary beach on the southeast side of the islet where sea lions had established a colony—nothing more than that. Neither the oceanographers, who understandably did not consider the islet significant; or the fishermen, who evaluated islands in terms of good anchorage or bad; or the remaining Aleuts, who no longer placed importance on the stories of their forefathers, could know that this island had been a Bogoslof in its day. Its birth had been as fiery as Bogoslof's, if one hundred and thirteen years earlier. More significantly, it sat midway between the Aleutian Trench and the approximate edge of the Bering Canyon, regarded as the largest ocean canyon in the world. Four times after its birth, in spectacular displays of protest, it had been pulled beneath the sea and thrust up again, vomiting lava and bellowing to be left alone.

The islet was the starting point of the catastrophe. At 0100 hours, 27 minutes, 4 seconds, plus or minus .2 seconds— not much more than an hour after the last minor protest supposed to have come from Bogoslof Island, 100 miles of rock structure along the Aleutian Trench collapsed. It was as though a guillotine wider than the horizon had dropped into the earth's belly. Up from the incredible wound came the gases and fluids, racing through channels centuries old, reaching the island's plug, straining at it, and then blowing out the side of the 7000-foot, semi-submerged volcano beneath it. Three hundred feet beneath the surface of the sea, the earth's guts spilled out white-hot and explosive. The plug, surmounted by the islet, undermined by a liquid sea of fire, toppled and fell, destroying the sea grasses and the sea lion ledges forever. Uncapped now, the lava fountain leaped upward, burning through the cold Aleutian waters like a welding torch, converting the sea into a cauldron and in later stages into a spectacular battleground. The lava build-up reached the surface of the sea to create rolling artillery bombardments as surface water turned instantly to superheated steam.

The volcanic island endured for seven hours until an explosion of gigantic proportions tore open an old vertical fissure halfway up the submerged slope on the south face, and in a matter of minutes the mountain was gone, fully half its bulk released as though cut through by a hot cleaver, sliding and tumbling to the bottom of the Pacific. But by that time the island's fate was irrelevant. The sea had been aroused and was attacking the coastlines of the Pacific.

The collapsing segment of the Aleutian Trench had done two things to stir the sea into vast motion; first the ocean poured in to fill the sudden depression in the Trench bottom; second, avalanches created by the sudden shock started clay-like accumulations 200 and 300 feet thick sliding down the nearly perpendicular walls of the Trench. At velocities of 60 miles an hour, the almost solid masses of sediment plunged 25,000 feet into the Aleutian abyss in a line ranging up to 100 miles on either side of the earthquake's epicenter. The resulting upheaval of waters was colossal, and the tidal wave —the tsunami—started its devastating journey across the Pacific—a wave measuring four feet high in the open sea, with a length between waves of 15,000 feet. The speed of the wave? Four hundred and thirty-five miles an hour.

The sequence of events as they appeared on official reports days later conveyed no impression of the human tragedy and the extent of the physical destruction incorporated in the charts and the computer-digested figures.

Honolulu Observatory received its first report of a large earthquake at 0100 hours, 52 minutes, 12 seconds, Pacific Standard Time. The alarm came from the seismological station at College, Alaska, where some difficulty had been experienced in clearing lines to Honolulu. College reported that its seismic instruments had been rendered unserviceable by the shock; in any event Honolulu's instruments had recorded a major shock by then:

0213 Honolulu sent out requests for seismic data to the Standard Seismograph Station network.

0221 Seismic data received from Hong Kong.

0226 Seismic data received from Guam.

0229 Seismic data received from Japan Meteorological Agency.

0232 Seismic data received from Berkeley Observatory.

0247 Honolulu Observatory established epicenter of earthquake.

52.5 North, 167.4 West. Approximate focus of earthquake, 37 Km. Force of earthquake, 8.9 on the Richter Scale.

0300 Bulletin issued to all agencies in the Warning System. "This is a seismic sea wave advice. A severe earthquake has occurred at 52.5 North, 167.4 West at 09.27 Z, 27 September. Vicinity south of Unalaska Island. It is not known, repeat, not known at this time that a sea wave has been generated. Its ETA for the Hawaiian Islands, Honolulu, is 1400 Z, 27 September."

Request issued to Tsunami Warning System for wave reports.

A ship at sea would have been scarcely aware of the wave's passage. Because of its relatively low contour and because of its velocity it would pass a ship's length in a second or less. But in shallower waters approaching coastlines, something else happened. The wave began to drag in the shallows, reducing its speed but increasing its height, as though the ocean bottom were thrusting the tsunami into view to reveal its awesome presence to the land it would engulf.

Long before the first wave report was received in Honolulu, the tsunami had claimed its first land victims. First of all the sea pulled back from the shorelines of the small coastal settlements on Unalaska Island, as though recoiling from the smoking matchwood left in the wake of the earthquake. It sucked with it numerous small fishing boats, floats and boat houses, and left the more securely anchored craft on the harbor bottoms and the shoals, their hulls embedded in the sludge and streaming sand.

In a few minutes the sea returned, the lunar high tide surmounted by a curling seismic wave. At Dutch Harbor the wall of water was 45 feet high. Eyewitnesses who survived it estimated the wave's speed at more than 100 miles an hour. It thundered into the town, carrying its upended burden of boats and floating debris, enfolding the pitiful remains of houses, schools, and office structures; scooping up the living with the dead and churning them into a grotesque flotsam. At its point of furthest advance it deposited a thin litter of dead and destroyed things, then pulled back again, taking most of the uprooted, dismembered town with it. When the wave returned again forty-seven minutes later it crested to almost 60 feet, creating absolute destruction.

The damage at Dutch Harbor was impressive, but its location, close though it was to the earthquake's epicenter, did not place it as directly in the wave's line of attack as certain other points along the coast of North America and Japan. Anchorage, badly damaged in the earthquake of 1964, suffered rudimentary trouble this time. Sitka, on the other hand, more directly in line with the radiating wave, suffered tremendous damage both to life and property. The population had virtually no warning before the first wave struck, hurling itself across streets in the early morning darkness to crush people in their beds and drag them back to sea.

Typically the second wave was higher and more destructive, and the following waves, while diminishing, each worked their own kind of chaos. Sitka's death toll, when the tsunami and its following seas had passed, was 417, and was not without its strange, apocryphal stories. The oldest inhabitant of Sitka, an Indian reputed to be 103 years old, was found alive, having been carried in the wreckage of her shanty for more than 2000 feet and deposited on the edge of a bluff. In her arms was the body of her great-great-grandson.

Masset, on the northern tip of the Queen Charlottes, was gravely hit, although the tsunami of 1964 had treated it lightly. Prince Rupert, British Columbia, suffered almost as much damage and loss of life as Sitka. In none of these places had there been time to issue adequate warnings. In the hour-and-a-half to two hours it took to alert even a fraction of the populations to the danger, the tidal wave had traveled more than 800 miles.

Two hunters camped on the beach at the end of Rennell Sound on the eastern edge of the Charlottes awoke to the rumble of distant thunder. Sitting up in their sleeping bags, they heard the noise approaching from the ocean end of the channel, building to a roar that bore no resemblance to thunder. In the split seconds before they died, their flash-lights played across a wall of water that wiped out the stars and filled the Sound from one edge to the other.

Communities and logging camps along Queen Charlotte Strait, both on the mainland and Vancouver Island were visited by the periphery of the wave. There was much property damage, but no deaths.

On the other side of the Island, however, the story was very different. The Civil Defense authorities would take perverse (but entirely justified) satisfaction, in the post-mortem days that followed, in pointing out that the probability of a major tidal wave on the West Coast had been drawn to the attention of both the federal and provincial governments on a number of occasions. With a proper warning system, backed up by adequate disaster resources, hundreds of lives could have been spared.

The governments, on the other hand, were able to argue that Hurricane Faith's depredations were at their height when the tsunami arrived. Official warning of the wave arrived a mere ninety minutes before the wave itself, and in that period of time with communications lines down and most radio stations forced off the air or operating on auxiliary power, only a fraction of the population learned of the tidal wave's approach and fled to higher land. Even the most superbly organized and equipped civil defense organization would have been ineffective under those conditions.

In the aftermath of the tsunami and the hurricane it would take weeks for the Coast Guard and Air-Sea Rescue teams to record the last official death. On that long list would appear hunters and late season campers, a group of seventeen dedicated hippies huddled in a shelter on Long Beach where they had come to pay their respects to Indian summer, and entire families riding out the hurricane in pleasure boats anchored "safely" in the shelter of inlets. The true death toll would never be known because the retreating waves of the tsunami took with them vast quantities of debris intermingled with the dead and the dying. Most of these were never found. In the reports they were listed as "missing, presumed dead." The presumption was correct in almost every case.

The wave station at Tofino was unable to alert the town of Port Alberni to the tsunami's arrival because the station was totally destroyed in the first explosion of the hurricane—tidal wave encounter. The wave continued on down the narrow, 40-mile passage cutting into the heart of Vancouver Island, its speed diminishing to 140 miles an hour, its crest rising to almost 50 feet—contributed to by a lunar high tide made even higher by the pressure effect of the hurricane.

The Royal Canadian Mounted Police and local Civil Defense officials had no more than an hour to warn the populations of the large mill town, starting at the waterfront and switchbacking up from there along the dark, storm-swept streets. Many sleeping residents failed to hear the loud hailers calling to them over the scream of the storm. The Civil Defense organized telephone teams to work methodically through the telephone book, starting with the hospital and other private and public institutions, but many telephone lines were down and this form of warning proceeded slowly.

Probably word-of-mouth proved to be the most effective method. Those telephoned were asked to arouse their neighbors and then proceed in an orderly fashion to high land. Some did this, but more yielded to panic and self-preservation and fled immediately with their wives and children, leaving their neighbors to sleep or toss until the wave arrived to claim them.

The estimated time of arrival of the tsunami at Tofino, as supplied by the Honolulu Observatory, was 0427 Pacific Standard Time, and the calculations were remarkably accurate. At 0431.4 the Wave Station at Tofino ceased to exist. Entering the Alberni Canal, its speed reduced, its crest more than tripled, the tsunami raced the forty mile length of the channel in seventeen minutes and slammed into the center of the town like a 50-foot wall of black, whitecapped granite. Entire streets exploded and were hurled to the surface of the speeding wave. Boats, automobiles, and entire houses torn loose from their foundations were catapulted as far as 2000 feet inland.

The big pulp and paper plant at Port Alberni, a virtual fortress of reinforced concrete, managed to withstand the first wave, although its interior was flooded and its machinery rendered useless. But that wave sucked ammunition with it when it withdrew into Hurricane Faith's howling blackness. Approximately one hour later, the second wave thundered in, the sound of it eclipsing the incredible discord of the storm, its crest reaching 65 feet in the confining walls of the channel, its surface loaded with the debris of the town. The pulp and paper plant could not withstand the barrage. Its chemical storage tanks and chip silos, broached in a dozen places, let in the multi-thousand-ton pressures of the wave, and blew wide open. The white towers and columns of the plant could be seen, even in that darkness, crumbling and sweeping away, like a child's sandcastle in an advancing surf.

The town was murdered and carried back to sea by that second wave. And there would be five more in the next six hours, each diminishing in force and size, but each exacting its own toll. After that the living would return and try to find the places they had known.

The story repeated itself with lesser severity as the tsunami sped south. Still, there were major tragedies to be reported. Crescent City, the target for many tidal waves in the past, was gravely wounded by a 40-foot wave. Small coastal communities ranging almost as far South as San Francisco stayed awake that night, warned in time of the approaching wave. Some were forced to evacuate as the sea retreated silently and then came in to flood streets and buildings.

Even in Hawaii, where there had been four hours' warning, people died although there was no excuse for their deaths. On the beach on northern Oahu the sea fell back quietly, leaving shellfish lying on the sand. Many of the islanders had waited for this moment, an opportunity too good to miss. They raced out to the new, unnatural tide mark with baskets and sacks and began to gather in the harvest. Those who placed caution before greed were able to return to high ground before the tsunami charged in. The others died.

18 . . .

It was Lindstrom's watch again, but *Haida Noble*'s entire complement stood watch that night. There was no way any of them could sleep. Hurricane Faith was testing the resources of the tug and the crew to the breaking point, and trying her best to destroy them.

At 0317 a particularly vicious wave reared high above the bow with the tug's 36-inch arcs boring triple holes of light in its black underbelly. Lindstrom cried out involuntarily, and Westholme lunged for a grip on the navigation table. Halfway along the foredeck the curling mountain broke with an impact as solid as though a 20-ton metal slab had been slammed down. *Haida Noble* shuddered along her full length. The wave parted at the forward mast house and raced along the main deck, port, and starboard, its passage marked by the ugly sound of metal ripping and abrading. The big tug rose from the blow, seawater streaming from her scuppers in long white veils.

"The Yokohama blow was nothing like this," Lindstrom shouted. "I'd like to see the eye of this thing pretty soon."

"Don't count on it," Westholme warned him. "She may be solid wind all the way across." He returned to the VHF set and tried once more to put a call through to the drill rig, but without success. "I don't think we're going to hear from them until this thing slows down some," he said. "They've lost their antenna, and no one would send a man out to fix it in this stuff."

As though to make a liar of him, a grotesque figure moved slowly through a bar of light on the boat deck, performing the impossible. Westholme stared incredulously through the salt-crusted glass and waited for the shape to reappear. When it did, he had difficulty identifying the face; the 100-mile-an-hour wind gusts were remolding the flesh on the man's face, penetrating the mouth and parting the lips back from the teeth.

It was Bibaud, he decided. The deckhand worked in a slow-motion nightmare, his body tilted at an impossible angle against the wind, water streaming from his rubber storm gear, as he passed a long coil of 1½-inch nylon rope around a stanchion, took up the slack, passed it around again and formed a clove hitch. Having done this he disappeared into the surrounding blackness of the deck, paying out the coil of rope as a safety line.

"Goddamned idiot," Westholme muttered. "No one's passing out medals."

Lindstrom had missed the action, his full attention on the wheel and the approaching seas. "I didn't hear you," he said.

Westholme didn't reply. He was pondering their last position, now marked with a neat X on the chart. The seas were pushing them back, which was good. *Haida Noble* was now 20 miles west of Cape Beal with the drill rig in their line of drift, 32 miles northeast. Plenty of distance between the tug and the coast, although the drift was in that approximate direction. In other weather conditions BUTCO 17 would be showing on the radar screen by now. In any event she would be in sight from the deck by sunrise if Hurricane Faith continued to close the gap.

Tait came into the wheelhouse, his storm gear dripping, his eyes blood-red and dazed looking. "We had a little trouble on the main deck. That last big one tore a life raft loose, davits and all. It was pounding hell out of things on the starboard side."

"Did you secure it?"

Tait nodded.

"What the hell was Bibaud doing up on the boat deck—trying to commit suicide?"

"Being useful," Tait said. "He had a notion we might be losing the lifeboats."

Westholme kept his satisfaction concealed. This was a good crew. "We don't pay heroes extra," he said.

"Maybe that wasn't Bibaud's thinking," Tait suggested. "He wants to make sure he can get off if the tug sinks. He says Quebec needs him."

Westholme and Lindstrom chuckled. It was a brief moment of relief. The only other one had been an hour earlier when the cook arrived at the point of hysteria and was found throwing crockery against the wall in the ruined galley.

Bibaud's observations, as he helped to clean up the mess, was fairly close to the truth:

"He should be in another business, that guy. He couldn't keep a coffeepot steady in a restaurant with two waiters holding him up."

"How's the cook?" Westholme asked now, suddenly reminded of him.

"In his bunk, planning tomorrow's meal I guess," Tait said. "We seem to be riding this thing out pretty good."

"We've taken the worst it can hand out," Westholme said with solid conviction, and he had a feeling that both Tait and Lindstrom believed him. They wanted to believe him. He crossed over to look at the barometer. It had risen a fraction but was still under 29. The wind and the sea hadn't subsided by a degree.

"Poor old Willie will be spitting diesel oil by now," he said with real compassion. An engineer's condition in a heavy storm was something less than comfortable.

"Thomson would spit diesel oil on a calm day, with a movie queen for his second engineer," Lindstrom stated. "He hasn't seen a decent engine room or a decent sea since he left Glasgow. That damn Lowlander isn't happy unless he's miserable."

"Then tonight he should be out of his mind with happiness," Westholme said, ". . . the second engineer too." He braced against the navigation desk again as another giant sea came over. Tait was thrown against him heavily.

Beside Lindstrom the ship-to-shore signal filtered through the general din filling the wheelhouse. Westholme struggled up the sloping deck toward it, fell back and then charged ahead as the tug leveled itself and prepared to plunge into a trough.

It was Alward on the other end, and the reception was incredibly bad. "Take it slower, Andrew," Westholme shouted. "The signal's terrible." In Westholme's memory this was the first time he could recall the president sounding excited— really disturbed.

Alward started to talk again, just as a burst of static issued from the receiver speaker and a voice made itself heard. "Hold it a minute, Andrew," Westholme said. "We've got something coming in on 1630." He motioned Tait to turn up the volume.

". . . severe earthquake has occurred at latitude 52.5 North, longitude 167.4 West in the vicinity of Unalaska Island at 0927 Z, 27 September. A tsunami has been generated and is spreading over the Pacific Ocean. It could cause great damage to all coasts and islands in the Pacific area. It is a series of waves and could be . . ."

"The ETA," Westholme said quietly. "Give us the ETA."

". . . Preliminary earthquake force 8.9 revised Richter. Reported wave heights: 60 feet Dutch Harbor, 62 feet Sitka, ETA information as follows: Pacific Standard Time conversion, Prince Rupert 0400; Tofino 0427; Port Renfrew . . ."

Tait turned the volume down, on Westholme's gestured instruction.

Into the ship-to-shore telephone Westholme said, "I just heard it, Andrew. What took them so long?"

"You've got to get the tug out of it," Alward commanded. "We're not going to put *Haida Noble* on the spot under these conditions. I want you to make for shelter."

"We've got less than an hour, Andrew. Time to go five, maybe eight miles in any direction, and then we're pushing our luck. Our best bet is to find deep water."

"It's a new ball game, Chris. The drill rig—uh—can take this better than we can . . ."

"I'm not too sure about that."

"Don't concern yourself about it, get *Haida Noble* into a safe situation. I want you to do that. Do you understand, Chris?" As a sudden afterthought he added: "We've got to think about the crew, their families. That sort of thing."

"I understand, Andrew. We'll find the deepest water we can in the time we've got left. You getting any wind in Vancouver?"

"Wind! My God, Christy, half the town is without power. Roofs ripped off. Trees down across power lines. Fires all over the lower mainland. It's a bloody mess!"

"Did anyone contact Lee?" He had deliberately held the question back until now.

"Jake tried two or three times. There's no one answering at your place. I'd say she was holed up with friends."

"Probably," Westholme said. "When you reach her, tell her everything is fine."

"I wish that were the truth," Alward said. "Don't forget now, Chris . . ."

"I've got to sign off," Westholme said curtly. "We're running out of time."

He placed the phone back into its cradle. Holed up with friends! The old Lee would have been sitting there at home waiting for the phone to ring on a night like this. Lindstrom was looking at him with an expression utterly serious and questioning. "You heard the same thing I did," Westholme said. "Have you ever been through a tidal wave?"

Lindstrom shook his head.

"I have—four hundred miles off the coast of Venezuela. Nothing to it. We had a swell running at the time and the wave itself wasn't much bigger than that—but it went deep, better than two thousand feet deep. What we have here tonight is different. We've got one hell of a hurricane sea moving north northeast and a seismic sea wave moving south. When those two babies meet"—he made a perplexed gesture—"your guess is as good as mine."

"We've got seventy fathoms under us," Lindstrom said.

"What are the chances of the tidal wave building up on that kind of bottom?"

"Pretty good," Westholme said. "Sixty-two feet at Sitka! That is one mother of a big wave. This coast is going to get clobbered tonight!"

He glanced at the chronometer. 0357. "According to Honolulu we've got thirty-four minutes to wait." He struggled back to the chart table and studied the fathom markings. "We'd have to run in the trough broadside to the sea to find ten more fathoms. It's not worth it, Eric. I want you to organize things below—a complete stem-to-stern check on stowage and loose gear . . . and before anyone starts anything I want lifejackets on. No arguments. At 0420 I want everyone up on the boat deck—except for manning in the engine room. Let Willie decide whether or not he wants to flip a coin. I want someone down there in case the remote fails."

He took the wheel from Lindstrom, calling over his shoulder as the first mate left: "No need for panic, Lindy. This is precautionary stuff. You know what I'm getting at. The last thing we want is the cook running amok."

Lindstrom nodded understandingly and fought his way out through the doorway. Tait remained behind undecidedly and then pulled himself up the tilting deck to take a position beside one of the engine room telegraphs. If Westholme noticed his presence he didn't indicate it. He stood, belly and chest into the wheel, bracing himself for the onslaught of a 50-foot wave picked out by the beam of one of the arcs. No sign of a let-up; if anything the seas were becoming higher, more powerful. Several had reached perilously close to the navigation bridge windows before they broke and fell away, the residue of their collapse sluicing across the glass and then whipping away in the keening wind.

There would never be another night like this; Westholme knew that. He thought he had faced everything, all the wicked combinations and permutations the sea and the weather could provide; icing and gale force winds on the

Murmansk run; tide and wind propelling an eleven-thousand-ton barge at him faster than his tug could tow it; the Yokohama hurricane with a tandem tow heaving on the end of the line; the night *Thrace* parted the line on the edge of Hurricane Farida—2-inch steel cable threshing like a live thing on the afterdeck, with two of the company's best men dead under its coils. But tonight had to take the cake!

He wracked his brain to recall all he had ever learned about tsunamis—which wasn't much. The chance of experiencing one in a lifetime was rare. The possibility of encountering one in a hurricane was extremely unlikely . . . and the odds of being caught in the confrontation of a tidal wave and a hurricane had to be astronomical. What was likely to happen? Some land-based oceanographic physicist would undoubtedly have a great deal to say about the dynamics of the two opposing forces. But damn it, what did that add up to in terms of *Haida Noble*'s chances?

There was no doubt that the tug would have to continue to ride into the hurricane. Coming about in these seas was now an invitation to disaster. So the tidal wave would take them in the stern. How big would it be—this big, bottom-raking curler? The hurricane waves, some of them exceeding 60 feet, were superficial—built up and projected by Hurricane Faith across the face of the ocean. The tsunami involved the entire mass of water through which it moved, top to bottom. There was going to be a crunch, but what kind of a crunch?

19 . . .

The chronometer showed 0402. Early morning; dawn two or three hours away, although the light would be delayed in showing itself, smothered on an endless horizon of scudding cloud and spindrift. At dawn, if visibility permitted, the drill rig would be large on the horizon—if the tsunami didn't prove to be too much for the steel island. He put that thought out of his mind.

At dawn perhaps Jake or Alward himself would telephone Lee again, find her at home and pass along some kind of encouraging message. If she wasn't at home, where was she? The house could be damaged and she injured for that matter; those big poplars in the back yard. Suddenly he was accusing himself bitterly for not demanding that someone from the company drive over and check the house out, hurricane or no hurricane. He supposed that every man in the crew was worrying about a wife or girl friend at this moment.

"What's the echo sounder reading?" he asked Tait abruptly.

Tait took his time checking it out. "Nudging sixty-seven fathoms."

"You a married man?" Westholme asked.

"In a manner of speaking."

"Kids?"

"Yeah."

The deckhand was making it plain that it was none of Westholme's business . . . and Westholme understood it, but a perverse streak of stubbornness wouldn't let it alone. Stubbornness? Or was it a growing suspicion that Tait had his own kind of misery—company for his own?

"What's her name?" he persisted, shouting to make himself heard.

"Who?"

"Your wife's name . . ."

"Lisa." Tait glanced pointedly at the chronometer. "Time's running out. Maybe I should be giving them a hand below."

"Stick around," Westholme ordered. "I don't want to be up here by myself if that ETA is wrong."

He wanted to say: "Tait, you're young and you haven't tried marriage the way I have, but you may have learned something that I missed. People learn sooner and younger these days. What do you do when your marriage turns out to be a twenty-year-old mistake? What do you younger guys know that it is too late for me to learn?"

Aloud, above the wind, he said: "I don't know how it is with your girl, but with Lee I would guess . . ."

"Mr. Westholme," Tait broke in, "are you trying to tell me something?"

"Shooting the breeze," Westholme said.

Tait held on tight as *Haida Noble* heaved herself against the sea. "My wife and me are breaking up . . . and it couldn't happen soon enough." He let go his grip on the engine room telegraph housing, waited for the moment and slid behind Westholme to take a position at one of the radar scopes. It was an abrupt, pointed movement, putting an end to that particular conversation.

Westholme had asked for it and he knew it. He stared ahead into the black nothingness of the storm and adjusted the wheel meticulously. Presently he said: "Do you see anything interesting on the scope?"

"There's some stuff almost off the screen to the west of us. Part of that Russian fleet I guess."

"And we think *we've* got troubles."

"They're in deeper water," Tait reminded him. "They're beyond the shelf."

Both men ducked involuntarily as a wave, fully 60 feet high, reared out of the darkness, appearing to overwhelm the wheelhouse. At the last minute *Haida Noble's* bow rode up on it and the wave parted, crashing thunderously on the deck and washing astern. The white, curling lip of the thing struck the glass with a solid, metallic blow.

"This is as hairy as anything I've seen," Westholme said. "There's a grab bag of stuff in the left-hand drawer under the navigation desk. See if you can find a couple of pairs of safety goggles. We could be traveling without glass before this is over."

Tait found the goggles and delivered a pair to Westholme. He tucked them into his jacket pocket, checked the chronometer and punched a button on the intercom. "O.K. down there. You've got two minutes left to make yourself comfortable on the boat deck. This isn't panic stations, it's action stations. There's just an outside chance we'll have to leave this tug. If that happens, action will be the name of the game. No lost motion, no holding back. Eric Lindstrom will be in charge of the operation, and my betting is he won't have to issue a command. Eric, are you getting this? Over."

"We're reading you, Chris."

"O.K. Have a couple of the boys bring up half a dozen sheets of half-inch plywood, a power drill and a half-inch bit, some quarter-inch nylon lashing material, and as big a sheet of Plexiglass as you can scrounge. We may lose the glass up here, and someone has left the storm panels ashore."

"Heads will fall," Lindstrom said cheerfully. "We'll be up there too de swee."

Westholme turned his mind to the tidal wave again. The earthquake would be like a gigantic pebble tossed into the ocean south of Unalaska Island. The tsunami would radiate from that central point like the ripple waves in a pool, filling the entire Pacific before it was finished. Its approach to the West Coast should be from the northwest.

He turned to Tait. "I want to take that wave, and the next one which will be even bigger, dead center on the stern. Just about everything we're going to do will be chancy. I'm going to alter course 30 degrees to port, banking on that wave approaching from west northwest—and we're not going to do it before we have to."

"We'll be taking a hell of a sea on the starboard quarter."

"And there's the chance we could broach." Westholme nodded agreement. "There's also the chance that we'll be sliding into a trough when the tsunami hits us. If it's a half-decent wave we could be flipped ass over teakettle— or broached. You've got your choice."

Tait was silent.

"You know what I think," Westholme said. "I think *Haida Noble* will have a lot to do with what happens. She's a lucky ship, George."

His voice shouting above the sound of Hurricane Faith had overridden Lindstrom's. Standing in the entrance to the wheelhouse, the first mate called again: "Christy . . . ready and waiting."

Westholme heard him but kept his eyes fixed on the approaching seas. "Have you got those panels, Eric?"

"Where do you want them?"

"I want them ready to board up this bridge if the glass goes on us. You know what to do."

"Sure thing," Lindstrom said.

"Who's in the engine room?"

"Willie. He wouldn't trust it to anyone else."

Westholme punched the intercom key to the engine room. "Willie, are you there?"

"Where else would I be?" the angry voice came back at him, the Scots accent bristling. "D'you know what they've done to us this time around, Mr. Westholme?"

"What have they done," Westholme countered. "They" was Thomson's word for the company.

"They've left off the boxes of wiping rags. The place will be a bloody mess in a day or two."

Westholme loved him for it. "Are you comfortable down there?"

"Aye, it's tolerable. But you'll talk to the proper authority about the rags?"

"You bet I will, Thomson. Look, we may have to aban-don . . ."

"Ah-h! I've heard all about it from Lindstrom. It's nothing compared to a good blow off the Hebrides. We'll manage fine."

"If I say 'jump,' you jump, Willie."

"D'you think I'd stay down here in a bog of bilge water?" the voice demanded incredulously.

"Hold on tight, Willie." Westholme shook his head and flicked up the button. The time was 0422. Five minutes to go if they were to trust Honolulu's ETA. "You'd better get Lindstrom in here," he said to Tait.

Lindstrom was beside him almost immediately. "Want me to spell you on the wheel, Chris?"

Westholme shook his head. "Stick around, just in case. I'm going to swing her 30 degrees to port at 0426. That's a pretty slim margin of safety, but I don't want to hold her on that course any longer than we have to. We could be dumped before the tsunami hits us."

"We're all ready for you," Lindstrom said. "The boys are wrapped around stanchions on the boat deck.

"If we run into trouble, you get back there and get them into the boats."

"I'll do that."

Together, with Tait standing behind them, they watched the hands of the chronometer move toward 0426. The mighty procession of waves mounting the bow was a kind of metronome throwing time out of perspective, establishing a gigantic beat of its own in which four minutes became forty—and yet when the long hand reached 0426 it seemed as though four seconds had passed.

"Here we go," Westholme said. He started the turn to port, letting the port engine do most of the work exerting some leverage against the overpowering waves. The first wave hit the starboard side as though it had a granite reef built into it. Even with power steering, the wheel tried to spin itself out of Westholme's hands. One more wave, just as large as the last, slammed against *Haida Noble*'s side, climbing the railings to the boat deck. In spite of Westholme's efforts and in spite of the efficiency of the Kort nozzles, the tug swung several degrees farther into the trough.

"To hell with it!" Westholme decided. "One more of those and we'll be in the trough and rolling over. The tsunami will throw two or three good waves at us, but this wind is going to pound us with waves for hours." He reached for the throttles on the remote console, adjusted the power and began to ease the tug's bow back into the oncoming sea. The next wave was somewhat easier, and the following one split itself on *Haida Noble*'s steeply rising bow.

"Come on," Westholme said. "Let's get this over with . . ." and at that moment the ship-to-shore telephone signal pierced the storm.

"Are they out of their skulls," Westholme exploded.

Lindstrom circled him to reach for it.

"Leave it alone," Westholme commanded. "We've got things to do."

The signal persisted until 0430, each of the three men on the bridge reading into it his own kind of foreboding. The voice waiting at the other end belonged to someone seated in a plush thirtieth-floor office in Vancouver. The voice had information to give them, orders to issue, warnings to convey. It didn't matter. Nothing the voice could tell them or demand of them at this moment could make any difference. *Haida Noble* and all the men on board her were committed.

After the signal stopped there was a moment when the combined rage of Hurricane Faith and the sea seemed to fill the wheelhouse, building up a pressure of sound and vibration that made thinking painful, destroying the impulse to utter intelligent words.

It was Lindstrom who made the attempt. "You know what I think? I think the tidal wave has passed us by. It's four minutes past the ETA. Honolulu didn't . . ."

He never finished. The movement of the hull was so incredibly swift and violent that the breath was jerked from his lungs. *Haida Noble* was lifted by the stern and tilted into an approaching trough, her bow swinging sharply starboard into a broaching position from which there could be no recovery.

Westholme had a fleeting impression of white water high above him a ship's length to port, the presence of something vast in the darkness to starboard. The tug was deep in the valley of two opposing waves, and then *Haida Noble* was picked up bodily by a force exerted along the full length of her starboard side, lifted toward the crest of the oncoming hurricane wave and tossed upward on the exploding elements of the two wave systems. The hurricane's attacking host of 60-foot waves racing across the ocean surface was ultimately defenseless against the unbelievable speed and mass of the tsunami; but in the shallows of the continental shelf the collision of the two forces was cataclysmic—two giant waves in headlong attack. The tug hung on the edge of vast, directionless turbulence, spinning in a pale phosphorous of white foam and spindrift, and then she began her stomach-wrenching descent into a bottomless trough.

Inside the wheelhouse the lights flickered and failed. Somewhere in the darkness Westholme thought he heard a man cry out in pain or fear, and then he was bracing himself for the impact that was to come, one hand darting up in an unconscious reflex to adjust the safety goggles he had clamped on minutes before.

It seemed to him the tug was plunging bow first, rolling to starboard all of 30 degrees, corkscrewing into the ocean. Beyond that his orientation and judgment failed him. All he could do was secure the wheel and maintain steerage in the event that *Haida Noble* ever emerged from the dive.

The bow went in deep. In the roaring blackness Westholme had no way of knowing how far or fast it went in until the bridge glass shattered in front of him and the sea entered. His impression was that the whole tug had gone under and was sinking, that he was pressed in by a solid wall of water forcing him away, and now was pinning him to the wheel. Shouldn't he be reacting in some powerful way at this moment, succumbing to the fear of death, struggling to escape the tug in a token attempt at survival, reaching out to secure Lindstrom? He did nothing. For the first time in his twenty-seven years at sea, Westholme stood outside himself and waited for his tug, his crew, and himself to die. There was no emotion or feeling attached to it.

Something in *Haida Noble*'s motion cleared his brain and jerked him back to reality. The bow was coming up, slowly, not nearly fast enough, but the deck was steadying and leveling out as the tug fought to surmount the tons of water riding on her bow, reaching for the slope of the next wave, breaking clear and shaking off the sea. Behind him he heard heavy, loose things tumbling and rolling to the back of the wheelhouse as the angle of inclination increased. The full force of Hurricane Faith was blasting into the wheelhouse past the shattered remains of the safety glass. There was rain mixed with it, and spindrift, but the sea was gone. *Haida Noble* had climbed out and was bow into the waves again.

Standing knee-deep in cold sea water, Westholme shouted for a light. "Break out some storm lamps, Eric, and check the situation on the boat deck."

Lindstrom didn't reply, but in moments Westholme saw the yellow beam of a storm lamp patterning the wheel-house wall as it approached. The face reflected in the light was Tait's. "Lindstrom's out cold," he said. "Pretty badly cut around the face." He held the lamp up to Westholme. "So are you," he added.

Westholme felt no pain. There was too much demanding his attention. "Get him out of this water and check him over. Don't move him to hospital. I want him up top in case we have to abandon later. Send the second engineer down to help Willie and tell Fenton I need him."

Tait stumbled away in the receding water, and Westholme pushed the engine room intercom button. "Willie? Willie Thomson?" There was no reply.

"Willie?"

The angry voice came through loud and clear. "I can't waste time talkin' now, dammit!"

"That's all I wanted to know, Willie. Stan Read's on his way down. We've lost the wheelhouse lights."

"If ye'd allow me I'd give 'em back to ye!"

Minutes later the lights came on again. Fenton stepped in to take the wheel, recoiling from the blast of wind howling through the window. He accepted Westholme's goggles. "You'd better have someone look at your face, Christy," he shouted.

Westholme turned away from the wheel clumsily, feeling bone weary and rubber-legged for the first time. Something like the fear he should have felt before began to take hold of him now, and he forced it away from him.

In the cramped boat deck shelter, little more than a partitioned extension between the radio room and the tug stack, he found most of the crew gathered. Lindstrom was seated on the deck with his back propped against the wall, turning his head groggily from side to side as Bibaud poked an ammonia stick under his nose. His face was a bloody pattern of glass cuts. Bibaud looked up as Westholme entered.

"My God, you're just as bad as this guy!" He passed the ammonia stick to Galbraith and stood up, staring intently into Westholme's face, reaching out to extract shards of glass embedded in the flesh. "Not even good hamburger."

Westholme backed away from him and held up a restraining hand. "We'll patch ourselves up later," he said. "We've got half an hour to get things back in shape. I want panels up over the navigation bridge windows for starters."

The men hesitated, the question in their eyes.

"That was the first wave," Westholme told them. "There will be others. According to the book the second one is always the biggest."

"I think you better take a look at Lindstrom," Galbraith interrupted sharply. "He's passed out again."

20 . . .

At 0332 Volkoff finally lost patience with Knight and attempted to straighten him out with some blunt talk. He interrupted the rig super as he began once again to pour his anger out on the radio operator.

"Son," the Texan was saying coldly and evenly, "you don't know what the hell you're doing. Far as I can make out you've been freeloading on this rig all summer. Right now I wouldn't trust you to fix a crystal set, and as far as that goes . . ."

"Lay off, Charlie," Volkoff called sharply from the other side of the room. He had been trying to concentrate on a game of draw with the geologist and a newly arrived roughneck. "The wind has taken out every antenna on the rig. It's as simple as that. Why don't you come over and help me lose some of my money?"

"Volkoff," Knight shouted above the hurricane sounds, his face reddening as he turned to him, "you're a company man, a head office watchdog. Everybody on this rig knows that!"

"Knock it off, Charlie."

"But until we leave this rig, I'm calling all the shots. Do you get my meaning? File any kind of a report you want, but you better believe my report is going to lay all the cards on the table. British United doesn't give a damn for us—for the boys on this rig. All the company wanted was that extra thousand feet of hole. If they lose the rig it's just another book entry."

"The rig's doing fine, Charlie. You worry too much." Volkoff turned away from him, feeling the super's angry eyes burning into him. The truth was that the drill rig was standing up to the seas remarkably well, in spite of the fact that several of the biggest waves had surmounted the deck in the past hour. He could sympathize with Knight, though. The man's strong awareness of responsibility was chewing at him like acid. He continued to pace restlessly back and forth behind the operator's chair, his eyes wandering over the maze of dials, lights, and wires, trying to dominate them into operation.

"Look at that, would you!"

Everyone in the radio shack heard his exclamation and turned toward him. He was pointing to the radar screen. For the past two hours it had been clear of anything resembling shipping, its field marred with the ripples and distortions created by the hurricane. Now a distinct blip had appeared in the center of the screen, its position in the lee of BUTCO 17, its movement imperceptible.

"The Russian," Volkoff said. "It's trying to move back, away from the rig."

"Bloody well time," Knight said viciously. "Come daylight we'd have fixed their wagon."

There was no way Volkoff could explain it. The Russian

skipper's logic in trying to find some kind of shelter in the lee of BUTCO 17 was acceptable. Audacious but intelligent and acceptable. Now he began to worry that the approach to the rig had not been to gain shelter, but for some other calculated purpose. It seemed impossible that the vessel, loaded as it was with valuable and delicate instruments and oceanographic equipment, would indulge in scientific snooping in weather like this. But then again why not? Under conditions like this, with communications out, the giant drill rig was like a mired-down dinosaur incapable of preventing any kind of an approach. With considerable courage, superior seamanship and the right kind of technical equipment it was possible to gain some kind of information, perhaps even install monitoring instruments. All of this was possible—but highly unlikely.

"Afraid of a collision," he decided. "They want to put more distance between them and us."

"That's a lot of distance," the geologist observed. "How far would you say?" he asked the operator.

"All of a thousand yards, I'd say."

"That's what you say, is it?" Knight said testily.

The blip was in the clear now, moving painfully slowly. "None of it adds up," Volkoff said. "She had some kind of shelter in the lee of the drill rig. Now she's facing a full sea again."

The geologist made an attempt at humor and failed:

"They've picked up a radio signal the wind is swinging. The waves are going to start coming the other way."

"Radio! That's what we need is a radio," Knight said, back on the subject again. "Hasn't anybody got a transistor that'll pick up Alberni, for God sake?"

Patiently Volkoff explained again. "We gave that up a long time ago, Charlie. The atmospherics are impossible, and the chances are most stations are knocked off the air or are running on auxiliary power."

Shortly after 0400 Volkoff and three of the others went back to playing cards. The blip on the radar screen was still easing north, but everyone except Knight had lost interest in the maneuver. He sat astride a chair with his chin resting on clasped hands across its back and glared balefully at the dot of light, his anger diverted from the radio operator to the trespassing Russians. From time to time the card players heard him explode into savage monologue in which British United and all living Russians suffered badly.

The poker game went on in spite of him, few words spoken because the high decibel roar of Hurricane Faith discouraged all but the most necessary conversation. No one played well; attentions were divided by the immensity of the wind, by Knight's troubled state of mind, and by the feeling of utter isolation that the blacked out communications imparted.

At 0430 Knight spun his chair in the direction of the operator. "It's 4:30, son. See if you can get a broadcast out of that bunch of junk."

"I've been trying for anything I can get, Mr. Knight. If I had a chance to get up to the antenna masts I could bring you in a signal just like that."

Knight flicked a disgusted finger through the orderly bundles of colored wires feeding into the back of the operator's console. "Spaghetti! Just so much goddam spaghetti." He directed an angry glance to the radar screen. "The Russians are getting radio signals, you can bet on that. One thing's sure, they . . . Christ!"

The others turned to see him standing beside the fallen chair, pointing his finger unbelievingly at the screen. Some of them, including Volkoff, were in time to see the small line of light spin sideways and plummet down the badly scrambled screen toward center. Before it disappeared Volkoff had guessed and was filling the room with his warning. "Cut the power, Ronnie! Hit the deck and hang on!" All around him bodies were diving for the floor, clutching for handholds. His own arms wrapped themselves around one of the legs of the console housing. At the same time the lights went out.

In the solid blackness, thick with the hoarse rage of Hurricane Faith's voice, they waited for something that only

Volkoff had any inkling of. In the dark, Knight's voice yelled plaintively. "What the hell is this, Mike? Some kind of . . ."

And then the impact occurred, so massive, so totally shocking that their senses refused for long moments to relay any kind of decipherable information.

It was more than a crushing broadside blow to BUTCO 17's northern perimeter. There was a lifting force coupled with it, a force so huge and effortless that one of the rig's fully ballasted tripod legs was lifted from the sea bottom, tilting the steel island alarmingly into the face of the hurricane. Beneath the deck, seismic sea wave and hurricane wave met in a gigantic explosion of opposing forces, buckling and tearing loose inch-thick steel plates. On the southern perimeter of the rig, Hurricane Faith's waves, rearing high against the attack of the speeding tsunami, raced across the drill rig's tilted deck and washed away installations as though they were made of cardboard. In the final analysis, it was the weight of these waves pressing down on the deck that saved the rig from total destruction. The displaced tripod leg was forced to the sea bottom again with an impact that was small compared to the blows that had preceded it—but even in this act of recovery, irreparable damage was done.

It was the cold water and the bite of the wind that shocked Volkoff back to reality. He lay with the others in the ruins of the radio shack, his arms still locked around the metal leg. Moments before he had been aware of water mounting over him, roaring in his ears, pounding him with all manner of floating things. So cold and water-laden was the wind that he was never clearly aware of the moment when the rushing sea retreated from the shack.

Still lying flat he craned his head around, trying to identify bodies lying close to him. "Charlie," he called against the scream of the storm. Some distance away, he thought he heard a voice reply. Much closer the radio operator shouted in a voice approaching panic.

"Hey! Mr. Knight? Mr. Volkoff? Gimme a hand, quick! I got something across my legs!"

Volkoff eased his grip on the post and slithered in inches of cold water toward the sound of the voice. "Coming over, Ron." He found the operator lying on his back, shivering with cold and shock, and began to explore the prostrate form, groping down past the waist to just below the knees; there his hand came up against solid wood and metal. A substantial portion of the heavy console had collapsed across the operator's lower legs.

"You feeling any pain, Ron?" he shouted in the injured man's ears.

"Nothing much. Something heavy across my legs. God I'm cold!"

Someone else crawled in alongside Volkoff. It was the roughneck, breathing heavily as though he had just completed a long race:

"You got some trouble here? I . . . uh . . . somebody hollering . . ." He broke into a violent spasm of coughing, trying to tear the salt water out of his lungs.

On the other side of the operator's body Knight's familiar voice cut in. "Isn't this beautiful, though. Isn't this beautiful! The whole damn rig falling apart! She can take anything! They said—any kind of a wind, any kind of a sea. Crap! I tell you, Volkoff, those people are going to get an earful from me . . ."

"Shut up, Charlie, and give us a hand here." The roughneck followed him as he eased ahead and came to a kneeling position with his shoulder against the face of the console. The roughneck imitated him. "Are you over there, Charlie?" Volkoff shouted.

"Tell me when," Knight called back.

Volkoff leaned close to the operator's ear and explained the situation: "We're going to lift this thing off you. As soon as you're free slide out from under. All right?"

"Sure," the operator chattered. "I'm freezing. It's the cold more than anything."

"Here we go," Volkoff shouted. "Heave!"

The heavy console came up slowly at first, then more easily as its point of balance shifted . . . and suddenly the operator began to scream:

"Please . . . no! No-o-o!" The sound became animal in its pain and faded abruptly to unconsciousness.

The three of them wrestled the heavy weight away from him and tumbled it back onto the deck, standing up in the full fury of the wind to do it. Back on his knees again, Volkoff made a tentative inspection of the injured man's legs. From just below the kneecaps, down to the feet, he felt nothing he could recognize as solid bone.

Knight and the roughneck were crowded in close to him now. "He's a mess," Volkoff reported. "He doesn't need first-aid, he needs major surgery."

"We'll take him to the infirmary," Knight said. "Get some morphine into him."

"No time," Volkoff told him. "If we're lucky we've got an hour before this rig breaks up."

The roughneck didn't want to share his opinion. "She feels real steady," he said. "I think she's going to make it okay."

The sound of something huge and metallic crashing in the outer darkness made a mockery of his statement. Other lesser sounds came to them from every direction, synchronized with the battering impact of each approaching wave.

"We were hit by a tidal wave," Volkoff told them, "and it almost knocked us out. The next one will be bigger. We've got to get off before that happens."

"The next one!" Knight shouted in disbelief.

"There will be several. The second one is usually the biggest. What we need right now, Charlie, is a light."

"I got a light, by golly!" the roughneck said in a startled voice. Almost immediately the substantial beam from a waterproof flashlight speared the blackness. Volkoff took the offered light and shone it in the operator's face. The skin was waxen and beaded with rain, but intermittent wisps of condensed breath from the open mouth were positive indications of life.

He handed the light back to the roughneck, the rays highlighting the gaunt, hollow-eyed look of strain on the man's face. "Do you think you can find your way over to the infirmary in all this?"

"I'll give her a try."

"Pick up an armful of blankets and ask them for some morphine ampules and some splint material. Better still, if the first-aid man can be spared, bring him back with you."

The roughneck rose into a crouching position, faced into the wind. Volkoff held him back a moment. "Tell anybody you see to get ready to abandon rig. They should start making their way to life raft stations now." The man nodded, struggled to his feet and was gone.

Only then did it occur to Volkoff that there had been others in the radio shack when the wave hit; the geologist, another roughneck. "We'd better round up the others," he said in Knight's ear.

"What?" Knight said in a thick voice.

"Freddy and the other roughneck. They're around here somewhere."

"That's probably so," Knight slurred disinterestedly.

Volkoff was aware that the super had lurched to a standing position. When next he heard his voice, it was a thread of sound under the wind. "Be right back."

"Where are you going, Charlie."

From far in the distance, miles away he heard ". . . send a telegram . . . company's going to hear about this . . ."

Volkoff scrambled in the direction of the sound, groping like a blind man to make contact. "Charlie! Wait, I'll help you send it. Charlie . . ." Only the wind, and the thundering sea, and the metallic death of the rig came to his ears.

He couldn't follow Knight without a light to point his way, or to be left as a marker to enable him to return. In that blackness there was no direction. The familiar hand-holds and building corners, the chunks of machinery in their roped perimeters that had once marked the way on blustery nights were all hurled together now in a tangle of destruction. He returned to the torn square of the radio shack, realizing that in his brief pursuit of Knight he had gone through a space once occupied by the south wall of the shack.

On his hands and knees he crawled looking for the radio operator, found him and checked briefly for the throbbing of a pulse in the man's neck. He was still alive. Proceeding methodically from there, he began to feel his way through the ruins, looking for the others. The geologist he found, glasses still intact on his dead face, his upper body projecting from the wreckage of a fallen wall. The other roughneck was either gone, swept away in the crushing wave, or buried somewhere under the timber and galvanized iron. He never had the opportunity to find out.

The bar of light from the lamp brought him around to face the returning roughneck, still wheezing and coughing fluid from his damaged lungs. He was totally exhausted, leaning heavily on Volkoff as he lowered himself to the deck.

"How did you make out?" Volkoff asked. It was a token question. He knew the answer from the man's silence, his broken attitude, slumped dejectedly among the soaked wreckage. Volkoff waited; gave him time.

Finally he raised his head. "We got to get off this thing," he said. "I didn't see no one. The infirmary is gone. I couldn't find it."

Although they would never know it, there were nineteen men alive aboard the rig at that moment. Knight was not among them. He had hurried over the south edge of the rig minutes before, intent on performing his errand. Of the living nineteen, seven had suffered serious injury; the other twelve were mobile but disoriented and panic-stricken. None of them knew there was worse to come, and only four of them ever made it to one of the rig's special, totally enclosed, untippable life rafts. Unfortunately it had been smashed when the remains of the helicopter were hurled upon it.

Volkoff shook the man roughly. Their paths had never crossed on the rig. There was no reason why they should have. Even in the card game tonight no names had been exchanged.

"My name's Mike Volkoff . . ."

The roughneck nodded, acknowledging that he knew. He lifted his head in the grotesque, yellow light. "Me, I'm Nick Bianco. I seen you around."

Volkoff took the light from him and turned it on his watch. Five minutes after five. Better than a half an hour had gone by: "Nick, we've got to get to the life raft as fast as we can make it, and we've got to take Ronnie with us. Okay?"

"Sure."

Together, they came to their feet, bracing themselves against the unrelenting wind, and moved into position on either side of the operator. He didn't move or make a sound as they stopped and lifted him, inexpertly and without ceremony, slinging one arm around each of their shoulders trying to lift his crushed legs clear of the shambles as they stumbled toward the ladder that would take them down to the raft deck.

They had no right to make it. The slashing wind bullied them savagely from behind, and the tangle of timber and steel was under their feet every step of the way. The beam of the flashlight was almost useless under these conditions, blinding them with its reflection as often as it showed them the way. Volkoff's lower limbs tingled sympathetically as the operator's terribly crushed legs struck one obstacle after another. There was no alternative but to lift and drag him along.

At the ladder it was a little easier. They were out of the direct blast of the wind as they lowered themselves, the roughneck first and then Volkoff, easing the unconscious body down and then following after.

The flashlight played over the streamlined contours of the life raft, a miracle of sea-survival design fashioned in reinforced Fiberglas and resembling a mammoth curling stone in the yellow beam. Volkoff climbed the boarding ladder and slid back the entrance port, shining the flashlight into the dark, dry interior. He scrambled in and turned to help the roughneck as he struggled up the ladder with the operator over his shoulder. They were going to make it!

Nick Bianco was wheezing like a drowning man as he dumped the radio operator into Volkoff's arms and fell into the safety capsule. Volkoff left both of them there and scrambled down the ladder again, circling the raft to throw off the mooring clamps. In the distance he heard, or did he imagine, the approach of a new, more ominous sound different in timbre and quality from the contralto scream of the wind? For the first time he felt fear, absolute, muscle-dissolving panic. He stumbled back to the ladder and started to climb, forcing his rubbery legs to move him up and over into the Fiberglas capsule. He reached up and slid the hatch closed; slammed down the two hatch fastenings . . . and a moment later the entire, dark, ear-shattering world turned upside down.

21 . . .

At 0617 the third wave in the tsunami system passed under and over *Haida Noble*. It was not as bad as the first, and in comparison with the second it was an anticlimax. Short of disabling the one remaining engine or breaching the leaking hull, not much more needed to be done to kill the crippled tug.

Westholme had learned a few things from the first wave and had *Haida Noble* in a somewhat better position to receive the second one, storm panels in position, both first and second engineers on station in the engine room, the crew deployed on the upper decks keyed up and ready for the unexpected. Lindstrom, protesting violently, was strapped into a stretcher on the boat deck and lashed securely between two stanchions with Galbraith detailed to keep an eye on him and cut him free if the tug started to founder. Westholme issued those orders in an offhand manner, but his crew was seasoned enough to know that tugs didn't founder, they sank with few preliminaries, like so much pig iron. Because of her size, *Haida Noble* might hesitate a few minutes longer than a smaller tug, but not long enough to make any difference.

Morale was good. All of them, except the cook, were holding together remarkably well. Perhaps it was the cook's abject terror that influenced them in the opposite direction. After the assault of the first wave he had been found on the floor of his cabin, lying on his side, eyes closed, knees tucked under his chin, screaming like a trapped animal. It was a disgusting sight. Even now, with a strong sedative in him, he remained curled in a corner of the boat deck shelter, eyes tightly closed to blind himself to reality.

There was no describing the tsunami's second blow. It didn't seem possible that a force that massive, involving as it did a 400-foot submarine wave whose upper limits peaked 30 feet above the surface of the sea, could strike with such suddenness. Violence of impact, yes—but with the swiftness of a boxer jabbing. Westholme, glued to the wheel, felt as though the blow had been delivered against him personally —that the sea's fist had slammed into his entire body, bruising the marrow of his bones.

Haida Noble's hull rang dully, like a broken bell hammered with a sledge and then she was propelled ahead and up, emerging on the furious peak created by the two opposing sea forces. The arcs were on at the time. Through the makeshift Plexiglas window Westholme caught an unbelievable glimpse of the entire sea beneath him for a thousand yards ahead. It was like looking down on a dark range of alpine mountains. Under him, unseen because they were on the edge of it, was the deep valley into which *Haida Noble* must plunge. Beside him, Bradley Fenton hunched his big shoulders and pressed in tight against Westholme. To give comfort? To receive it? It didn't matter; every man on *Haida Noble* was alone when the big tug pointed her bow into that dark valley.

Afterward none of them remembered too much about it,

least of all Westholme. The tug was in command in those lost minutes, even though both men managed to stay at the wheel. *Haida Noble* came through it. Crippled and leaking, with stunned and injured men aboard her she rose once more from the sea and lifted her bow to the next attack from Hurricane Faith. And Westholme's only feeling at that moment, as he swung the wheel and reached tentatively for the remote controls, was gratitude. Once again he owed his life to *Haida Noble* and their relationship became, if possible, closer and more profound.

The damage was extensive and some of it serious, particularly where the water poured in around the cracked stern gland on the port engine shaft. Willie Thomson called for help as soon as the main tsunami turbulence passed by, and Bibaud and Galbraith went below to rig auxiliary pumps in the event that the main engine pumps couldn't cope.

The forecastle deck was a shambles of mast lengths, broken booms and the remains of radar and wireless installations, all wrapped together by the sea and tied with the tangled remains of guy lines and stays. The side band radio and ship-to-shore communications systems were out, although the tug's intercom was still working. Tait was the first to use it, calling the bridge to report water entering the crew's quarters through fractured plates around the toppled forward mast. Life rafts and one lifeboat had been carried away, and sundry portholes stove in; in the wire room, despite precautions taken before the hurricane hit, a 3-ton anchor had broken its shackles and punched a hole through the bulkhead leading to the engine room.

Westholme let Fenton make the general damage survey and supervise the emergency repairs. Until the third and fourth wave passed by, his place was in the wheelhouse.

Tait had joined him again in time to help him with the third wave, which was damaging enough but manageable.

"Is this thing slowing down," he said, "or is it my imagination?"

Westholme had sensed a different feeling to the sea, a different sound to the wind for some time now. The barometer had been up over 29 inches for at least a half an hour, but that didn't mean anything necessarily. "Let's call it imagination," he shouted. "How do things look down there?"

"Like a bulldozer went through."

"Lindstrom?"

"He rode it out pretty good. Wants to go back to work."

Westholme shook his head in the negative and concentrated hard on the next approaching sea. The view through the streaked and scratched makeshift screen was less than perfect. "George, I think you're right. This thing *is* slowing down some."

Had *Haida Noble*'s radio been working, he would have had confirmation. The weather report was at that moment issuing a revision. The meteorologists, right in their theory and wrong in their timing, were able to report that the arctic cold front—the front which was supposed to have subdued an upstart of a gale three days ago—had finally succeeded in shouldering a full-scale hurricane off course. Faith was moving out to sea, having sated herself in an unprecedented march of death and destruction along the Pacific Northwest coast of North America. The tidal wave had helped, of course, but the two in opposition, working together but against each other like the jaws of a vice, had crushed life and property into a common tangle of ruin. Cities, towns, communities, and isolated dwellings were not spared from the vice, and the emergency resources of the entire Pacific Northwest, land, sea, and air, were taxed to the limit for days to come.

The sea and the wind had abated dramatically by 0800 hours. The fourth of the tsunami waves created no real problems, and returned Bibaud to a semblance of his old clowning self. "After you get hit with a sledgehammer two, three times, a tap from a baseball bat feels real good."

It was now Westholme's watch officially and he took it automatically, unthinking, until Fenton persuaded him to get some rest. "You haven't had any sleep since you came on board as far as I know."

"Neither has anyone else."

"Sure they have. I think you should have a few hours in the sack, Christy. Things are under control."

Westholme looked around the wheelhouse skeptically; the shattered glass, the dripping and battered storm panels, radar scopes drenched with water and unserviceable, the port engine room telegraph signaled to "Stop." "Things look great," he said.

"There's nothing we can do about the port engine," Fenton persisted. "The pumps are working fine and we'll be able to get at that stern gland in another hour. Willie's in his bunk."

"Willie is?"

Fenton nodded.

"Well," Westholme decided. "Things must be better than I think."

"With any luck we'll be back in Vancouver this time tomorrow."

"No we won't," Westholme said. "The instructions were to pick up the drill rig."

"There's no way we can handle her with half power," Fenton protested. "We've got trouble of our own."

"Not as much trouble as that rig. It's daylight. We should be in visual contact with her right now. Have you taken a look this morning?"

Fenton nodded slowly. "There's nothing out there . . . but then our position . . ."

"Brad, you know as well as I do that we're ten, maybe fifteen miles off the mouth of Barkley Sound, dead center. Look . . ." He called off the names of the major islands lying to port of them in the gray, obscure distance. "Effingham, Dodd . . ." *Haida Noble* dipped into a trough of the huge swell running, and the landmarks were lost to sight.

"That's so," Fenton admitted.

"Then somewhere ten miles astern there should be a drill rig. I'll take you up on that bunk time, but I want you to come about and start a search. Begin with the drill rig co-ordinates and work shoreward from there following the line of drift. When you spot anything I want to hear about it."

Fenton nodded and turned to the wheel.

As Westholme left, he had another thought. "Keep a sharp watch posted port and starboard, and keep your eye on the echo sounder. There may be an unmarked navigational hazard closer than we think." Fenton knew he meant the drill rig.

He didn't go to the master's stateroom immediately. First he made it down to the engine room and said a few words to Read and the deckhands sloshing in ankle-deep water at the base of the engine installations. The sounds of the pumps and the main engine undoubtedly rendered anything he said unintelligible, but all three of them nodded cheerfully, and he gathered that they were reasonably satisfied with their lot.

Before he was through, he had prowled all the trouble spots on the vessel, from the hold on up to the main deck. *Haida Noble* had taken a terrible beating. For the first time since he had captained her, he saw the visible signs of the sea's massive punishment in her buckled plates and battered bulkheads. The anchor that had broken loose in the wire room now rested against the ruptured engine room bulkhead with one great fluke hanging down into the engine room itself. The possibilities of recovering and securing it before they got back to port were remote.

The galley was much worse than he had imagined. One table, tearing loose from its floor bolts, had ripped its way through benches and set them free to pound the interior of the area to splinters. There was literally no place to sit or to set a cup. In spite of this the electric galley stove was glowing red. A large pot of coffee simmered at the back of it, protected from upset in its metal grid. In the center of the stove above the red glow a two-gallon pot of water sat and bubbled. Westholme went over to investigate, lifting the lid to peer into the steaming interior. The aroma was beautiful: meat, barley, split peas, a touch of tomato catsup perhaps, and enough garlic to make it interesting. He picked up the ladle hanging on the pot edge, dipped it in and tried a careful sip of the scalding mixture. A little thin yet, but coming along. It would be a shame to eat it before it was ready.

He looked around for something to stave off the hunger pains. He was damned hungry! On the galley's cutting board a cold roast of beef had been pinned to the wood with a knife to keep it from rolling onto the deck. A loaf of bread had been secured in the same manner. He made himself four mayonnaise-dripping, beef and cheese sandwiches, filled a plastic carafe with hot coffee, topped it with an inverted mug and headed for his cabin, halting whenever he sensed a violent movement building in the tug.

Arriving in his quarters, he deposited the sandwiches and the coffee on the floor by his bunk where they stood least chance of upending, and then cut through the bathroom to Lindstrom's adjoining cabin. He opened the door carefully, allowed light from the bathroom to spill across the first officer's face briefly, and then shut the door. Lindstrom was asleep and breathing strenuously.

Passing through the bathroom again, he stopped to examine his wounded face and grimaced at the sight. His skin was pock-marked and slit with glass wounds, many of them still oozing blood. He moistened a clean cloth with hot water and green soap and sponged away some of the mess before he returned to his banquet.

Seated on the floor with his back comfortably settled against his bunk, he poured coffee into his cup, tasted and savoured it. Delicious! No need to rush things. He would have to find out from the cook, if the bastard lived, what kind of coffee that was. He contemplated his sandwiches, spreading them out like a deck of cards and choosing the biggest and fattest, raising it to his mouth and taking a whole quarter of it in one bite. Great! And he had three sandwiches to go!

Tait found him there two hours later, lying on his side asleep. There were three good-looking beef and cheese sandwiches close to him. Tait took one of them before he woke Westholme up.

Heaving himself back into a sitting position, Westholme shook his head violently and stared up at Tait, the sleep still dark in his eyes.

"We thought maybe you should come up on the bridge, Mr. Westholme."

"Sure . . . sure." He hauled himself to his feet. "What's the trouble?"

"Looks like the rig may be gone. The way Fenton figures it we should be over the co-ordinates now."

Westholme stooped and picked up the two remaining sandwiches, paying elaborate attention to the one Tait had in his hand. Tait grinned and took a large bite. "Have you been watching the echo sounder up there?"

Tait stood aside as Westholme stepped through the doorway and headed for the wheelhouse. "So far we're picking up twenty fathoms. It looks clean down below."

On the bridge Fenton was dividing his attention between the wheel and the echo sounder. When Westholme entered he turned the steering back to Tait. "The rig could be drifting, Christy. There's always that possibility."

"Slim chance," Westholme said. "What's your procedure?"

"We're on the second leg of a one-mile-square search. If it's down there we're bound to pick it up."

Keeping his eyes on the echo sounder, Westholme asked more questions. "The leak in the engine room under control?"

"The best they could do. We're shipping ten or fifteen gallons an hour."

"Has anyone checked on Lindstrom?"

"Sleeping like a baby, last time I heard. The cook's something else again. He has enough pills in him to put a gorilla to sleep, and still he hollers!"

Tait said quietly, but with a note of apprehension in his voice: "We're over something . . ."

"Dead slow!" Westholme cautioned. He had seen it at the same time. The jittery line on the echo sounder which had been tickling the mark at twenty fathoms, had suddenly jumped to ten; then eight; then abruptly back to fifteen fathoms.

"That's as far as we go," Westholme said. "Reverse engine, dead slow, George." To Fenton he said, "Get a sea marker out before we move off."

Fenton issued brief instructions into the intercom and a moment later Bibaud hustled out on the forecastle deck, his arms wrapped around a fluorescent red sea marker and its neat coil of anchor rope. He tossed the coil over the side followed by the sea marker, waved jauntily up at the bridge and scuttled out of sight.

"I think we'd better make a turn to starboard," Westholme decided, "circle around and then follow the line of drift toward Amphitrite Point."

Fenton had remained silent, not necessarily agreeing with the move.

"We couldn't take a chance on proceeding farther, Brad. There's a hundred and twenty feet of water under us. The deck of that rig is four hundred feet across. The legs are more than a hundred and fifty feet high. Even if she's tipped or broken up the chances are that part of her is just under the surface. In this swell she'd go through our bottom like a razor blade."

"You think that was BUTCO 17?"

"I hope it wasn't, but if it wasn't then she's drifting, and the line of drift is toward Amphitrite, making some allowance for last night's wind direction. The job now is to find her—or her survivors."

"Man!" Fenton said in frustration, "What a little bit of radar could do for us now. Get back to the sack, Christy. You've got a few more hours coming to you."

On the way back to his quarters he looked in on Lindstrom and found him half asleep and groggy, his bony frame seeming to lose itself under the blankets, his eyes looking heavy and doped.

"They said you were asleep," Westholme accused him. "You could be up chipping brightwork or nailing the galley back together again."

"That's what I've been telling everyone," Lindstrom protested. "I feel great!"

There was a large contused bump on the side of his skull just above and behind the right ear. Westholme leaned over and studied it closely. The protrusion had parted the salt-and-pepper hair on Lindstrom's scalp. "If you got it brass plated it would be a doorknob," he said. "Any idea what did it, Eric?"

"I don't know . . . Who knows!" he said impatiently. "Christy, I'm going to climb into my pants and walk out of here."

"Have you tried to do any reading?"

"What's there to read? I don't want to read."

"Stay put until 1200 hours," Westholme instructed. "We don't need you for anything right now and I'd like you to take your watch tonight. Curl up with a good book until we give you the signal."

"What about the rig, Chris? Are we in sight?"

"She's not where she's supposed to be," Westholme said carefully. "There's a strong possibility she went down. The echo sounder picked up something near her co-ordinates. All we can do now is follow her probable line of drift in case she's still floating, pick up survivors if she isn't floating."

"The rig gone down," Lindstrom said in disbelief. He stared up at Westholme with realization beginning to return. "This whole goddam coastline must be . . . the wind and tidal wave together. Chris, how bad are things?"

"Chances are they couldn't be any worse. We'll finish the search and then duck into Ucluelet for information—if Ucluelet is in shape to tell us anything."

"Remember when Alberni got hit in '64? That was tame compared to this. Shipping destroyed; half the town washed away. People are going to need help."

"That's why we're staying out here," Westholme said. "Nobody is likely to come looking for that drill rig until the towns and settlements have been taken care of. Now lie back, you lead swinger. We may need you sooner than you think."

He shut Lindstrom's door behind him and crossed to his own cabin, uneasy about the first officer's appearance. It took a lot to shake this man; but this time he was hurt. His eyes showed it.

In his bunk and under the covers, he tried to turn his mind to normal considerations. There was nothing normal, he decided. If the drill rig had gone down then most of its crew were down there with it. The chances of anyone abandoning the rig successfully were slim to impossible. Beyond that, along the tortured sweep of the West Coast, there would be death and destruction in every inlet, on every stretch of shallow coast leading to a habitation. Vancouver? Mostly hurricane damage, he decided. But how much, and where had it hit hardest? Was Lee safe in the house endangered by the line of poplars? Was she at home at all? It didn't matter where she was, he wanted her with him right now, close to him in the bunk, bringing him her special kind of comfort, listening to him try to explain that she was the only reason he went to sea—and the only reason he came back.

22 . . .

Fenton didn't send for Westholme until the life raft was almost alongside. To begin with, sighted at a distance it could have been just one more piece of incredible flotsam like the stuff they had spotted along the line of drift in the past two hours; mostly wooden wreckage impossible to identify as part of BUTCO 17. There were steel fuel drums, a wide variety of floats, the forward section of a gillnetter—empty and gutted by the sea.

Galbraith spotted and identified the life raft, its orange Fiberglas lid almost totally camouflaged with broad strips of kelp. Floating in the big swell it resembled a giant lacquered bowl inverted on the surface of the sea. Fenton didn't want to launch a boat unless he had to. Chances were the raft was empty, leaking and ready to sink. He edged *Haida Noble* toward it cautiously, avoiding the possibility of the raft being swept against the tug's hull. Fifty yards away from the bobbing capsule, Tait, balancing in the debris of the ruined foredeck, employed a loud hailer to test for life:

"Hello, life raft. Can you hear us? Hello, life raft."

Haida Noble drew nearer, closing the gap to 25, then 15 yards, Tait continuing to use the loud hailer as the distance narrowed. Finally he shrugged his shoulders in a gesture of futility and looked up to the bridge for further instructions.

"We'd better try and get it alongside," Fenton told Galbraith. "Hustle down there and give Tait a hand to put a hook on it. I'll come about and place it in our lee."

It wasn't until the raft was almost within pike pole distance that they heard the rappings, weak but persistent and unhalting. Tait waved violently to the bridge to stand off and Fenton swung the tug to starboard, opening the gap to a safe distance.

At that point Fenton summoned Westholme to the bridge.

Westholme stared at the bobbing capsule speculatively while he listened to Fenton's plan of action, which was simply to lower one of the boats, place *Haida Noble* between the rescue operation and the swell and then transfer the occupants of the raft to the boat.

"I don't know, Brad," he said finally. "The people in that thing are either too weak to open the hatch, or the fastenings are jammed. We'll have a devil of a time trying to work on it with the sea running like this. I'd feel a lot better if we could take the raft on board."

He reached for the binoculars Fenton had been using for the search, and went out on the navigation deck for a clear view of the problem. A distance of 25 yards separated the tug from the raft. The raft's restless movement and the broad ribbons of kelp concealing much of the structural detail made it difficult for Westholme to find what he was looking for— some kind of provision for attaching towing or lifting ropes. Finally he spotted it, a kind of pad eye consisting of a heavy metal plate with a ring molded into its upper surface. It was riveted into the raft's fender ring. Moving the glasses slowly around the fender, he found the outline of another under a slick strand of kelp. There should be at least one and possibly two more.

Returning to the wheelhouse he handed Fenton the glasses. "The raft is fitted with lifting rings. We'll take it aboard with one of the stern booms. You'll still have to use a boat to fit the lifting hooks. Will you see to it, Brad?"

Fenton nodded and draped the binocular straps around Westholme's neck. "Keep between us and that swell."

"I'll do my best. We won't lift the raft on board until you've got the boat back in the davits and all the crew aft to fend off. The folks inside that thing are going to appreciate it if we give them a soft landing."

Fenton departed, and minutes later Westholme heard the sounds of the davit blocks rumbling as the boat eased down the port side of *Haida Noble*. In order to make a quick escape from the tug, the lifeboat's engine was turning over before the boat hit the water, and in a moment Westholme saw the boat pulling away toward the raft with Fenton at the tiller while Galbraith held the line from the tug's afterdeck boom.

Just before the lifeboat arrived alongside the pitching orange disc Fenton cut the engine to idle and let the next swell carry the boat precisely on target with Galbraith fending off and at the same time looking for an eye into which to insert his pike pole. He worked quickly and expertly, finding the eye and pulling the raft alongside long enough to insert the first hook of the bridle, then swinging the raft to bring the next eye into position to receive its hook. There were three eyes spaced around the raft's fender, and Galbraith made a brisk thumb-and-finger gesture when the third hook was in place, attached a nylon towing line to the raft's third eye and began to pay the line out as Fenton made the turn and started back to the tug. Behind them the towing line took up the strain seconds after Galbraith had whipped several turns around a cleat. In this manner they towed the raft back to within 30 feet of the tug, with Bibaud on the afterdeck taking in the slack of the boom cable.

At this point Galbraith cast loose the towline, and the lifeboat returned to its retrieval position under its davits, leaving the raft secured to the barely slack boom cable. On the intercom Westholme called for Tait to come and take the wheel. By the time the deckhand arrived, the lifeboat was up and swinging into a secured position on the boat deck. Both Fenton and Galbraith scrambled out and fell into step behind Westholme as he made his way down to the afterdeck to size up the situation.

The raft was floating at a safe distance several yards beyond the tip of the extended boom. Bibaud had the winch power on and was standing beside the control levers with a look of impatience on his face.

"Come on you guys. You want them to die from old age in there, damn it!"

Both Fenton and Galbraith had armed themselves with pike poles; Westholme did the same, turning to Bibaud to give him the signal:

"Slow and easy, Ernie. Like a crate of eggs."

The machinery took up the strain; gears engaged, and one of the winch drums began to rotate smoothly, drawing its line back through the boom tackle. The slack bridle pulled taut above the dome of the life raft, hesitated a moment and then drew the capsule clear of the ocean surface, not before a partially subdued swell struck the underside of the raft and set it swinging alarmingly.

"Start her coming inboard," Westholme shouted above the machinery sounds.

"Okay, okay," Bibaud grumbled. The boom rotated around the Samson post as the raft rose higher above the water and began to swing closer to the edge of the tug. All three men reached out and up with their poles to stop the pendulum action of the big, orange disc, its surface the color of a boiled crab, mottled and streaked with seaweed and oil scum. Bibaud maneuvered the raft dead center above the cleared stern portion of the afterdeck and lowered it to a resting position on the deck, the impact cushioned by the steadying arms and shoulders of the three men.

The French Canadian cut the power and came over to join them as they circled the raft looking for the best means of entry. At first glance there was no visible hatch opening, so streamlined and well-fitted was the capsule. Brushing away the strips of kelp, Westholme found the thin, oblong line marking the entrance. He slapped his hand, palm-downward, against the smooth surface.

"Hello, in there! Can you hear us?"

Immediately they heard the sound of a muffled voice. A hard object beat slowly and methodically against the inner shell.

"Can you open the hatch?" Westholme shouted.

This time words could be understood without question. "No . . . Stuck."

"Galbraith," Westholme instructed. "See if you can hustle up the tools we need to break into this thing. Ask Stan Read to come up and give us a hand."

It took the better part of thirty minutes to drill holes into the entrance hatch sufficient to gain leverage to pry it open. It yielded slowly at first and then sprang open as though spring-loaded, releasing a thick cloud of incredibly foul air. It was a mixture of human sweat, and breath, and the un-mistakable stench of putrefaction.

Over his shoulder Westholme said: "Someone fetch a couple of stretchers and an armful of blankets."

Stan Read handed him the flashlight he unhooked from his equipment belt, and Westholme shone it into the fetid interior, playing the yellow beam over the tangled mess in-side. As far as he could make out there were three men in there, although there could have been others in the heaped mass of water-soaked blankets, broken ration boxes and first-aid supplies.

"Okay," Westholme assured them. "This is the end of the line. Can any of you get out under your own power?"

"Sure," a husky voice said. "Reach me a hand."

Westholme shone his light toward the voice and extended his arm, feeling the wet, cold fingers curl around his. He took up the strain, felt the body tense and move forward, then fall back again with a cry of frustration as much as of pain:

"I'm hurting too much, damn it!"

"Relax," Westholme told him. "We'll get you out. What condition are the others in?"

"One of them is in very bad shape. Critical I'd say. He hasn't moved for hours. The other has breathing troubles. Pneumonia, maybe."

Westholme shone his light around the edge of the raft's dome and spotted the hand clamps at spaced intervals. "Does the top come off this thing?"

"Supposed to. Although you'll probably have the same trouble as you did with the hatch. Maybe I can loosen some of these off for you?"

"Don't move," Westholme instructed. He clambered inside the shell, his feet going ankle-deep in seawater and sludge, his nostrils tightening against the stench of the confined interior. His fingers ripped down on the spring-loaded clamps, releasing every second one and then completing the freeing of the raft cover by releasing diagonally opposite clamps in order to take off the pressure equally. He kicked the debris away under his feet, spread his legs slightly to take up the strain, placed the flats of his hands against the raft top and pressed upward, applying his full strength. Nothing much happened, and then the left-hand edge of the lid began to slide free, letting in a thin slice of daylight. He scrambled over to that side and applied full pressure. Stan Read and Galbraith helped from the outside, sliding screwdrivers into the widening gap and prying downward. The top popped suddenly like a pressure lid on a jar of preserves, spinning off to one side and landing on the deck. In the full light of day Westholme stared at the faces of the rescued.

The three men lay sprawled on plastic-covered foam-rubber mattresses in man-sized "bins" which were molded into the ledge that circled the perimeter of the raft's interior.

Two of them looked dead, although the rapidly heaving chest of one of them, accompanied by snuffling, congested breathing, indicated that he was still fighting for life. The other lay with his legs encased in two badly applied splints, his head tilted back, his upper lip stretched thinly across his bared teeth in a frozen grimace of agony. Westholme crouched beside him and checked for the pulse he knew he wouldn't find.

"I knew he was gone," the third man said. "I think I've known it for at least two hours. A man couldn't live with pain like that."

Westholme eased himself out through the raft entrance and glanced at Fenton. "Do you think you can take care of things here? Move the two up to the infirmary. I'll go ahead of you and get things ready. The third one . . . wrap him up in something and put him on the floor of the freezer."

He thrust his head back into the life capsule. "We'll talk later," he told the haggard, youngish-looking man with the black thatch of hair and the sooty pattern of whiskers. "Just one question. Are you from BUTCO 17?"

"We are. She's on the bottom . . ."

"That's all we need to know for the moment. You're on the tug *Haida Noble*. My name's Christy Westholme, skipper. See you up in the infirmary in a little while."

On the way to the room that had been equipped by the company as a miniature ship's hospital, Westholme stopped off at the cook's cabin, knocked once on the door and opened it without waiting for a reply. The cook was lying on his side, face to the wall in the semi-darkened room. A Gideon Bible lay opened and face down on the cabinet beside his bed.

Westholme leaned over and shook the man's shoulder roughly. "Come on, get up. We need you."

The cook rolled over immediately, his eyes widening apprehensively. "What's happened. Are we . . ."

"We've got sick and dying men on board. Get on your feet."

"Captain, I can't. I just can't. I'm not up to it. Ask the other fellows; they'll tell you . . ."

"What's your name?"

"Telford, sir. You ask any of the crew. They'll tell you I shouldn't be on this tug. I've never been on anything bigger than a 200-tonner since I started with the company."

"You're on *Haida Noble* now, Telford. Get out of that bunk and start pulling your weight." He reached down and ripped the blankets away in a cold, deliberate movement. The cook lay there curled up in shock, his fat thighs and buttocks bulging the pale fabric of his thermal long underwear.

"I want you in the galley in five minutes. I want a good beef broth for the two men in the hospital . . . and I want a square meal for the entire crew. And I don't care if you die in the process, Telford. The next time you lie down it'll be because I told you you could, or you're sick, or you're maimed . . . or you're dead!"

Westholme left abruptly, turning hard right and walking three paces to the door giving entrance to the hospital. Inside, it was as he had expected; hastily reassembled after the ordeal of the hurricane. He checked the compartmented medicine cabinet and found liquids oozing from its bottom. The smell was like concentrated drugstore. The three fixed bunks on one side of the room were a shambles of buckled mattresses and scrambled sheets. He straightened out two of them, and then returned to Telford's cabin; this time he opened the door without knocking. The man was into his trousers and buttoning up his shirt.

"Telford, when you're finished in the galley, I want you to straighten out the hospital. There'll be two men in there. Sick men requiring your attention . . ."

"Who, Captain? What's happened? One of them is Lindstrom, isn't it? He's dying! I knew when I saw him that he was finished!"

"Neither of them is Lindstrom," Westholme said in disgust. "They're men—people who've been through worse hell than any of us, and you're going to take care of them. If they need their teeth brushed, you brush them. If they need an enema you do the job."

"Are they that bad?" the cook said in an appalled voice.

"Worse," Westholme assured him, and he said it with conviction. He turned to leave.

"Captain Westholme," the cook said behind him in a tight and righteous voice. "I am a ship's cook. I signed on as a cook.

I pay my dues to the Guild as a cook, and I don't have to nurse anybody."

Westholme turned and tried to hold the man's darting eyes with his own. "Telford, if you don't do what I tell you, the chances are you won't return from this trip. Is that clear?"

"The Guild is going to hear about this!"

"Not if you don't get back, they won't. Now hustle!"

Telford dropped the shoe he was trying to fit on his foot, and Westholme departed for the bridge.

23 . . .

Tait was doing all the right things on the bridge, but with that same, strange air of detachment. Calm sea, cruel sea, it apparently made no difference to him. It wasn't just a matter of cold efficiency, Westholme knew that instinctively. He had seen other men like this. They were glaciers trying to cap active volcanoes.

"Where are we, George?" he asked.

"About six miles southwest of Amphitrite Point. Lots of stuff in the water."

"That raft has been knocked around some."

"So I saw."

"Three men in it. One dead. One close to it. The other seems to be in reasonable shape."

"How are we making out in the engine room?" Tait asked. "It would be nice to have the other engine turning over again."

"Not a chance," Westholme said. "That's a job for home base." He returned to the immediate concern. "With Lindstrom under the weather, and the two from BUTCO 17, I think we'd better make our approach as close to Amphitrite Point as we can get and then swing into Ucluelet for medical help and company instructions. It'll give all of us a chance to check with the home front—if the telephones are working."

Tait said nothing, and Westholme suspected that the man would not be telephoning anyone when they reached Ucluelet. On the other hand he would be phoning. He would pull rank, if necessary, to telephone Lee and tell her what he felt and how he felt about her.

"Come home," she would say. "Please come home, Christy."

From Ucluelet it would be tough to get back to Vancouver, with every float plane requisitioned by Civil Defense and Air-Sea Rescue. He would explain that to her. He would explain that *Haida Noble* would be needed along that coast to bring help to the injured, to round up the dead, to do whatever needed to be done.

"I need you here, Christy," she would say. "The poplar trees have fallen. The garage is flat. Christy, please come home!"

"Lee, you know I'd rather be with you than with anyone else in the world. We haven't been together enough. It's been one of those things. I chose the wrong business, I guess. But, Lee, I can't come home now. A terrible thing has happened on this coast. I can't tell you how terrible! Lee, I love you so much I wish you were here with me sharing it. I wish you had shared the hurricane and felt the blow of the tsunami, standing beside me and helping just with your presence. Lee . . . I told you this after I came back from the Yokohama blow, after the *Thrace* tow. I told you I wanted you to share the danger, because a man and woman sharing danger are expressing love!"

"I've been watching this for a few minutes now," he heard Tait say in a new tone of voice. "With the size of the swell and this goddam Plexiglas abortion to look through, it's hard to tell which end is up."

Westholme returned to the reality of the tug with a feeling approaching guilt. He peered through the stained, abraded Plexiglas panel, his line of vision directed above the black line of the enormous swell, sighting just above it and dipping when that line dipped. He saw what Tait had seen and reached unconsciously for the binoculars around his neck. Was it one of the sea's illusions or something more substantial? His first glimpse of it gave him the impression of an island with torn trees leaning across its spine. Then he was certain he had seen nothing but the strange optical effects of the swell.

Tait said: "I think it's a hulk. Too big to be anything else."

Westholme went out on the deck and drew the binoculars up to his eyes, trying to home in on the spot where he had seen the island. There was nothing but the huge, silken gray hump of the swell shouldering its way to the rocky beach of Amphitrite—and then he didn't need the binoculars. In the gray overcast of the midafternoon he read the plain language of the Aldis lamp, and heard Tait's voice at the same time.

"Distress!" the deckhand called. "There's a ship close in to Amphitrite."

The distant light continued to flash its call for help, the signal obliterated at regular intervals as the disabled vessel disappeared in the troughs of the advancing swell. Westholme lifted an Aldis lamp from its bracket and went out to the bridge rail where he repeated an acknowledgment of message several times before returning to Tait at the wheel.

"They're in real trouble, George. Another hour and they'll be on the rocks. Sooner than that if they come up against the north edge of George Fraser Island or some of the smaller stuff in there."

"It could be *Tahsis Ranger*. She'd be in the neighborhood just about now."

"Too big for the *Tahsis Ranger*. Look, George, go below and tell the boys to start gearing up for a towing job. Tell them we can't waste any time getting a line on board. Brad Fenton should be in the ship's hospital attending to the BUTCO 17 survivors. I'd like to see him up here as soon as he can manage it."

Westholme took the wheel and nudged the throttle ahead on the remote control, feeling *Haida Noble*'s good engine respond almost immediately. Running at three-quarter speed, he estimated the tug was making better than 9 knots which would place her in line-firing range within half an hour. Squinting ahead through the Plexiglas he could see no sign either of the ship or the distress light, and was concerned for

135

a moment that the vessel had foundered; but then the low, cluttered silhouette appeared again on a heaving dome of the sea and he was able to adjust his course to center on it.

Hard to tell what she was under these conditions. Lying low in the water like that she could be a tanker or a seriously leaking freighter. If she was a tanker there would be hell to pay when she hit the beach and spilled her cargo.

Fenton entered the wheelhouse inquiringly and Westholme explained the situation to him briefly. "It's a routine salvage job as these things go, Brad, with the one difference that we can't waste a minute and we can't afford any foul-ups. If the first line misses or breaks I doubt that we'll have time to put on another."

"The boys are getting things ready now," Fenton assured him. "The recovery chain is just about ready to go on deck."

"That's fine," Westholme said, "but chances are we won't be able to use it." He punched the button for the wire room. "Tait?"

Tait's voice replied on the intercom speaker.

"We may have to use a wire bridle instead of a recovery chain, George. Better have one ready just in case. One-and-a-half-inch wire."

Tait acknowledged and Westholme switched off.

"How are the BUTCO 17 people?" he asked Fenton.

"One of them appears to be all right. A few cracked ribs maybe; bruises on him like big tattoos." He shook his head doubtfully. "I don't know about the other one. His lungs are full of stuff. His friend is certain it's pneumonia."

"What we need right now," Westholme said, "is a good doctor. I'll go down and have a look. Hold her on this course until we're in line-firing position. I'll probably be back up before then. If not, give me a call."

Telford gave him an aggrieved look as he entered the ship's hospital. The cook was trying without success to get some hot broth into the mouth of the comatose roughneck.

"Forget it," Westholme told him. "He's too far gone for that right now." The man's breathing was alarmingly congested.

Even Westholme's unpracticed hand could feel the fever in the dirt-streaked forehead.

"Clean him up," he instructed.

"We've put him in pajamas already," the cook protested.

"Get some hot water and soap and sponge off the worst of it. My God, look at that crud!"

The other patient was in his bunk propped up against pillows, his hands wrapped around a mugful of beef broth, his eyes following the action silently.

Westholme turned to him. "Feeling better?"

"Back from the grave? I couldn't feel better. My name's Mike Volkoff. I'm with the BUTCO people."

"Fenton tells me you're bent but not broken."

"I'm hurting where there aren't places to hurt. Nothing more serious." He lifted the mug. "This brew is going straight into the bloodstream."

"There's lots more," Westholme said. "Maybe you'd like something solid?"

Volkoff shook his head.

"If you want anything at all you ask Telford here." With his back turned away from the cook, he winked at Volkoff. "He's got his doctor's degree. You need a bed pan or anything?"

"I'll call as soon as I do."

"What happened on the drill rig?"

Volkoff shrugged. It was a gesture of futility. "I don't suppose anyone will ever know for sure. She was taking the hurricane without any trouble, but the first of the tsunami's waves started to break her up and . . . the second finished her. We were in the life raft by then. It was like being in the middle of a cement mixer. The people who build those rafts deserve a citation, but I think I could give them a few pointers on shockproofing."

"I'm sorry we didn't make it in time," Westholme said, "but we were having our own problems. At one point we were hoping to ride in the lee of the rig and take advantage of the shelter. That was before the tidal wave changed our minds."

Volkoff sat up suddenly, wincing as his battered muscles tortured him. "It had gone right out of my mind! I suppose I'll be remembering details for the rest of my life. One of the Russian ships tried to ride in our lee. Charlie Knight was all for dropping sticks of dynamite on her—poor old Charlie."

"She was in a bad position when the wave hit?"

"The worst, although she was moving back just before it happened. I'd say she was a thousand yards north of us. And then everything started to move. The last thing we saw on radar she was coming straight at us. If she weathered the first wave, the second would have brought her up against the rig."

"Probably," Westholme agreed.

"BUTCO 17 has got company down there," Volkoff said. His eyes had become distant, remembering the final moments of the giant rig—the men who had died.

"Get some sleep," Westholme advised. "If you feel up to it later, take care of your friend here, if he appears to need anything."

"A couple of suggestions," Volkoff said. "Prop him up in more of a sitting position. It'll help his breathing. If you had some oxygen . . ."

"Better than that," Westholme said. "We've got a tent to go with it. "Telford, give me a hand here."

Together they rigged up the heavy plastic tent over the unconscious man. They mounted the oxygen tank in its rigid housing, fitted the hose into the tent's adapter, and started the gas hissing softly into the tent's interior. "Nobody smokes in here," Westholme warned Telford.

He rummaged through the medicine cabinet, found an untapped vial of penicillin, filled a disposable hypodermic carefully and returned to the sick man's bunk with the injection and an alcohol-soaked wad of cotton. Telford winced as Westholme swabbed the roughneck's muscular arm and plunged the needle in. When the cylinder was empty, he withdrew the needle, bent it and tossed the whole outfit into the disposal bag clipped to the bunk.

"That's all we can do for him now," he said. "Keep your

eye on him, Mike. Shout if you want help. Telford is needed in the galley. He is also a gourmet cook."

"I appreciate everything he's doing," Volkoff said earnestly, and produced a wan smile on the face of the cook.

Westholme returned to the bridge just as Fenton was preparing to call him. The crippled ship lay directly ahead of them, dead in the water, and listing seriously to starboard. It was no ordinary vessel. Even in its crippled condition, with the larger portion of its superstructure smashed and collapsed, the ship had impressive lines. Its hull was black with a sharply raked bow. The remains of the superstructure were a pleasant, sandy color surmounted by a squat, yellow funnel with a black crown around it. Positioned in the center of the funnel, the clean red standing out in contrast to the yellow background, was the hammer and sickle of the USSR. Even taking the combined effects of Hurricane Faith and the tsunami into account, it was difficult to understand how the ship could have suffered such massive damage. Both forward and afterdeck masts had been carried away. Seventy feet back from the bow, on the starboard side just forward of the superstructure something had dealt the hull a crushing blow, pushing it inward and tearing a ragged hole in the plates. Across the superstructure itself was an indentation reaching from the stack to the bridge, collapsing decks into one another. At some point fire had broken out amidships and swept aft before being extinguished by the sea and the rain, or by human effort. The two lifeboats visible on the starboard side were charred black, as were unfamiliar installations on the afterdeck. Blistered paint and large patches of heat-patterned metal on the ship's side gave evidence of the fire's intensity.

The identity of the ship and the appalling extent of the damage arrested Westholme's attention for a long moment and then he turned his mind to the problem of the tow. No more than half a mile from the crippled vessel the Pacific swell was grounding itself on the rock-studded shoals of Amphitrite Point, building a white crested surf all of 30 feet high that pounded at the granite buttresses rising out of the shallows.

The echo sounder indicated thirteen fathoms under *Haida Noble*'s bottom. There would be even less under the Russian. The combined effect of the swell and the incoming tide were pushing the vessel inexorably toward destruction.

"We'll have to tow her by the stern," he decided. "She's down by the head and taking seas through that hole in her side."

Fenton nodded in agreement. "What the hell did she run into, a battleship?"

"Just about as bad," Westholme said. "She collided with BUTCO 17. You'll have to go aboard her, Brad. Take Galbraith and Tait with you and organize some muscle from the Russian crew. I'm afraid you're going to have to hand-haul the bridle lengths into position."

"I wish to hell one of us spoke Russian," Fenton grumbled.

"I wouldn't worry too much," Westholme said. "Someone over there is bound to speak English. Better get moving. Take the rubber dinghy and don't forget the walkie-talkie."

"The fellow from the drill rig. Volkoff. That's a Russian name, isn't it?"

"He looks like a clean-cut, fourth generation American to me. I don't think he's fit to travel, Brad. You'll manage fine. Take a look in Lindstrom's cabin before you go below. Ask him if he feels up to giving me a hand for an hour or two."

Westholme took over the wheel as Fenton departed. Up until now he had been barely aware of the Russian crew members scattered along the upper decks of the vessel. Some of them were waving violently. There were bandaged arms and heads among them. He held *Haida Noble* on a position parallel to the Russian and a hundred yards off its starboard side, bow pointed into the swell, dividing his attention between *Haida Noble*'s steerage and a new detail that had caught his attention. At a hundred yards he couldn't be positive; the uniformly dark attire of the Russian crew, and the knitted toques worn by many of them made identification difficult; but it seemed to him that a good many of the watching figures were women.

24 . . .

Lindstrom's voice behind him held an incredulous note. "That's a *Russian!* Man, what's keeping her afloat?"

"God knows," Westholme said. "We're going to have to hustle if we're going to hold her off the rocks. Take the wheel for me, will you, Lindy?" His eyes made a swift appraisal of the mate's condition. Not good. Still the dullness in his pupils, a sagging expression in the lines of his face. "How are you feeling?"

"Never better."

"I think you can use some more time on your back, but we're shorthanded for the next hour or so and I've got a soft job for you."

"Cut it out!" Lindstrom said, and his voice was surprisingly angry. "I'm in no worse shape than anyone else. Look at you! Your face looks as though it had been worked over by a cougar."

"All right," Westholme said drily. "We're both candidates for plastic surgery. First I'd like you to hold the wheel while I take a quick look at the boys in the hospital. Then I want you to supervise the transfer of the bridles onboard that ship. Brad is taking Tait and Galbraith with him to handle things from that end."

"That's all I need to know," Lindstrom told him with the same irritable note in his voice. Westholme ignored it. The man must have a headache big enough for the whole crew.

He went below to the hospital where he found the condition of the roughneck unchanged, although it seemed to him that the fever might have dropped a degree or two. Volkoff was sleeping, or appeared to be, but when Westholme turned to leave, he stirred and opened his eyes.

"Didn't want to wake you up," Westholme said.

"I don't think I was asleep. I'm afraid to—in case I wake up and find myself on that damned raft."

Westholme grinned. "Not a chance," he said. "By the way, do you speak any Russian?"

"Some," Volkoff said. "Why?"

"We may have need of it in a little while. In the meantime, get some sleep."

Volkoff's questioning eyes followed him out of the room.

Back in the wheelhouse, Westholme slipped into his insulated jacket as he talked to Lindstrom. "I'll take over on the aft controls now. You're going to need more than Bibaud to help you, Lindy. Better give Stan Read a shout."

Lindstrom was summoning Read from the engine room as Westholme made his way aft to the remote control station located on the stern of the boat deck. *Haida Noble* had four remote control positions, enabling the captain to work her from the best point of view, depending on the operation to be performed. In this case, the relation of the tug to the disabled Russian was going to be stern-to-stern, and Westholme was going to have to hold her there as though she were at anchor.

Below him on the afterdeck, one of *Haida Noble*'s big inflatable life rafts was ready to go, its outboard motor fastened into place and tilted out of harm's way until after the launching. The crew was busy attaching the launching sling, but Bibaud had time to look up at him with an aggrieved look.

"How come these other guys get all the good chances? There's girls on that goddam ship. All kinds of girls!"

Westholme grinned at him and said nothing.

"If I change my name to Smith, can I go along?"

"Better you should change it to Lenin," Galbraith shouted. "For God sake, Ernie, lend a hand here."

The French Canadian returned to his task with an exaggerated expression of sadness.

Westholme checked out the gear assembled on the deck. The two bridle legs were there, a bucket of heavy grease, rubber chafing tubes, two coils of floatable, polypropylene line ¾-inch and 1½-inch. Fenton had taken the precaution of hauling six, gasoline-powered bilge pumps up from the wire room. From the looks of the Russian's waterline, they were going to need all those pumps and more.

The tools, two portable walkie-talkies, and extra cans of fuel for the pumps were all there, laid out as neatly as surgical instruments for an emergency operation—leaving nothing to chance. Ocean salvage called for that kind of planning. More often than not it was impossible for a salvage team to return for the equipment they had forgotten.

The small manageable items were being stowed in the rubber raft now, including a waterproof case of rations. "What's the matter, Brad?" Westholme called down. "They'll feed you caviar and champagne."

"Chances are they don't have a wet soda cracker," Fenton said. "I've been disappointed before."

Bibaud was at the winch, manipulating the levers and controls expertly as he swung the raft up and over the rail into the lee of *Haida Noble*. The others manhandled a cargo net over the side. Fenton, Galbraith, and Tait, in waterproofs and lifejackets, got ready to follow one another into the raft while Read and Lindstrom held it and fended off with long pike poles. It was a dangerous operation in the swell, which was one reason why an inflatable raft rather than a rigid whaleboat was customarily used.

Fenton went first, waiting until the sea lifted the raft as high as it could toward the tug's deck, and then releasing his handhold on the net in order to drop aboard. The other two did the same, and then all three picked up the short oars and pushed away hastily, putting a safe distance between the raft and the crushing weight of *Haida Noble*.

The next great swell picked them up like a cork and carried them ahead toward the Russian, Galbraith sitting in the stern to position and start the outboard. Westholme waited until he saw the blue puff of exhaust smoke and the white turbulence signaling that the raft was under power, and then proceeded to maneuver the tug into position.

Down by the head, its bow section weighted down with seawater, the Russian rode with her stern away from the advancing swell—which was a small blessing Westholme could be thankful for. At least *Haida Noble* would be able to work in comparative shelter, her stern as close to the

Russian's as safety would permit. He swung the tug into a careful turn and cut across the swell toward the listing ship, waiting until the rubber raft and its salvage team were alongside the vessel before he began to position *Haida Noble*. Fenton and his crew secured the raft to a cargo net let down by the Russians and clambered up to the rail, with walkie-talkies and other gear slung over their shoulders. Boarding a crippled ship was seldom a happy assignment. Westholme could remember some of the close calls he had had in the days when he was in Fenton's shoes. He caught a glimpse of them as they were hauled on board by a multiplicity of reaching arms. At least one of the boys—Galbraith he thought—was roundly embraced as he was dragged onto the deck.

Below him he heard Bibaud's elaborate protest. "Damn it to hell. The party, she's started already!"

"Cut it," Lindstrom growled. "In Russia everybody hugs everybody. Get that heaving line ready to go aboard."

Bibaud trotted to the stern with the carefully coiled circle of the weighted heaving line. The other end had already been attached to a heavier polypropylene line. He stood waiting, the weighted end of the heaving line dangling in his hand, as Westholme brought the tug broadside to the stern of the Russian and two hundred feet beyond it. Pushing the throttle on the stern control console ahead, he waited for the surge of power and then put the tug into a sharp turn, the Kort nozzle steering installation making it possible for the tug to turn virtually in its own length. *Haida Noble* was now stern to the broken ship's stern and slightly more than one hundred feet out with the gap closing steadily as he reversed the engine. The swell was traveling the full length of the Russian, reaching *Haida Noble* and lifting her so that her stern rode above the Russian's for a few moments with each passing sea. Westholme's task was to bring the tug close enough to transfer the heavy bridle legs, the pumps and other gear, without being lifted into the ship's overhanging stern by the heaving sea. Once he was there he would have to keep the tug on station.

Fifty feet now separated the two vessels. Westholme watched the gigantic ripple of sea snaking along the sides of the Russian ship, barely lifting its waterlogged weight, and then it slid under *Haida Noble*'s stern and she started to rise. He saw Fenton and Galbraith positioned at the stern rail, with Tait probably farther back on the deck among at least twenty Russian crewmen. Now he was above them looking down. The moment was right. "Let her go," he shouted to Bibaud.

The deckhand had anticipated the command. The whirling heaving line straightened into a flat arc, arrowing toward the Russian's stern, its weighted end landing a good 10 feet inboard. At the same time, *Haida Noble*'s stern began to drop until the tug sat well below the Russian ship's afterdeck. There was no doubt that they were busy up there; the heaving line was whipping up from *Haida Noble*'s deck at a great rate. By the time the next swell raised the tug into a dominant position, the end of the polypropylene line had been dragged aboard.

"By God," Stan Read marveled. "They've got everybody on the line . . . women and all!"

It was true. The rope was being passed down a double rank of Russian crew members, a number of whom were unmistakably female. Some of them not bad looking either, Westholme decided. The work force was pulling in the line with a rhythm and a serious intensity that was some indication of their desire to be saved from the beach.

Down below Bibaud hammed a baritone version of the Volga Boatmen and waved wildly at the Russians before the swell passed and dropped the tug out of the line of sight.

In spite of the foreground noises, Westholme could hear the sound of the surf clearly now. He could see the breakers drawing a line as white as chalk against the rocky coastline approaching Amphitrite Point. Fifteen minutes left. No more.

The polypropylene line was all up, its end attached to an eye in the first leg of the bridle. It was the time-tested method of manhandling heavy cable aboard a dead ship where no motive power existed—a light line hurled aboard, capable of pulling in a heavier line which, in turn, was capable of taking the strain of a steel cable. Polypropylene was a modern boon to this kind of operation. If it fell in the water it floated and was easy to retrieve.

Haida Noble was riding high again and the first few feet of heavy bridle began to move off the deck. Fenton would see to it that the work party conserved its strength for the moment when the tug's stern rode above the crippled ship's. That way gravity would be helping the transfer of the one hundred-foot length of inch-and-a-half steel wire.

Down into the ocean's slick trough and then up again, rising to a position where, to Westholme's mind, the furious action on the Russian's afterdeck was like watching a theatrical spectacular from a balcony position. The Russian crew members were chanting now—a kind of melodic grunt timed to the moment of greatest effort. Others of the ship's company had gathered to watch; and many of these, Westholme noticed, were wearing bandages. There were perhaps fifty people gathered within his view, some of them dressed in officers' uniforms, and more than one of those uniforms worn by women.

As the tug began its next descent, Lindstrom looked up at Westholme, bemused: "Now what kind of a ship's company is that, do you think?"

Westholme shook his head. "Have you got the other leg of the bridle ready to go?"

"All set."

A new length of polypropylene line had gone aboard, piggybacking on the first bridle leg. It was detached and began to move down the ranks of a second crew of volunteers, pulling the other section of the towing bridle aboard. Every effort was swift and calculated. The entire operation was governed by a kind of desperate efficiency in which every individual knew his place and his role.

"Those guys want to get out of here so bad they can taste it," Bibaud chuckled. "By God, this calls for a party! What do you think?"

Lindstrom turned on him in an explosion of rage that

146

shocked even Westholme. "Can't you keep your mind on the job, you bloody frog clown! We're not finished! We're not even started, and you're calling for a party."

"Sorry about that," Bibaud said in a low voice. His gaze flickered toward Westholme and there was black anger in his eyes.

"Lindy," Westholme said. "We can manage fine here, if you'd like to have a breather. We'll have her on the line in a few minutes."

Lindstrom glared up at him and then back at Bibaud. His throat tightened convulsively and he ran to the rail to vomit into the sea. He returned with an expression of unrelieved embarrassment on his face, and glanced obliquely at Bibaud.

"I don't know what came over me, Ernie," he said. "Whatever it was, it's gone over the side. I'm sorry."

"Back to the bunk, Lindy," Westholme commanded. "Nobody's blaming you."

"Let's get her on the line," Lindstrom said. "Then I'll go back to the bunk. That's a promise."

Westholme's face granted reluctant approval. Then his attention was drawn to the controls on the remote console as a particularly heavy undulation of the sea moved toward them. To stay in position he had been going astern slowly throughout the operation; now he was obliged to increase power to hold the tug against the pressure of the swell. He didn't move a moment too soon. The tug was carried a good 15 feet ahead as the swell hit and lifted them. Both bridle lengths, secured to the tug's main towing cable, began to pull away from the Russian. At the peak of the swell, Westholme looked down at a score of bodies sprawled on the deck, trying to recover the two loose ends of moving steel. The movement stopped as the tug's new power compensated and it began to ease back to its former position.

Back in the valley again, Westholme took a deep breath and glanced down at the rest. Bibaud still had his hands over his face. "All right," he said. "Brad should have those bridle legs secured before the next swell. We're just about ready to move off."

And not a minute too soon, he thought. Perhaps too late. The surf crashing on Amphitrite was loud, but his anxiety made it deafening; his ears were tuned for the first sound of keel metal rubbing on the sea bottom.

25 . . .

They had done the best they could in the time they had and with the ship in the condition she was. The Russians had made it possible to put the bridle aboard in record-breaking time—but still time might have run out. What they had now was a standard bridle towing arrangement: two 100-foot lengths of heavy towing cable, each fastened to a mooring bollard on opposite sides of the afterdeck, and fed through greased and rubber-insulated fairleads to the afterdeck of *Haida Noble* where they met and were shackled to the tug's big towing cable.

It wasn't ideal. It was far from ideal. No one on the tug had any illusions about that. They should have been towing the ship by the bow, heading straight to sea, using its own massive anchor chain as the point of connection for the towing line. But none of this was possible, and time was running out.

On the peak of the swell, he looked down and judged that Fenton was ready. The second mate hadn't used the walkie-talkie yet, but he had to be ready! Galbraith was smearing heavy grease over the bridle cables where they passed through the Russian's stern fairleads.

As the tug descended into the next gray-green trough, he and the others heard it simultaneously and winced. It was like their own bones being dragged across the bottom. Lindstrom had his palms pressed to his ears as though the sound had pierced his eardrums. The last, passing swell had dropped the Russian ship—some substantial part of the Russian ship—on the bottom. It grated and shuddered with the impact.

"To hell with it," Westholme said. "Give us some line, Ernie," he shouted. "We're going out."

Bibaud worked the towing winch like an artist, matching the speed of the cable drum to *Haida Noble*'s smooth acceleration forward. They had to get at least 600 feet of towing cable out before the tug could take up the strain, otherwise the angle between the ship's high stern and the tug's relatively low stern would be acute enough to break the bridle.

Westholme covered the 600 feet angling out from the rocky shore at three-quarter speed, taking a chance on the cable drum overcoming the braking system and running out of control to create a backlash of devastating proportions. Bibaud and the equipment stood up to it.

Close to the 600-foot mark Westholme braked the tug with a full speed astern maneuver that shook her already battered length. "Put her on the line, Ernie," he shouted.

Slowly *Haida Noble* eased forward, taking up the strain on the towing cable, lifting it out of the water in the first critical effort to start the Russian ship moving, trying to overcome the inertia of the dead ship and the friction of a hull beginning to ground on the bottom. The next swell made the difference. As it passed under the scarred ship's hull, Westholme felt the barely perceptible difference and pushed the power up to full speed. The Russian moved! All of them saw it; all of them felt it—and in the distance all of them heard the thin sound of people cheering on the decks of the ship. *Haida Noble* was away and moving, drawing her cable as tight as a fiddle string, but with the Russian following behind her angling slightly away from the shore. In a few minutes or so, with the ship in deeper water, they could increase the length of the cable and thereby improve the safety factor.

Lindstrom cheered loudly and ran up to slap Bibaud on the back. "We did it! Ernie, you were right—this calls for a ding dong of a party!" Then he lurched over to the rail and got sick again, his hands pressed feverishly to his head.

Westholme inclined his head toward Stan Read in an imperative gesture, and the second engineer crossed the deck to stand beside Lindstrom as he tried to heave up the non-existent contents of his stomach. The mate stood back from the rail finally, turned and shrugged up at Westholme as if to say that it was ridiculous and unexplainable.

"We're on the line," Westholme called to him. "Back to your bunk."

Lindstrom nodded and avoided the helping hand Read extended to him. "I'm going to stand my watch," he warned Westholme, and left the deck, handing the walkie-talkie to Read as he passed.

Westholme tuned up the volume on his own set, becoming increasingly impatient with Fenton's silence. He should have been in touch by now, with some kind of report on the situation. As he had expected, the tow was showing all the signs of being a nightmare. Towing by the stern was never easy under the best of conditions, but the Russian vessel, unbalanced by the tons of seawater in her forward compartments, and rendered even more unstable by a rudder which Westholme now suspected had been jammed to starboard, was beginning to yaw off the line of travel. The motion would become more pronounced when the line was lengthened to a safer fifteen hundred feet, but there was no alternative. Running with a short line, it was only a matter of time before the bridle weakened and snapped.

He gave Bibaud the signal to pay out more line, and reached out to switch to "send" on the walkie-talkie. "Fenton? Brad? Westholme here . . . are you receiving me? Over."

Immediately Tait's voice came back. "Fenton's talking to the captain. Things are bad over here. They've lost half the ship's company."

"Have they got any kind of power at all?"

"No power, no heat. She's dead."

"Still taking in water?"

"Not as much, as far as I can make out, but we're going to need all the pumps and more if we want to keep her head above water."

"Tell Fenton . . ."

"He's here now. Tell him yourself."

The next voice was Fenton's, out of breath and suppressing excitement:

"Christy? Sorry we couldn't make contact sooner. Things are in a hell of a mess over here. People dead and injured. Men and women both!"

"Okay, Brad. What do you need?"

"The pumps, for starters. And, Chris, the captain asks permission to transfer five or six injury cases to *Haida Noble*, along with a doctor."

"You know how we're fixed, Brad. We're not set up to take care of that many people. We haven't got enough medical supplies to . . . Hold it a moment, Brad."

Below on the afterdeck, Telford had appeared and was talking animatedly to Read and Bibaud, his gesticulating hands trying to encompass some kind of emergency. Westholme leaned over the rail:

"What's up, Telford?"

"Lindstrom, sir. I told you he was serious."

"What about Lindstrom?"

"He's on the deck outside his cabin, Mr. Westholme. He's not in his right mind, and his arm and leg are gone. He just can't seem to move them."

Westholme went back to the walkie-talkie. "Tell the captain we'll take the injured aboard as soon as he can arrange for the transfer. We'll run for another fifteen minutes into deeper water, and then shorten up to transfer the pumps and take the injured on board. Are you receiving me, Brad?"

"I'm getting it."

"The doctor is essential. Tell them that. Tell them we've got a case of pneumonia, and something that looks like brain damage . . . Lindstrom."

"My God! Lindy! I'll take care of it. We'll be ready for transfer in fifteen minutes. The pumps will have to go up by block-and-tackle."

"Details are up to you," Westholme said, and signed off.

"Stan, you and Telford go and take care of Lindstrom. Slide him onto a stretcher and support his neck all the way.

Ease him onto a bed in the hospital. No pillow—and strap him in. How are the others?" he demanded of Telford.

"The one in the tent is breathing easier. The other one's asleep."

"Get a move on," Westholme said. "I'll need you back here as soon as possible, Stan."

He turned his mind back to the problem of the tow. *Haida Noble* was making painfully slow progress; her speed was under two knots, and it wasn't likely to improve because of the virtually unmanageable action of the helpless ship at the end of the line. Still, the white line of surf on Amphitrite was receding and the sound of its destruction was more distant.

Westholme had contended with clumsier tows in the past. The leaking drill rig in the Caribbean took the prize; three weeks of steady towing at a speed never exceeding one knot. This tow? With any kind of luck, and barring the possibility of the bridle snapping, they'd have the ship in safe shelter at Ucluelet in five or six hours; expert hospital care for the serious cases, sleep for everyone. Sleep. The word held a new meaning for him suddenly. He felt the fatigue enveloping him like a leaden garment, and thrust the sensation away from him. The others were as tired as he was and none of them had complained. They were a great crew. Given a choice he wouldn't change one of them—Telford excepted.

Bibaud was leaning on the winch brake control, staring moodily in the direction of the Russian ship. Lindstrom in his burst of temper had called him a clown. Westholme didn't think so; this man and others like him concealed some deep feelings under the clown's façade. Humor—the talent for diverting the deadly serious into the safety of laughter—was at once their mask and their armor. He liked Bibaud, and respected him.

"Don't worry, Ernie," he called down. "All those women put together don't have the style of one Montreal girl."

"Style!" Bibaud exploded theatrically. "What is that? They are women, and that's all the style a man needs. Hey, that face of yours don't look too good."

Westholme's face wasn't giving him pain so much as discomfort bordering on pain. From hairline to chin it was uniformly angry and sore. He could tolerate it. He grinned at Bibaud and felt the tightness:

"When we have that party with them, you've got the advantage."

"I got the advantage anyway," Bibaud told him. "They find out I'm a bachelor from Quebec and I've got my choice."

"You're sure you don't want to change your name to Smith?"

"You kidding? Bibaud suits me just fine."

Westholme had been hearing the sound in the corner of his consciousness for several moments. It was an indication of both his and Bibaud's fatigue that neither of them reacted until now. His gaze went south, searching the sky, and almost immediately he located the plane—a PBY wearing its big wing like a plank across the top of its pregnant fuselage. It was flying at about five hundred feet and losing altitude as it approached. The sight of the ancient flying boat warmed Westholme's heart. He knew the plane and probably knew the pilot.

"The Air-Sea Rescue boys," Bibaud shouted enthusiastically.

Westholme put the tug on automatic pilot and ran into the wheelhouse to find the Aldis lamp. By the time he got back to the stern remote console the plane was down to two hundred feet and no more than a half mile away, beginning to level out. They would be trying to make radio contact, Westholme knew that. He knew as well that they would fly over low and see the condition of both ships, then circle to exchange Aldis messages. He wished the swell were lighter, to enable the flying boat to land and pick up Lindstrom and the roughneck; but the very fact that the plane was there and in contact was good enough. *Haida Noble* was no longer alone.

The PBY did exactly as he had predicted, coming in low between the two vessels, going into a slow circle and returning with its Aldis lamp beginning to flicker from one of the opened gunner's blisters. It was the International Code message immediately recognized by Westholme. "Can we render assistance?"

He countered with the letters TA—"I can proceed"—considered sending the further message "injured on board" and then decided not to. The plane had its work cut out for it. Scores, perhaps hundreds of vessels and communities had worse problems than did *Haida Noble* right now. He would be in Ucluelet with the Russian in five or six hours, and the plane would have relayed the information and prepared the town for the arrival. He repeated the simple message "I can proceed," and waved cheerfully at the lumbering plane as it made a final low pass and continued north. In a few minutes Ucluelet would know, the company would know, and Lee would know that *Haida Noble* was still afloat and earning her money.

26 . . .

Ten minutes later, with nineteen fathoms under her, *Haida Noble* began to shorten her line again, drawing in toward the stern of the Russian and keeping the towing line slack in the final stages of the approach, to avoid placing undue strain on the bridle. Stern-to-stern, the difficult business of transfer began. The walkie-talkies were an invaluable aid.

"We'll take the pumps first," Fenton's voice instructed. "They're still moving the injured on deck."

Rising on the swell, Westholme could survey the arrangement on board the Russian. One of the fire-charred booms had been rigged for hand-hauling. A set of rollers had been clamped to the deck astern, along which the heavy nylon rope from the boom would travel. As the tug began to drop, Galbraith stepped to the rail and hurled a heaving line onto *Haida Noble*'s stern. Bibaud leaped on it, trapping it with his foot and then grasped it with both hands to haul it and the larger boom rope in, struggling ahead with the weight of the rope over his shoulder until he was able to stoop and hook it into the lifting eye of one of the portable pumps. He began to drag the pump to the extreme stern of the tug, to allow the lift up to the afterdeck of the Russian to be almost vertical. Westholme stopped him:

"Ease off, Ernie. Wait for Stan."

"Two hundred pounds! No sweat," the deckhand said. But the second engineer's appearance back on deck at that moment saved him from having to prove his strength. Together they lifted the pump onto the edge of the cable roller housing and waited until they got the hand signal from Fenton directing the operation from the stern rail of the Russian. With the boom rope drawn tight, and the tug's stern beginning to descend again, they pushed the pump over the side and watched it rise immediately to the rail of the crippled ship, its pendulum motion reduced to a minimum by the almost vertical angle.

In this fashion, all six pumps were lifted to the Russian with only one casualty. A larger than usual swell moved the tug out of position during the transfer of the fourth pump, which dropped away from the tug at the end of a long and angled rope, swung toward the ship, and struck the hull solidly. Bibaud cursed in fluent French.

"It's all right," Westholme said. "They're built to take punishment."

There was no need to transfer the gasoline cans, Fenton informed them. The ship would be able to supply additional fuel.

Now began the transfer of the injured Russian crew members to the tug, and Westholme approved of Fenton's solution to the problem. Making use of the vessel's one, undamaged lifeboat, he carefully put the injured into it, two stretchers at a time and slowly lowered the boat to *Haida Noble*'s waiting life raft. There Galbraith and Tait slid the stretchers aboard and conveyed them to *Haida Noble* where they were lifted on deck, this time by the tug's lifeboat, sliding up and down on its davits like an elevator.

"Technically, this is damned efficient," Westholme ob⌐ to Bibaud. "Medically, I'm not so sure."

There were six stretcher cases in all, most of them with heavy head bandages; four of them with splinted arms or legs as well. On the third and last trip the doctor, a short figure bundled up in heavy jacket and oilskins, accompanied Tait and Galbraith, assisting the two deckhands substantially as they struggled against the motion of raft and the tug to slide the clumsy stretchers into *Haida Noble*'s lifeboat.

Bibaud, working the davit tackle, stared down with an expression that was half amazement and half reverence. "A woman, by God!" he said to Read. "That doctor's a woman!"

She came aboard behind the stretchers, handed onto the deck by Galbraith, although she gave the impression of being able to manage it by herself. "You are the captain?" she asked of Bibaud in a level, but definitely feminine voice.

Bibaud stared into the serious, very tired, but decidedly attractive face . . . and said nothing.

"He's aft ma'am, at the controls," Read said. "What can we do for you?"

Tait eased past them and went to relieve Westholme at the controls. "They seem to be a nice enough bunch," he told him. "The woman speaks better English than Bibaud."

Westholme was convinced of this as soon as the brief introductions were made.

"I would like to install these men in a warm place, Captain Westholme. I understand there is a hospital—a treatment room."

"Not too adequate, I'm afraid," Westholme told her. "We've got three people in there now. Two of them can use your help."

"I will do what I can, Captain. Our people can go, perhaps some there. Some elsewhere."

"The crew's quarters will be the next best thing," Westholme decided. "You'll have them all together where you can keep an eye on them."

Telford had arrived and was hovering uncertainly in the background. "Mr. Telford here will take charge of the hospital arrangements. Ask him for anything you need."

She smiled fleetingly in Telford's direction. "I will be grateful to you, sir."

The cook almost wept with gratitude.

"Show the doctor to my cabin, Mr. Telford . . . you may want to organize yourself, Dr. Davodov. In the meantime we'll see to your injured." He looked at his watch. Three forty-five in the afternoon. "I think I can promise you we'll be in Ucluelet by no later than nine this evening. There are proper hospital facilities there."

"Thank you, Captain Westholme," she said. "May I also say that Captain Kutskov wished me to convey his profound thanks to you and your crew for what you have done . . . and are doing."

Westholme grinned. "I won't say it's our pleasure," he said. "You'd know I was lying."

"It has been a sad time for your people and for ours," she said, and reached to take up her large bag of medical supplies. Telford darted in and captured it.

"Would you like to come this way?" he inquired tentatively. She turned and followed him.

Galbraith drew his hand across his sweaty, exhausted face. "Amazing how much more I feel like working for her than I do for you," he told Westholme.

"Grab the end of one of those stretchers," he instructed the deckhand. "Show her how much you like working for her."

Back beside Tait at the stern controls, Westholme heard a little more of the story while he signaled Bibaud to begin letting the line out again:

"The ship really got clobbered," Tait said. "The way they figure it, the tidal wave carried them up against one of the rig's legs. The gouge aft of the navigation bridge happened when the top of the drill tower fell on them. Part of it is still there."

"How many hurt?"

"There were a hundred and eleven people on board. As far as they can make out sixty-two are dead or injured. Eleven are missing—probably overboard or up forward in the flooded

157

compartments. They had a good fire through the crew's quarters and out onto the afterdeck."

"All the women," Westholme said. "I know some of the trawlers carry women, but I've never seen anything like this."

"It's quite a usual thing to have women deckhands, women technicians, scientists—even captains and ship's officers—on Russian oceanographic vessels."

Both Westholme and Tait turned to see Volkoff standing behind them bundled in an overlarge insulated jacket, the hood pulled up over his head. He was squinting in the direction of the crippled ship now riding at the end of the fifteen hundred-foot line. He continued to talk:

"That is the *Irkutsk*, a *Nikolai Zubov* class oceanographic research ship." The words emerged tightly, as a threat rather than a statement.

"What are you doing out of bed?" Westholme demanded. He was on the edge of anger. They had gone to great pains to drag this man from the sea—to give him a second chance.

"Other people need my bed worse than I do," Volkoff said. "More than that, suddenly I've got an ax to grind." He said it coldly and incisively.

"How's that?" inquired Westholme. The American had lost his friendliness—become belligerent. The pain and shock were catching up.

"That bastard sank BUTCO 17."

"Probably contributed. I wouldn't want to say one way or another."

"Okay. I'm not about to argue with you. Let's just say that ship is the *Irkutsk*. It says so in good Russian characters on the stern. I know the ship by reputation."

"Is that so? Who are you, Mr. Volkoff?"

"I told you. I work for British United Traction. I'm an oceanographic mining engineer, and my opinion is that you are towing a piece of very hot merchandise."

"It's a ship," Westholme said. "I've towed a lot of them, all nationalities. This one has had more trouble than most."

"You could be some kind of a hero when you deliver this one in port. Where are we heading?"

"Look, Mr. Volkoff . . ."

"It's Mike Volkoff."

"I've got a ship on the line. We found her disabled in the water, with injured and dead aboard. This is a salvage tug designed to tow ships in trouble. That's about all there is to it. Now I'd suggest that you find yourself a bunk somewhere and sleep it off until we get to Ucluelet."

"I just wanted you to know what you've got on the end of that line. It's a Russian oceanographic vessel rigged to gather special information. Call it a spy ship."

"Thanks, I appreciate it." Westholme turned his back on the American, dismissing him with the gesture. He stared hard through the gathering dusk, watching the blind, staggering movement of the ship as she yawed at the end of the cable. It wasn't any of his damned business what she was, or who the people were on her. Let the Canadian authorities figure that one out when he got to port. In the meantime, there were injured and dying people to be taken care of; there was Lindstrom to be taken to the hospital . . . and he liked the straight honest look in the green-gray eyes of that doctor.

Behind him, Volkoff said, "Look . . . I'm sorry. I'm taking this pretty damned personally."

"That's all right," Westholme said. "I can understand how you feel. Let the experts sort it out later. Okay?"

"That suits me," Volkoff said shortly. He turned to leave.

The walkie-talkie began to crackle and Westholme turned it up.

"Brad? Is that you? Westholme here . . . over."

The voice emerging from the speaker was not Fenton's. It was deeper, more precise—with a vocabulary more carefully selected:

"Captain Westholme? Captain Mikhail Kutskov here. Are you receiving me?"

"Loud and clear," Westholme said. "What can I do for you, Captain?"

"I wish to thank you, Captain, for the assistance you have rendered to us. The situation was very serious, as you can appreciate."

"I'm glad I was at this end, not yours," Westholme said. "How is that bridle riding?"

"Very well I believe. Captain Westholme . . . may I ask, is this the best speed we can make?"

"I'm afraid so," Westholme told him. "That bridle hookup is second best. I guess you know that. Also your ship has zero steerage."

"What power have you, Captain?"

"We're running on one engine—5000 horsepower. Why?"

"Captain Westholme, I would like to make a salvage contract with you."

"Under the circumstances I don't think that will be necessary. You can make your own arrangements with my company when we arrive in port."

"That is something I must avoid, Captain."

"I don't read you," Westholme said.

"I don't recognize that expression, Captain."

"I don't understand what you're saying. Do you mean you want to avoid a formal salvage contract with my company, because . . ."

"No, no, no!" the captain of the Russian ship said almost apologetically. "What I mean is that I do not wish to enter a Canadian port. I would like to commission you to tow my ship back beyond your country's Twelve Mile boundary. For this I will pay you whatever reasonable amount you ask."

Westholme wasn't certain that he had heard it right. He glanced at Tait and Volkoff for confirmation and found them as confounded as he was.

"You want us to tow you out to sea?"

"Under the circumstances, Captain . . . yes."

"No deal," Westholme said harshly. "We'll be in Ucluelet by 2100 hours at the latest. You can battle things out with the authorities after that. It's not my business."

The voice at the other end was patient—almost soothing. "Captain . . . what I am asking is necessary, you must understand that. I mean no harm to you, or your vessel. In this troubled situation it will be no more difficult to tow us back to our fleet than it will be to reach a Canadian port. I would

160

hope you would co-operate—and I am prepared to reimburse you for this service."

"Don't goddam listen to him," Volkoff hissed in Westholme's ear. "That guy is in deep trouble and he knows it. There's more to this than just the BUTCO 17. He had enough electronic intelligence gear on top and under the hull to make the *Pueblo* look like a ferryboat."

Tait said, "He doesn't mean it! You should see the condition of that ship. Christ, the captain himself is supposed to be injured!"

Westholme made up his mind. "I want you to understand this, Captain Kutskov. For the good of your ship's company; for the good of your ship and mine—and all the people I have on board—I am taking you into Ucluelet. I understand you have been injured, and I can guarantee . . ."

"There is no time left to argue. Here is what you must do . . ." The voice was now more intense, crisper, more imperative. "You must tow my vessel as far as the Twelve Mile limit. There you may leave me if you choose, but for every mile you tow my ship farther I will reimburse you to the amount of one thousand dollars."

"You're out of your mind! You're sick!" Westholme was convinced of both charges.

"I apologize for not being more explicit. I would suggest a fee of ten thousand dollars to tow my ship to the edge of the Twelve Mile limit. You need not concern yourself after that— unless you want to."

"He may be sick, but he's not crazy," Volkoff said loudly. "That baby can't afford to be caught inside your line. Tell him to go to hell."

Westholme's inclination was to push Volkoff away. Tait accomplished the same thing by moving in between them while Westholme turned back to the walkie-talkie:

"I want to talk to my second officer, Mr. Fenton."

Almost immediately Fenton's voice came on, anxious and incredulous:

"Christy . . . I can't believe it! The people here need us. I mean it! They need us. Up until now I thought it was a straight salvage operation. Captain Kutskov needs help as much as . . ."

Obviously he had been taken from the set, or the set had been snatched from him, because the next voice was the Russian captain's:

"Captain Westholme, your officer means well, but I must insist that you tow me as I demand. I intend no harm to you, your ship, or to anyone else. Simply tow me beyond the Canadian line and leave me there. It is a very simple request."

"He'll have the whole fleet waiting for him," Volkoff said. "That's the last you'll see of any of them. You've got yourself a spy ship, Westholme, and he's wriggling to get off the hook."

"Get off my back," Westholme told him coldly. "This is none of your business. You're nursing a grudge."

To the Russian captain he said: "I'm sorry. We're taking you in. I've got critically injured men in my own crew, and I've got six of yours. This is no time for politics, Captain."

"You have your responsibilities and I have mine. I am sure we will both try to live up to them, Captain Westholme." The voice receded from the microphone and broke into a brief staccato of Russian.

"You've got him buffaloed," Tait decided. "He's having a conference."

"Like hell he is," Volkoff exclaimed. "He's issuing instructions on another wave length . . . and you're goddamned right I'm nursing a grudge. That Russian has a lot to answer for."

27 . . .

"They don't have any radio equipment working," Tait said. "Maybe some walkie-talkie equipment, but everything else has been knocked out."

"He's telling someone to put a plan into action," Volkoff insisted. "The odds are he's in touch with the Russian fleet— even a submarine." His voice tripped on itself, and he stopped talking.

Kutskov's deep, unruffled voice was back again, as placating as ever. "Captain Westholme, you leave me with no alternative except to borrow your vessel for the time it will take to tow us to the Twelve Mile line. You will be paid, of course, but my crew will man the tug."

"Not a chance," Westholme said angrily. "I don't understand you. You're not making any sense at all. What you're doing is refusing our salvage services which are to tow you safely to port for repair and medical attention. I've got the right to cut you loose."

"I don't want you to do that, Captain. What I have done is take the responsibility for any decision out of your hands. My people will manage your vessel. They are excellent seamen."

Westholme turned away from the speaker, two red spots of anger beginning to show high on his cheekbones. "I don't believe this! The man is stark, raving crazy!"

"He's been through a bad time," Tait reminded him.

Volkoff's opinion differed. "I think he's desperate—but he is also smart. He wouldn't be playing for time like this, making these demands, if he wasn't . . ."

The Russian captain's voice interrupted. "I want you to understand, Captain, that I will not willfully hurt either your vessel or any member of your crew. It is highly unsatisfactory negotiating with you over this intercommunication system. I would like you to join me aboard my ship."

"That does it," Westholme said tightly. "We're going to set you adrift, Captain. When you come to your senses, fire a flare. And just remember that the longer you wait the more your people and mine are going to suffer."

Behind Westholme and the others, a thickly accented voice commanded overloudly: "You will turn around from there, please."

In a reflex motion Westholme switched to automatic pilot and swung around to stare at the two bandaged figures confronting them. Not twenty minutes before these two had been brought aboard on stretchers, critically injured. One of them still wore a bloody head bandage. They were about

Tait's age, in their middle twenties; of medium height but husky and well-muscled. Both of them held automatic pistols of unfamiliar design and deadly looking. The one with the bandaged head had a compactly constructed walkie-talkie slung across his shoulder. Still keeping his weapon steadily aimed, he ducked his head toward the set's mouthpiece and spoke a few words in Russian.

Volkoff began to say something and Westholme stopped him. "Too bad none of us speak Russian," he said with deliberate emphasis. "Stick around, Mike."

Kutskov's voice began again. "You have been boarded, Captain. For a few hours you will not be responsible for your vessel, and then you may have it back again, together with the salvage fee agreed upon."

In Westholme's advanced state of fatigue, the entire scene became dreamlike: the bandaged gunmen, the outlandish demands of the Russian captain delivered in this conversational, conciliatory manner, the thirty-six hours of incredible ordeal that had preceded this were all part of the same nightmare. He took a long moment to collect his thoughts and discovered that he had little to counter with:

"You know this constitutes an act of piracy?"

"Perhaps not. I would like to discuss it with you, Captain. You will come aboard, please. Your second officer may then return to your vessel and assist my crew if he is inclined to."

Westholme saw no way to refuse. The danger to Fenton and the others was obvious. He glanced at Volkoff and then said: "I have one of my top salvage people with me. I'd like to bring him along."

"That could prove useful, Captain. By all means."

The feeling of unreality was departing, replaced now by a cold and contained anger. Westholme saw the need to match the Russian captain's impressive degree of control. "You're taking a lot on your shoulders. Are you aware of that? This is piracy in any court of law. You are deliberately endangering the life of my first officer and an American citizen on board. Both must have expert medical attention. The chances of your ship being caught inside Canadian waters are still good . . ."

"And yet none of this would need to have happened, Captain Westholme, if you had simply agreed to tow us a few miles west. We will discuss this matter of responsibility shortly if you wish . . . by the way, it should be understood that Dr. Davodov is a highly competent physician. She has been sent aboard solely to treat your people, and is not a party to the game I am forced to play."

"You expect me to believe that?"

"It doesn't really matter whether you do or not. You and your colleague must join me at once. It is getting dark. My crew will help you to embark."

Westholme hunched his shoulders in profound frustration, then inclined his head toward Volkoff. "I haven't any cards to play. Have you?"

"He's bluffing! He's nothing but a damned hijacker."

"Hijackers have a way of meaning everything they say these days. Come on, let's go." One of the Russian crewmen was beckoning impatiently with his pistol.

"I'm not going," Volkoff protested. The suggestion had shaken him.

"You're my salvage specialist," Westholme told him in a low voice. "I'm going to need you to—interpret a few things for me."

"Look, Westholme, I'm an American citizen, and none of this mess is any direct concern of mine. Once we're in that Russian's hands . . . I can't hack this." The punishment of the past hours was showing on his face.

"We are in his hands," Westholme said, "no matter how you look at it. Come on, Mike. Let's see what you know about salvage."

Under the unwavering muzzle of the Russian crewman's gun they made their way across fifteen hundred feet of pitching sea to the battered and blistered side of *Irkutsk*, Westholme handling the outboard motor and the steering while Volkoff sat and glared at the Russian.

The man was determined to carry out his instructions. At

the same time, he made several efforts to put his prisoners at ease, all of which were rendered ineffective by the presence of his slim-barreled weapon.

"You don't worry," he assured them in his bad English. "Soon everything be good again."

On another occasion he offered them cigarettes from a battered package he pulled out of his jacket. "We be friends," he encouraged, and then glanced ruefully at his gun and settled back to concentrate on his guard assignment.

Fenton was waiting at the rail of the Russian ship when Westholme clambered up the net and over the side. He looked and sounded stunned:

"There was no way I could guess this, Christy. They were so glad to see us. Friendly . . ." His voice trailed off.

"They're still friendly," Westholme said, "but with just a little twist. Better get back to the tug, Brad. Take care of our boys the best way you can. And, for God's sake don't try to be a hero. The way things stand now, this ship is going back over the Twelve Mile and there's not a thing we can do about it, except relax and protect our backsides the best way we know how."

When Fenton went over the side to the waiting raft, he was cheered on his way by several demonstrative crew members, his jacket pockets bulging with Russian cigarettes and two cans of caviar. He shook his head in disbelief and failed to return Westholme's wave as the raft began its journey back to *Haida Noble*.

Now it was the turn of Westholme and Volkoff to receive the welcome of the ship's company. Westholme heard the word "captain" being passed along the deck. Hands were reaching out to shake his, to thump him heartily on the shoulders. One giant of a man encircled his waist with a massive arm and squeezed him affectionately. Very few of them appeared to speak English, although there were several attempts at it—mostly memorized colloquial expressions:

"Good guy! Okay! Good guy Captain!"

A girl in her early twenties, dressed in crew dungarees and jacket, pushed forward and gave both him and Volkoff circular tins of sweet chocolate, then darted back into the crowd following them. They were moving behind the officer assigned to lead them to the captain's quarters. In the confusion, Westholme was able to lean over and voice a message into Volkoff's ear:

"Remember, you're one of my crew. You don't speak or understand Russian any more than I do."

Volkoff nodded. Tension had tightened the muscles of his face. He was limping slightly as he kept pace with Westholme.

At a roped-off section along the deck, the welcoming party stopped and formed a ragged gauntlet of well-wishers, hands still reaching out to touch and pummel as the officer passed the two men through into the off-limits area, and then refastened the rope. If he spoke English, he gave no evidence of it.

"I'd be willing to bet," Westholme said quietly to Volkoff, "that crowd thinks it's heading for port."

"You'd win," Volkoff said, so positively that Westholme knew he must have heard statements to that effect. "My God, what a shambles!"

They were threading their way over and around the remains of a collapsed ship's deck, chunks of twisted structural steel, and splintered timbers. At one point a man with an oxyacetylene torch was trying to cut away a riveted grid of metal that projected several feet over the ship's rail. Volkoff nudged Westholme as they approached the obstruction of steel junk. Near the deck, disappearing in the maze of girders and metal cross-beams, was a piece of half-inch plate perhaps three feet deep. The characters stenciled on it in black marine paint read: *TCO 17.*

The guide made an abrupt right turn and passed through a doorway leading into the ship's main deck interior, taking a flashlight out of his pocket to light the way. It was cold in there with the peculiar chill of unheated, moisture-beaded steel. There was an all-pervading stench of scorched things, blistered paint, incinerated cloth, charred steel—and the other smell Westholme would never forget from his Navy days; the smell of burned flesh, made more cloying in the fumes of a Lysol solution intended to mask it.

Up companionways and along corridors they went with the stench following them and the cold striking into their bones. It was very much like walking through a gigantic tomb.

"You people have had a very bad time of it," Westholme decided to say.

"A tragedy, Captain," the ship's officer said in quite good English. "It would be difficult for you to understand how terrible. Captain Kutskov has many problems to contend with at this time."

Westholme interpreted it as an attempt at a defense for the Russian captain's indefensible position. He remained silent and felt Volkoff's black eyes turned to him, registering the same thought.

Ahead of them, the uniformed Russian parted a heavy tarpaulin, and stood like a theater usher beckoning them ahead with his flashlight. "You must watch your footing here," he warned them.

They were outside again. Westholme stood on the edge of a jagged canyon slashed into the ship's superstructure and tried to grasp the enormity of the destruction. The drill rig tower, or a portion of it must have gone right through the ship's quarters, the galley, God knows what else! A gangplank had been jury-rigged to bridge the terrible gap and along this Westholme and Volkoff picked their way toward a tarpaulin wall on the far side.

"Right through," the Russian instructed. "Just a short distance after that."

Parting the heavy canvas, Westholme found himself in what must have been the forward portion of the radio room. It had been neatly halved by the falling steel, the afterportion crushed to smoking wires and rubble. The ship's officer hustled past them, shining his light to reveal a heavily paneled wood door with impressive brass fittings. He knocked twice and then, with his head to the door, said loudly:

"Captain Kutskov . . . they are here."

"Please come in," a deep, placid voice replied. And the ship's officer opened the door.

Westholme entered a handsome, elaborately appointed navigation bridge and felt the wave of comfortable heat surround him. The guide, unsmiling and somber, beckoned the two men ahead past a massive chart cabinet. Turning hard right, Westholme came face to face with Captain Mikhail Kutskov.

The man sat, semi-reclining, in what looked like a heavily constructed deck chair on which some foam rubber and blankets had been arranged. He wore the dark blue trousers of some kind of an official uniform, black silk braid running down the outer panel of each leg. His stockings were black and with a silken sheen, and his feet were fitted into plain capped, black calf shoes polished to a handsome lustre. From the waist up he was naked except for a heavily quilted red smoking jacket draped over his shoulders. The reason for the bare torso and arms was readily apparent.

The man's left arm, side and face extending right up into the scalp were swathed with some kind of wet, medicated gauze, appearing at a distance like white, dead skin peeling from his body. In fact, the gauze held intact the skin and tissue destroyed by the fierce heat that had swept across the captain's body. Unless the medication soaked into the cloth was pain killing, Captain Kutskov was suffering.

Whatever he felt or didn't feel, he was the first to break the silence. "Well, Captain Westholme. It would appear that we have both been through the wars." He was staring appraisingly at Westholme's lacerated face.

"I'd say you got the worst of it," Westholme said. "I'd like you to meet Mr. Michaels." Volkoff tried not to react to the sudden coining of the name.

"Ah-h!" Kutskov's expression was one of satisfaction. "The man who is expert in the saving of ships. We can use you, Mr. Michaels. Your last name strongly resembles my first."

Volkoff smiled humorlessly. "I guess it does at that."

Westholme was trying to read the Russian, get some clue to the man's thinking processes—his real state of mind—but it wasn't possible. The good side of his face was impressive enough, strongly molded. Eyes almost the same shade of gray as Westholme's, but with a trace of a slant to them; hair almost entirely gray but wiry and curling. He would put the Russian's face at fifty years, but the well-muscled torso looked younger than that. As for the man's attitude, his frame of mind? He was meticulously relaxed and friendly—like a genial host welcoming friends.

"I'm having some food served in a moment," he said. "I hope sincerely that you gentlemen are hungry?"

Suddenly Westholme realized that he was ravenous.

28 . . .

Fatigue and the mind-numbing events of the day were the enemies Westholme had to guard himself against . . . and they were almost too much for him. Take danger and nullify it with the outward appearances of security and conviviality; take physical pain and discomfort and cancel it with warmth and good food; take violence and death, symbolized by the aimed weapons of *Irkutsk*'s crewmen, and erase it with the genuine welcome and the gratitude of the ship's company; take all of these extreme opposites and let bone-numbing tiredness throw them slightly out of focus, place them just beyond the edge of judgment and rationality and the brain begins to doubt its images.

Fortunately, Volkoff succumbed rapidly to vodka and the surprisingly good food placed before them. The warmth that suffused the entire bridge, generated by kerosene heaters distributed through the area, had as much to do with it as anything. It was a deceptive, disarming, hospitable warmth against which tired, threatened men should arm themselves. Volkoff gave in, and it was just as well that he did because he was becoming quarrelsome, beginning to assert his rights as an American citizen, the liquor overcoming his physical depression.

He managed to get through the vodka apéritifs, the caviar and anchovy appetizers washed down with more vodka, and then the fine borscht. But when the ocean perch in egg batter was brought onto the bridge by two exhausted-looking stewards, Volkoff was asleep. Westholme and Kutskov had the conversation to themselves, and Westholme was glad that he had nursed his vodka.

"He is a very tired man," Kutskov observed.

"I guess we all are," Westholme said.

"Quite right . . ."

There was a knock at the door at this moment and the captain gave permission to enter.

It was the ship's doctor, once again a woman. She was somewhat older than Dr. Davodov, with a trace of gray in her hair; becoming slightly plump but still impressive in her bearing. She was all business. Standing in the doorway, she addressed a few brisk words to the captain in Russian, and advanced upon receiving his nod of agreement.

He introduced her courteously while she removed items from her bag and placed them on a sterile cloth spread out on the deck beside him:

"Dr. Lebedovitch, I would like you to meet Captain Westholme, master of *Haida Noble*. Captain Westholme, my ship's doctor."

Westholme inclined his head toward her and smiled. "I thought we had your ship's doctor."

Kutskov chuckled. "This is a rather unusual ship. I believe we have four medical doctors on board. Is that not so, Dr. Lebedovitch?"

"Two now, Captain," she said in an emotionless voice. "Dr. Davodov and myself remain." She crossed to a large, stainless-steel container steaming above an alcohol flame in a corner of the bridge, picked it up by its handles and carried it over to the captain's side. Deftly, she began to lift the soiled gauze from the captain's burned body, employing a pair of forceps. She worked an area at a time, removing gauze, spraying the lacerated and blistered skin with fluid from an atomizer, then covering the treated area with saturated gauze from the sterilizer. During this procedure the captain talked, with time out to breathe deeply when sections of the soiled gauze tore rather than slipped from his burns. It was an impressive demonstration of stoicism which Westholme chose to believe was being performed for his education.

"For a ship in distress, you run a good galley," he observed.

"Our main galley is non-existent, Captain. It was totally destroyed together with most of the officers' and scientists' quarters. But my feeling was that this little effort at hospitality should be made. It enables us to take the measure of one another under pleasant and civilized circumstances. Neither one of us has forgotten that ultimately we must come to the point." He stiffened slightly as Dr. Lebedovitch worked to release a stubborn piece of gauze from his earlobe.

"I think probably that time has come," Westholme said.

"I agree. And as soon as this excellent doctor has finished with me, we can get down to business." He said a few words to her in Russian, and she replied briefly.

"Apparently I am mending reasonably well. The problem seems to be one of infection. Another drink, Captain?"

Westholme raised a restraining hand, and watched Kutskov pour one for himself. "You have quite a few women on board."

"Not unusual for an oceanographic research vessel. Not unusual, in fact, for women to serve most professions and trades in my country. Is that not right, Doctor?"

"Seventy percent of all doctors are women, I believe," she said in her uninflected voice, as she continued to apply the dressings.

"I know for a fact that at least thirty percent of all people presently working in the sciences of oceanography are women," Kutskov said. "The *Vitiaz*, for instance—that is the flagship of the Institute of Oceanography—quite often sails with a full ship's company of women. Captain, crew, scientists—everyone."

"There's an old sailing superstition in our part of the world," Westholme said. "A woman on board a ship is bad luck."

"One of ours too. But just a superstition, a pleasant myth.

Things have changed greatly, Captain, and are continuing to change. In your country as well as in mine, I am sure."

The doctor had finished her dressings, and was placing instruments back in her bag. She spoke once more to Kutskov in Russian.

"An excellent idea," he said. "The doctor suggests that she examine the cuts on your face. In her opinion some of them appear irritated."

"I'd appreciate that," Westholme said. The vodka was making each small wound in his skin pound individually.

She worked quickly with probes and cotton wads soaked in a soothing fluid with an aromatic scent strongly resembling juniper. "You are fortunate that stitches are not required," she said. "It would be well if you did not shave for several days. You must not disturb the healing." She gave him a white tablet with a glass of water, left half a dozen more with him to be taken at specified intervals, and departed quietly.

"An impressive woman," Westholme observed.

"In the past thirty-six hours she has seen as much of mass suffering and death as any military surgeon with the strongest stomach. I would agree with you that she is an impressive person." He paused and adjusted himself more comfortably on the tilted chair. "Now then, should we discuss our mutual problems? Not at great length I suggest, because sleep will be the best medicine for both of us."

"This ship is moving at less than two knots," Westholme said. "We've got time to make a few decisions."

"Still we must not slow our thinking processes to two knots. We don't have that much time. May I tell you what I believe the position to be, Captain Westholme?"

"Go ahead."

"While matters have taken a somewhat unusual turn, basically what we have here is a salvage operation." He held up a hand to prevent Westholme from interrupting. "My ship's owner, the Academy of Sciences, USSR, represented by myself under these circumstances, has contracted with your company, Oceanlink Pacific Limited, to tow *Irkutsk* to a position of safety. The position of safety designated by my company is a position beyond the Canadian Twelve Mile limit . . . in international waters, to be exact."

"There is no contract," Westholme said abruptly. "The only position of safety is a port where you can get major repairs and adequate medical attention."

"But that is not your decision to make. Under standard salvage arrangements, as I understand it, the owner reserves the right to state how his ship will be disposed of. In this case we have elected to have our ship towed into international waters."

"Do you consider that we are working under some kind of a contract?" Westholme demanded.

"I have said as much, and have stated that we will pay you a salvage fee."

"Okay, Captain Kutskov, if we have a salvage contract— a standard salvage contract—then I am in charge of this tow, and I will be until your ship is delivered to safety. I have the right and the responsibility, under the terms of the contract, to decide what that safe destination will be—and it is not some Godforsaken point out in international waters!"

"I hope we are going to be able to discuss, rather than argue."

Westholme lowered his voice and settled back in his chair. He wished Volkoff were involved in this conversation instead of sprawled asleep in his own leather chair. "My first responsibility as captain is to my crew and my ship, then to your crew and your ship—in that order. In the interests of all those responsibilities, this tow should be going into Ucluelet." He looked at his watch. "I would have been there half an hour ago, at 2100 hours."

"Perhaps we have begun this badly. Let me state the position another way, and I must add that the commissar assigned to this ship—Commissar Volkonski—might not agree in every respect. Let me say that my ship's owner, the Academy of Sciences, now represented by myself for purposes of negotiation, is concerned that this vessel be returned to international waters. As the salvor, you need not know what those reasons are. Your only concern is to do what the owners are paying you to do."

"Double talk!" Westholme said angrily. "What you have done is pirate my tug, without concern for the lives of the people aboard her—or the people aboard this ship for that matter. The decision to tow into international waters is yours, and the responsibility for whatever happens is yours too. By every law of the sea, and by every responsibility of your command, you are wrong . . . and you know it!"

"Perhaps your summation is more realistic than mine. Blunter in any case. Captain Westholme, I admire you and have respect for you. Quite honestly I do not expect you to reciprocate. But we do have a common ground of under-standing. Both of us command ships. Both of us have orders to follow, no matter how odious they may appear to be. I respect you for the importance you place upon your respon-sibilities. Perhaps you may come to respect me for the same thing."

Westholme hunched his shoulders ahead in frustration. "Talk! Let's forget about the diplomacy, or the politics, or whatever the hell else you're trying to pull. What's this all about, Kutskov? What's driving you to do it. Are there orders you are bound to follow? Is this your own crazy idea? Do you think that what's left of your fishing fleet is going to be able to help you once you make it out beyond the Twelve Mile? If I knew some of the answers, perhaps I could help."

"Knowing the answers would not be good for you, believe me. I have done all I can to help you, Captain. I have re-moved from you the responsibility to make a decision. You cannot be blamed for what might yet happen. I assure you that you, your crew, and your tug will be safeguarded and that your company will be paid for services rendered. There is no need for you to know why I have taken these actions. It is much better, much safer for you if you do not."

"The commissar—what did you say his name was?"

"Volkonski . . ."

"Let me have a word with him. If he speaks for the owner . . ."

"The State. Volkonski would speak for the State."

"The same thing, I guess," Westholme said impatiently. "Does he share your plan of action?"

"Unfortunately," Kutskov said, "Commissar Volkonski was consigned to the sea along with thirty-four others of the ship's company this morning. He was an understanding man, and would have been able to help me substantially with my decisions."

Westholme sat with his head in his hand, completely at a loss, his brain refusing to come to grips with the situation, feeling the tight bands of fatigue closing in.

"You are not to concern yourself beyond the safety of your ship and your crew," the Russian captain said earnestly. "You have worries enough, and you cannot share mine. We have managed to build an impasse between us. Quite possibly sleep will reduce it to nothing by morning."

He picked up a makeshift microphone hookup attached to the arm of his chair, pressed a button, spoke into it in Russian, then turned to Westholme.

"The officer of the watch will escort you to your quarters. Not too comfortable, I am afraid." Westholme stood up wearily and went over to shake Volkoff awake.

"By the way, Captain Westholme, I inquired as to the power of your vessel earlier today. Five thousand horsepower, you said?"

"Ten thousand if we had both engines working."

"But five thousand should be sufficient to tow this ship at considerably more than two knots?"

"Not with the towing gear we're using, and the yaw this ship is developing. Two knots is pushing it."

"I would like to be in international waters by dawn."

Westholme looked at his watch. "Eleven or twelve hundred hours will be more like it," he said. "Push it any faster and you're in trouble."

Kutskov laughed with what sounded like genuine humor. "No matter how we look at it we are in trouble. No?"

The officer of the watch knocked and entered, a young, clean-cut man in a well-tailored uniform and sea jacket. He was almost military in his manner, directing his questions to the captain in brisk Russian. Captain Kutskov replied in the same tongue and gestured toward the still-sleeping Volkoff. The officer marched over and helped Westholme pull the American to his feet. The man came up grimacing as his sore muscles unwound.

"God in heaven! I feel as though the drill rig landed on me when it went over," he groaned.

"What did he say?" Kutskov asked pleasantly.

Westholme grinned and shook Volkoff roughly. "He's back in the Caribbean somewhere towing a drill rig. He's the only one I know who works in his sleep."

"Good night, gentlemen," Kutskov said.

Westholme said good night and nudged Volkoff to do the same. As he rounded the corner of the chart rack, he looked back and saw that the Russian captain's eyes were closed. In the light of the lanterns strung across the ceiling, his face had sagged and become very old.

Their cabin, as Captain Kutskov had warned them, was anything but pretentious. It was a small one on the upper deck, containing two bunks, one above the other. A kerosene lamp hung from the ceiling, providing the only heat and light. There was a cramped bathroom containing a sink and toilet but no shower. The single port was covered with a dead light, locked in place. The ship's damp coldness pervaded the room and helped to deepen Volkoff's growing mood of depression.

"You shouldn't have involved me in this," he insisted again. "None of it is any of my business."

"Keep it down!" Westholme warned sharply. "The walls aren't that thick." He went to the door and tried it. As he expected, it was locked from the outside.

"Locked!" Volkoff said tautly. "We're locked in—right?"

"What do you think?" Westholme retorted. He was too exhausted to be tolerant.

"We're prisoners?"

"I suppose so. Frankly, at this moment I don't give a damn.

I wouldn't walk out of that door even if it was unlocked and there was a taxi waiting to take me to the Department of National Defense. I'm bushed."

"Something like this separates the men from the boys."

"What the hell do you mean by that?"

Volkoff decided to switch the subject to safer ground. "Do you actually believe any of us are going to get out of this alive?"

"As a matter of fact I do. If we keep our noses clean and don't do anything foolish, I think we'll be back on *Haida Noble* by noon tomorrow, heading for Ucluelet."

Volkoff stared at him in disbelief. "I don't know how you can be as casual as that, with your tug and crew at stake, your own life—mine! This is an ELINT vessel, a spy ship. Can't you get that through your head? Do you think they'll let any of us free to tell what we saw?"

Westholme rubbed a perplexed hand through his hair, and started to take off his clothes. "Mike, we haven't seen anything. We don't know anything except that a Russian ship was tossed inside the Twelve Mile in a hurricane."

"It came in under its own steam. It sank BUTCO 17! I can testify to that."

"There was a collision. The ship damn near sank herself."

Volkoff moved in closer, his eyes gleaming like a conspirator's, but circled with tiredness and pain. "We can't let them get away with this, Westholme. They've broken every rule, every law . . ."

"They've also got us by the short hairs," Westholme reminded him, and climbed into the lower bunk. "Better keep the lantern on. It throws heat."

Exactly what wakened Westholme was not certain. Possibly it was the new motion of the ship, which became his main concern as soon as his brain began to function again. The lantern was flickering low in the dark room, its fuel almost exhausted. Volkoff was snoring lightly in the upper bunk. Westholme himself should have continued to sleep, because the warmth of the blankets and fat quilt the Russians had provided was wonderful. But there was something wrong.

He lay there and tried to analyze it. *Irkutsk* was rolling. Either the course had been changed, or the wind had changed. Neither! New course or new wind, the ship should still be yawing, zigzagging ponderously at the end of the line. Either the tug had stopped towing—or the bridle had snapped. He pulled his arm out of the warm covers and studied the luminous markings on his watch. 0517. Not long before dawn . . . and the ship had stopped.

The other possibility, and there was no way it could be possible, was that the tow was completed and the ship now rolled aimlessly beyond the Twelve Mile. He hoped it was so. He wanted someone to open that door and tell him that *Haida Noble* was waiting to take him aboard again—that the whole bloody nightmare was over.

Seconds later, a key did rattle in the door and it swung open, letting in the strong beam of an electric torch. Westholme couldn't see the man standing behind it, but the voice was friendly enough, even though the English was twisted.

"Captain says, for you and your friend, coffee with him. In a minute, please. You dress. Yes? Outside I wait."

"Anything wrong?" Westholme had to ask.

"Captain says you come. Coffee."

Westholme eased out of the bunk and reached for his clothes; then rumpled Volkoff's thick hair until he snorted and came awake.

"Who is it? Westholme?" He sat bolt upright, revealing his fully clothed body. "Westholme, is that you?"

"It's me," Westholme said as he buttoned himself into his shirt.

"What's happened?"

"We'll find out on the bridge. The captain is pouring coffee. One thing is certain; this ship has stopped."

"We're over the line. Now they've got to decide what to do with us."

"Oh for God's sake," Westholme said in disgust. "We've got enough trouble without you inventing more. Put your shoes on." He was lacing himself into his own, pulling on his jacket, trying to find a pocket comb to straighten out his hair.

"Look," Volkoff said, "don't read me wrong. I'm not scared. I'm mad; I'm suspicious, I'm uptight, but I'm definitely not frightened. We've got to second-guess these bastards. That's all I've been trying to say from the beginning."

"I'll go along with that," Westholme agreed. "What are you guessing?"

"Not so much guessing as thinking that we've got to take a stronger stand."

"Fine," Westholme said. "I'd like to show a little strength. What do you suggest?"

"We've got countries behind us, man! We're not fighting this thing alone. I'm an American citizen. You're a Canadian citizen. Your tug is Canadian property. The boys in your crew have got the same rights you have. Westholme, you seem to think that we're fighting this thing all by ourselves."

Westholme pulled the zipper up on his jacket. "I gave that some serious thought last night. The hard truth is, Mike, that we *are* fighting this thing by ourselves. We have been for the last twenty-four hours. We may be for the next forty-eight. The Russian is in the same position as we are."

"I'm not sure I know what you're getting at."

"Yesterday, when we took this ship on the line, we signaled to an Air-Sea Rescue plane that we could proceed—that everything was fine. With the destruction from the tidal wave and the hurricane up and down this coast, you can bet we're on the bottom of the priority list right now. *Haida Noble* is proceeding, and every serviceable ship on this coast is busy with its own kind of trouble."

Volkoff was getting the message. "No way to communicate. We're on our own for a while, that's true."

"And true for Captain Kutskov too, don't forget that. He's holding a lot of good cards, but he doesn't have his country kibitzing over his shoulder to tell him what to play."

"That could be good or bad, depending on the man."

"So that's all we have to go with—the man. So far I trust him. Let's continue to play our little game, such as it is. Keep your ears open whenever they're talking Russian. Pick up clues. Try and find us an advantage."

"I'll do what I can," Volkoff said, "but I still think we can play a tougher game."

"Okay, Mike," Westholme said as he opened the door. "You be the United States. I'll be Canada. Let's go up on the bridge and talk it over with Russia."

29 . . .

The master of *Irkutsk* seemed not to have moved since Westholme's discussion with him the night before. A young, broad-cheeked girl wearing a clean blue smock had just finished shaving him, and was gathering in her equipment. The gauze bandages had been changed again recently, and Kutskov's entire appearance was alert and efficient. A low table with a compartmented top had been moved in beside him. On it were arranged tea and coffee decanters, cups and saucers, and a plate of sweet biscuits. Incongruously, a walkie-talkie set, similar to the one employed by the Russian crewmen on board *Haida Noble,* was lying at the end of the table within easy reach. *Haida Noble*'s own set was hanging by its strap from a hook above the navigation desk.

There were two others with Kutskov, both ship's officers, middle-aged, well built and with uniformly rigid features. It wasn't that these two lacked friendliness. Rather their manner was that of men concerned with issues much larger than social pleasantries. In Westholme's opinion both were functioning under severe strain.

Kutskov introduced them pleasantly and properly, and Westholme promptly forgot the difficult names, remembering only that they were the ship's second and third officers. Both understood English and spoke it reasonably well, further evidence of the training and capabilities of this ship's company.

"Perhaps you would like to serve yourself," the Russian

master invited. "I believe there will be something more substantial later on."

"The ship has stopped," Westholme said abruptly.

"That is why we were obliged to call you on deck. Possibly you would like to help us with this matter. As you may have guessed, the towing bridle has broken."

"You increased the towing speed," Westholme accused without hesitation. "I warned you about that."

"The towing bridle has broken," Kutskov repeated patiently. "That is the immediate problem. There is no time to explore the reasons. I am afraid the cable has worked a considerable amount of destruction on your vessel."

Westholme knew exactly what must have happened. Someone—undoubtedly Kutskov—had issued orders to the tug to increase speed, probably within the past hour. It wouldn't be long before the new strain on the cable took effect, accentuating the yawing motion of the crippled ship, stretching the steel-cored wire to the breaking point, rubbing metal on metal where the bridle legs passed through the fairleads. Then, without warning, the dull twang of a multi-ton towing cable snapping back like elastic toward *Haida Noble*'s stern.

"At this moment," Kutskov continued, "your crew is giving us some trouble. The attitude is understandable, but it is extremely important for them to render whatever assistance they can in putting a new line aboard us. By my reckoning we have slightly less than six miles to go before your assignment is completed."

"How much damage to the tug?" Westholme asked.

"I would suggest that you talk to your second officer, Mr. Fenton. I am sure he will tell you everything. We have not been able to reason with him." Kutskov nodded to the *Haida Noble* walkie-talkie set, and one of his officers reached for it and handed it to Westholme. "The object of your conversation, of course, is to obtain his co-operation."

Westholme pushed the button to transmit. "Brad. Brad Fenton? Westholme here. Are you receiving me? Over." He repeated the message several times, and then looked at Volkoff as though searching for the reason for the silence.

"I should explain, as well," the Russian captain said, "that there were casualties. I believe we have both lost a man, Captain Westholme."

Westholme took one swift step toward Kutskov and felt restraining hands on his shoulders, holding him back.

Behind him, Volkoff exclaimed, "All right, Westholme! *Now* what do you think!"

At the same time the speaker in the walkie-talkie rattled into life: "Westholme?" the voice inquired. "Are you receiving? Over."

"Brad? Brad, what's going on over there?"

"It's goddam awful! Poor Bibaud . . . Tait has blown his stack and tried to fight all the bastards at once. He's out cold and locked in your cabin. It's a mess, Christy, just a . . ."

"Okay, Brad. Slow down. Now what's the situation?"

"The bastards increased the towing speed. The cable kicked back and . . . Bibaud's dead, along with one of them. There's cable all over the afterdeck."

Westholme turned to the Russian captain. "Safeguarding my tug and crew, are you!" His voice was dry with anger, disbelief—and sorrow.

"I can't persuade you to believe that I am as distressed as you are, Captain. Perhaps you will understand later. I elected to take a risk—and a heavy price has been paid."

"Like hell it has," Volkoff said furiously. "Everyone has paid but you. The drill rig, your own ship, the tug. How much more?"

Captain Kutskov rubbed his knuckles across his broad forehead, eyes closed momentarily as he searched for the restraint to frame his words. "Let us grant that we have personal feelings. They must not be allowed to surface now. Later, all right. The objective—and it is my objective—is to return my ship across into international waters." He looked at Westholme squarely. "I have made a number of mistakes in the past few days. I admit this readily. But I do not intend to make any more. I am determined to retrieve my position, and I will proceed from risk to increasing risk until the objective is achieved." The words were not delivered as a threat, but as a statement of absolute and irrevocable fact. Westholme knew he could not be shaken.

He went back to Fenton: "Brad, I can't believe this has happened. It's a terrible thing. Bibaud was . . ." He didn't finish the sentence. There was no way he could express how he felt about Bibaud. Tough, unemotional Tait had expressed his sorrow with violence—and paid for it. With luck and the right moves now, there would be a time and a place to pay proper tribute to Bibaud.

"Brad, I don't want any of you to put up any more resistance. You've got to believe that it can only lead to more serious trouble. I don't want anyone else ending up like Bibaud. Is that understood?"

There was silence at the other end.

"Are you receiving me, Fenton?"

"I hear you."

"Is the towing winch still operating?"

"How do I know, with a thousand feet of cable lying on top of it!" There was rebellion in the second officer's voice.

"Start Stan Read cutting away that cable. Drop the whole works overboard, and while that's happening get the boys to pull a new bridle out of the wire room. Tell them I don't want any heroes, and no more dead men. We need to put the new line aboard within the hour. Possible?"

"I don't know about that until . . ."

"Make it possible, Brad. The way things are shaping up, all our lives could depend on it."

"I'll have to talk to the others."

"You do that. You tell them that we're dealing with a man who has wiped out more than thirty of his own people. Now Bibaud. He'll go the limit if he has to."

"I read you," Fenton said. "I'm on my way."

Westholme put the walkie-talkie on the table beside Kutskov's. "You heard my orders," he said. "That's the best I can do."

"I am grateful for that," the Russian said. "Your bluntness may have persuaded him—although I think you misjudge me. I am in an extremely difficult position, Captain."

"So was Ernie Bibaud when that cable hit him in the face," Westholme said harshly. "Your orders killed him! That's your trouble; you're hooked on orders. This isn't war, it's peacetime, and the master of a ship can countermand orders in the interest of human lives. My God, Kutskov, you've got circumstances ten times over that justify taking your ship and crew into port."

"I don't expect you to understand," Kutskov said. "Under other conditions I think I could convince you I am not inhuman. Now, Mr. Michaels," he said to Volkoff, "it may be that you can turn your skills to the saving of our ship."

Volkoff shrugged. "It looks as though all the arrangements have been made."

"I want you to know," Westholme said deliberately, "that your orders killed a good man—a man I valued as a friend."

"You have made your point," Captain Kutskov assured him, "and I have told you I am deeply sorry. Now I must ask you to help me with my ship."

"Okay," Westholme said, "let us below. Give us a chance to do a damage survey, stem to stern. Maybe we can do something about the leaks—or are there things down there you don't want us to see?"

Kutskov glanced at one of his officers and spoke to him inquiringly in Russian. The man seemed to be considering a question—his expression dubious. His fellow officer interjected a comment, shaking his head in the negative.

The ship's master listened carefully and then turned back to Westholme. "Our own people have gone over the ship rather thoroughly. Apparently you can be of most use in the transferring of the new cable."

"Okay, let's get started."

"There is time for both of you to have your coffee, or your tea, as you prefer."

"I don't have the appetite for it," Westholme said. Quite obviously no one on the bridge had an appetite. The cups remained nested in their compartment, untouched.

"Captain Kutskov," he said deliberately, "do the people

on board this ship know what you are doing? Do they know you could be making a life-or-death decision for them?"

"That needn't concern you," Kutskov said sharply.

"Do they know that you broke one of the cardinal laws of seamanship when you brought this vessel within six miles of a lee shore with a hurricane blowing?"

"I am on the best of terms with my ship's company," Kutskov said loudly, beginning to raise himself from his reclining chair. He stifled a groan and fell back. For the first time his anger showed. "You are in no position either to bargain or pass judgment. Now I can be blunt. You are the master of a tugboat, nothing more. You are under my command until I release you."

"Now you're talking a language I understand," Westholme said.

"I have done everything I could to demonstrate goodwill under impossible circumstances. If I must take a stronger position, you have only yourself to blame."

"Who the hell do you think you are?" Volkoff demanded. "You're not dealing with individuals, you're dealing with countries—with Canadian and American citizens, with Canadian property, inside Canadian territory!"

Kutskov threw up his one good arm in a gesture of hopelessness. "I have been trying to convey to you that I respect your persons, your country—everything. When my ship is back in international waters, everything will be as it was before. You will have been paid . . ."

"Nothing is the same," Westholme told him. "My deckhand, Ernie Bibaud, is dead."

"As are many of my own ship's company—including good and close friends."

"Who would be alive if you hadn't moved this ship in behind BUTCO 17," Volkoff accused. "You helped to sink that drill rig!"

"You believe yourself to be well-informed, Mr. Michaels," the master of *Irkutsk* said in a cold, speculative voice.

"Take a tour of your own ship," Westholme interjected

swiftly. "The evidence is spread all over hell's half acre. One of your crew is cutting pieces of the drill rig away right now."

"There was a hurricane force wind," Kutskov said wearily. "There was a tsunami. All of us are victims of the sea. Circumstances have brought us together. Why are we not working together to safeguard our individual interests?"

"Because only your interests are being served," Westholme stated flatly. "You talk like a Philadelphia lawyer, but it all boils down to the simple fact you are going to get your own way, if it kills us."

"Perhaps. Perhaps that is so. Go now, both of you! Take them to the afterdeck," he instructed his ship's officers. "Put them to work at the thing they understand."

"You are involving yourself too much, Captain," he called after Westholme's retreating figure. "You too, Mr. Michaels. Simply do your job as you would in any other salvage circumstance and everything will go well."

Not until they had been escorted to the ship's afterdeck, submitted once more to the earnest and genuine camaraderie of the crew members selected to haul in the bridle legs, were Westholme and Volkoff able to exchange conversation, and then it had to be guarded and cryptic. One of Kutskov's somber ship's officers remained close at hand, presumably to act as liaison in the cable hook-up.

Haida Noble lay one thousand yards astern and in line with *Irkutsk*. At that distance it was possible to see with the naked eye the bright blue flame of Stan Read's cutting torch working to free the tangled cable. Binoculars brought the scene up close, and Westholme discovered two torches working in close proximity, Read using one and a Russian crewman employing the other—their identical welder's masks making twins of them. Two other Russians stood by, one at the stern control console looking down on the scene; the other against the stern rail on the afterdeck. Neither of the two were holding guns, although Westholme had no doubt they had them ready in their jackets or their belts.

Three other members of the boarding party remained to be accounted for. One was dead and lying somewhere in the bowels of the ship with poor Bibaud. Logically the others would be deployed in the engine room, navigation bridge and probably the hospital. Dr. Davodov? Taking care of Lindstrom and the roughneck, he hoped. Strangely, he continued to trust Kutskov in many ways. He still believed that the doctor had been sent aboard *Haida Noble* as a gesture of goodwill, just as he had absolute confidence in the friendly attitude of the Russian crew now assembled around him to pull the bridle on board.

They were young, most of them in their early twenties. Good faces behind two-day growths of whiskers. Female members of the crew stood at the rail aft on the upper deck and looked down, for the most part conversing among one another; some of the more outgoing ones calling down to members of the work party. It was a peculiarly healthy and encouraging scene; incongruous, out of context in a ship on which death had left its mark, but these people, young and with much yet to expect from life, had turned their backs on the hopelessness of the previous two days. *Haida Noble* and her lifeline were all the hope they needed.

At an opportune moment, he said to Volkoff: "Too bad we couldn't do that damage survey."

Volkoff picked up the lead smoothly. "I don't think we need to. It's absolutely clear that they don't need us to look at anything below." Moving in closer, he said. "This ship is exactly what I said she was, and I think I know what she's up to—among other things."

"That's fine," Westholme said easily. "We'll do our job and get out. Nothing more."

"I'm with you," Volkoff said earnestly. "All of a sudden I understand that old saying 'curiosity killed the cat!'"

The booms on *Haida Noble* were beginning to swing as Galbraith worked the winches. Grapnels on the boom cables dug into the mass of tangled wire on the deck, lifted it clear and swung it over the side, returning for additional loads. In a very few minutes the deck was virtually clear. The big tug made a turn across the diminishing swell and approached *Irkutsk*, performing basically the same maneuver as before, swinging her stern around to meet that of the Russian ship. Fenton was a good man at the wheel, even going astern with one ship's engine out.

Galbraith stood with the heaving line in his hand, just as Ernie Bibaud had done the day before, swung and threw it unerringly onto the stern deck of *Irkutsk* where half a dozen of the crew pounced on it. There was loud cheering when the line was captured. Once again Westholme and Volkoff received hearty congratulations and handshakes, as though they had personally landed the line. A few minutes later Galbraith heaved the second thin line on board, and the two work parties began the task of hauling in. After yesterday's experience, they were familiar with the job, and the operation proceeded swiftly in an atmosphere of celebration. The two work parties were hauling with gusto to a half-grunted, half-chanted phrase repeated over and over again in rhythm with their effort. The women on the upper deck had started a song of their own in counterpoint with the chant of the work crews. The total effect was impressively melodic.

"I'd call that whistling in a graveyard," Volkoff observed flatly.

"Makes nice listening though," Westholme said. They had turned and were watching the bright, animated faces of the women on the upper deck. Arms locked together along the rail, the entire group was moving in unison to the song, heads moving to left and right in perfect time.

"I just don't believe it," Volkoff muttered. "You don't know whether to hate them or love them."

Westholme felt the American's hand tug quickly on the pocket of his jacket, saw him turn back abruptly to face the stern of the ship, and decided to hold his own position continuing to scan the singers on the upper deck. In his ear, above the singing and general confusion he heard Volkoff say:

"The two in uniform on your left, up above. I know one of them . . . and I think she knows me."

Westholme let his eyes move slowly left past the line of singers, registering finally on two uniformed figures at the end of the rail; one male, the other female. The woman, in her late twenties, was pointing toward him and talking animatedly to her companion.

"I see them," Westholme said, forcing his eyes to move to other faces on the upper deck. "Who are they?"

"She's an oceanographer, and a good one. I met her at the Oceanographic Congress in Moscow in 1966. We saw a lot of one another, if you know what I mean."

"Friend or enemy?"

"Now? God knows. Then it was friendly enough."

"I have a feeling," Westholme said, "that the fat is in the fire." He turned around slowly to survey the progress of the cable transfer. The heavier polypropylene ropes were being hauled in now. In a few minutes the bridle ends would come aboard.

"I shouldn't have come with you," Volkoff said harshly. "It's the worst possible thing you could have done."

"Cut it out," Westholme ordered him flatly. "The worst thing either of us can do is to lose our control."

"What control?" Volkoff demanded. "We don't hold a card. Not a card!"

The ship's officer stepped in close to them, his eyes narrowed and questioning. "You are troubled?"

"No trouble," Westholme said. "We were just arguing about the best way to secure the bridle. We don't want it breaking again."

The Russian nodded and appeared satisfied.

The first of the bridle ends was on deck and being dragged toward a mooring bollard. "Come on, Mike," Westholme said. "It's time we went to work."

Volkoff fell in beside him unwillingly. Westholme could feel the tension in him. He beckoned the American down beside him as he stooped to examine the condition of the bollard.

"All we want to do," he said, "is save the tug and the people aboard her—and our own skins while we're at it."

"No chance," Volkoff raged softly. "What's your plan? Where's that beautiful plan of yours?"

"What's yours?" Westholme flashed back. "Stand off the ship's company with a monkey wrench?"

"I'm an American citizen," Volkoff's voice remained low, but thin and strangled. "I don't have to take this."

"Knowing Kutskov, do you think your chances would be any better if you had a U.S. destroyer alongside right now."

"You're goddam right I do!"

The work party was upon them, struggling to aim the bridle eye at the bollard. Westholme stood up and took a purchase on the cable, helping to guide it ahead until it could be positioned over the bollard. Volkoff stood by and watched, hands in pockets, eyes smoldering. He remained unco-operative as the second leg of the bridle was fitted into place.

Seventy-five feet astern, *Haida Noble* began to move ahead, her winch paying out the new cable, taking up the strain, increasing the distance between the two vessels to five hundred, a thousand, fifteen hundred feet. Westholme felt the attitude of *Irkutsk* change. The helpless stern swung around ponderously, aligning itself with *Haida Noble*'s towing cable, and beginning to move. The Russian ship was under way again.

Taking the in-going tide into account, together with the prevailing current, Westholme estimated that the ship had lost three miles in the almost two hours it had taken to hook up the new cable. The Twelve Mile limit was nine or ten miles away—say ten hours away—he estimated. The rising tide would hold them at a standstill until it went slack and began to ebb. Ten hours, if all went well. If the weather changed; or if the cable broke again; or if Volkoff or his own tug crew precipitated trouble then it would be longer than ten hours—a lot longer.

A friendly Russian crew member offered him a cigarette which he accepted gratefully. Volkoff refused with a terse shake of his head. The man struck a match and held it for Westholme. He was young, out of breath from the hauling of the cable, his forehead liberally beaded with sweat. "We go Vancouver, yes?" He answered his own question with a nod.

"My brother, Vancouver . . ." He held up two fingers on his hand. "One—two time. Trawler mate."

The ship's officer interjected himself into the conversation, said a few words to the crew member and sent him away on an assignment. The boy left, waving cheerfully.

Beside him Westholme heard Volkoff say. "Brace yourself. Here it comes." Out of the corner of his eye he saw the two ship's officers shouldering their way through the crowd. The one in the lead confronted Westholme coldly. "You will come to see the captain . . . and your friend too."

The officer reached out to take him by the arm.

Westholme avoided the hand. "There's no need for that," he said. "Let's keep it friendly." He plunged his hands deep into his jacket pocket and walked beside his escort, Volkoff following behind sullenly. Just as before, they passed through a gauntlet of well-wishers; tired, battered, smiling faces; hands reaching out to touch; voices trying to express gratitude to the men who had snatched them from the rocks, to the crew of *Haida Noble* who were towing them to safety. The irony of the situation was overpowering; Westholme could feel himself drifting into Volkoff's unreasoning frame of mind. He was beginning to understand what the death of BUTCO's crew and the ordeal in the life raft had done to the American. The nightmare was getting to him as well.

30 . . .

Captain Kutskov had a tribunal waiting for them, or so it appeared to Westholme. There were the two oceanographic scientists, dressed in well-fitting uniforms which were almost civilian garb; blue blazer and gray skirt for the woman; blue blazer and gray trousers for the man. She was a singularly attractive brunette, out of her twenties and into her early thirties, Westholme decided. The man was older, balding, a little heavy in the paunch but with bright, dark eyes that probed and measured. Her smile when she saw

Volkoff was tentative, nervous, disappearing quickly. In the entire group, her manner was the only one approaching friendliness.

The others: three ship's officers, consisting of their escort of the morning and the two who had summoned them to the bridge, were uniformly cold and wary. Two enormous crew members stood restlessly in the background.

Mikhail Kutskov had wilted considerably since the early morning meeting. The pain and tiredness were showing in his eyes, and he still reclined in the tilted-back position on the chair. An effort had been made to fit the upper part of his body into a light, woolen pullover cut away to avoid the burned portions of his side and arm, but in spite of the heavy, stuffy warmth in the area, the chill of shock was beginning to tell on him. Westholme thought he could smell the faint, sickly aroma of suppurating tissue. Areas of the gauze dressings were showing blotches of yellow.

"I believe introductions are unnecessary," Kutskov began abruptly. "Mr. Volkoff, you are apparently acquainted with Miss Baliuk, scientist on staff, Institute of Oceanology, USSR?"

Volkoff looked at her without smiling. "Hello, Serafima."

She inclined her head toward him in an uncertain greeting.

"This, of course, changes the nature of our relationship," Kutskov said to Westholme. "I have dealt with you honestly, and with a sincere wish to demonstrate goodwill under the most difficult of conditions. On the other hand, Captain Westholme, you have chosen to practice deceit. Two simple tugboat men is it?" He pointed a finger at Volkoff. "This man is an oceanographer of sufficient capability to have attended Moscow in 1966."

"I didn't know that," Westholme said.

"You knew he spoke Russian?"

"I knew that. I brought him with me for that reason. It was one of the few advantages I thought I had."

"And it turns out to be a serious disadvantage, Captain. How long have you known him?"

"Not long . . ."

"Since the sinking of the British United drill rig number seventeen. Is that not true?"

Westholme nodded. "We picked him up. He was one of two survivors."

"Out of more than fifty," Volkoff cut in. "Two out of fifty. And you can hold yourself responsible for . . ."

"You are in no position to comment or to bargain," Kutskov said sharply. "To all intents and purposes you are a spy doing your best to discover what you can about us. We are no longer concerned for your welfare, Mr. Volkoff—or for yours, Captain."

"A spy," Volkoff said incredulously. "This whole damned ship is rigged for spying—and I didn't *ask* to come aboard her." He glanced at Westholme. "I was brought aboard."

"Nevertheless you came under false pretenses, and you have had an opportunity, no matter how slight, to draw conclusions, to report inaccurately and alarmingly on the purpose of our ship in these waters."

There was a brisk knock on the door, and Kutskov's involuntary jerk was indicative of the strain building in him. At his signal, one of the crew members went to the door and opened it. It was Dr. Lebedovitch. She stepped through the doorway and advanced toward the captain.

He waved a protesting hand at her. "Not now, please. We will be finished shortly."

"Now," she said firmly, lapsing into impatient Russian.

He argued with her angrily, but her firm hand was on his forehead as she countered his objections in her cool, uninflected voice. He glared at her but conceded abruptly, and she moved unobtrusively in beside him, her head, with its slightly graying hair, bent over his burned arm, her entire personality seeming to blend into the background.

Volkoff grasped the opportunity she had unwittingly provided. "You're sick," he said. "In pain, running a fever. How do you expect to make a rational decision in your condition? She said . . ."

"Quiet!" Kutskov roared in a totally surprising display of rage. For the second time, Westholme saw him try to raise himself from the chair and fall back in pain. The man was suffering from more than burns; a back injury, possibly.

Volkoff was not to be put down. He switched to animated Russian and continued until Kutskov called over his shoulder to one of the crewmen. The man advanced threateningly and Volkoff decided on the wisdom of silence.

Kutskov addressed Westholme. "I presume you know these waters well?"

Westholme nodded.

"Knowing the condition of this ship, the technical difficulties of towing it, the currents hereabouts, how much time do you think it will take to reach international waters?"

"I've thought about it," Westholme said. "It will be a minimum of ten hours."

"That is a reasonable estimate?"

"I'd say it was optimistic . . . Captain, can I make a couple of comments? They may not prove to be practical, but I'd like you to hear me out."

The Russian tilted his head back and shut his eyes momentarily as the doctor worked patiently to release an encrusted piece of gauze. When he opened them again, they were black with pain.

"What is it, Captain?"

"In my first discussion with you, I admired your logic—your ability to keep emotions out of the picture. For a number of understandable reasons, emotions are starting to influence all of us more than they should. You might say the danger is escalating."

Kutskov chuckled without any trace of humor. "Spoken like a diplomat." He glanced at the others and translated the gist of Westholme's statement.

"Then I'll speak like the tugboat skipper you say I am," Westholme said. "From where you sit, there may be larger issues—bigger orders issued by your Academy, your Navy, the State. I don't much care. The only issue that really counts is that I have sick and injured on my tug; you have even more aboard this ship, unless I miss my guess. If you don't want this ship to go into a Canadian port, let me take all of you aboard *Haida Noble,* and let this ship go up on the beach or down to the bottom. That's where she's going to end in any event."

"It is a generous offer," Kutskov said wearily, "but it won't do. It lacks understanding of the true situation. I won't explain it to you. I think Mr. Volkoff can do it for me."

Volkoff looked perplexed, and then understood and took up the Russian's challenge. "I'll make an intelligent try, Captain. This is an ELINT vessel; something that could be classified as a spy ship. The USSR has scores of them; so has the United States . . . and the orders are the same on both sides: if your vessel is in danger of seizure, you must destroy it. The *Pueblo* is a classic example of what can happen if you can't or don't follow the destruct order. Am I close?"

Kutskov's silence was permission to continue.

"All right. Supposing I'm correct part of the way. Your country doesn't have any equipment or device on your intelligence collection ships that the United States doesn't have. I speak from a fair depth of knowledge. Oh, you may have a temporary advantage in one or two areas; but then we make up for it in others."

"That is not true!" For the first time, the middle-aged oceanographer entered the discussion, and his attitude was vehement. "We have led the way in the application of science to the study of the oceans. The United States of America has lagged far behind—more concerned to rape the sea bottom than to perpetuate it for mankind."

"You're changing the subject, professor," Volkoff said sharply. "I'm talking about intelligence collection ships. I'm saying this ship is one of yours, and I'm saying that under the rules of the game it has got to be destroyed before it is captured. All right? Then accept the Canadian's offer." He chucked a thumb at Westholme. "Put your people on board his tug and destroy this goddam hulk!"

"Transparently clever," the oceanographer said. "Destroy it here on Canada's continental shelf, in twenty or thirty fathoms of water. How long do you think it would take to bring up the pieces and fit the story together?"

"So that is the situation, isn't it?" Captain Kutskov said to Volkoff. "The ship must be demolished and sunk. Faced with the same problem, the Americans would do the same . . . and the ship must be destroyed in international waters deep enough to prevent the possibility of anyone retrieving any significant part of her."

"Why? What do you think you will be concealing?" Volkoff insisted. "The chances of your having something on this vessel beyond the imagination or even the knowledge of the United States is pretty slim. Let me try guessing. Serafima . . ." He turned to the strained and silent women. "The paper you delivered in Moscow was on the feasibility of underwater storage depots for everything from foodstuffs to fuel oil. It was the best work on the subject I've ever seen. So . . . this ship is surveying for or perhaps is installing underwater storage depots for future military purposes. No? Then your partner here could be an expert in the establishment of atomic caches, or submarine detector networks, or atomic submarine maintenance facilities—or simply the farming of kelp for the starving populations of the world. The point is that anything you are doing, we are doing too—give or take a few sophisticated twists on either side."

"I'm afraid," Kutskov said, with what sounded like genuine regret, "that you have expressed much better than I could the fact that our problem encompasses more than the destruction of the ship now."

"How's that?" Westholme said.

"Your friend, and by association you yourself, have become too knowledgeable."

Volkoff swung toward the Russian. "If that's a threat, forget it. Neither one of us can make your position any worse than it is."

"You know," Westholme said, shaking his head in slow disbelief, "what we're having here is a kind of a summit conference; three or four of us trying to throw our weight around, trying to figure out some kind of power play, and the people who stand to lose most, if not everything, haven't a clue what we're deciding for them."

"The subject is closed," Kutskov said. The doctor had finished with him and was putting away her bottles and bandages.

"How many of your ship's company believe they are being towed to a Canadian port? How many know this ship is going to be blown to bits in international waters?"

"Before that they will have been transferred to other vessels in the fleet," Kutskov said.

"You hope! What vessels? What fleet? I haven't seen anything shaping up on the horizon." Westholme tilted his head toward the starboard bridge window in the general direction of the sea; several others looked instinctively.

The taller of the two large Russian crew members forgot his attempt at a military at ease stance, executing a complete turn as he craned to get a better view of something he could see starboard of the ship. With his back turned to the room, he spoke rapidly in startled Russian, only to be interrupted by another voice in the same language emerging from Captain Kutskov's walkie-talkie.

Volkoff turned to Westholme, his eyes suppressing excitement. "There's a Canadian vessel approaching!" To Kutskov he said. "There was no way you could get away with this."

"At this moment nothing has changed," Kutskov said. "See if you can identify the vessel for us, Captain Westholme."

Westholme crossed to the starboard side of the bridge and let his eyes travel across the gray, restless line of the sea until they came to rest on a medium-sized craft some three miles distant, approaching from a northerly direction. He turned back to the others, looking for binoculars, received a pair from one of the ship's officers and trained them on the approaching vessel:

"It's *Blackfish*," he confirmed. "Canadian Coast Guard vessel."

31 . . .

"Talk about luck!" Volkoff exulted.

Westholme returned to stand in front of Kutskov. His manner, in contrast to Volkoff's, was restrained and earnest. "This is the chance we've been looking for, Captain—you as well as me. No one can fault you for surrendering to one of our Coast Guard vessels. You and your ship's company will be better off in every way, and later on if there is a need for me to testify, I think I would have to come to your defense on a number of issues."

"And would your American friend here come to our defense? I think it is unlikely. I am sorry, Captain, but nothing has changed. We will proceed on into international waters."

Volkoff's expression, as he stared at Westholme, was one of complete disbelief. "Now come on! Tell him he's out of his mind!"

"Not in the least," Kutskov said sharply. "I have the advantage over both of you in that I know exactly what I must do, and I continue to possess the means to achieve it. The Coast Guard ship will approach the tug, is that not true, Captain?"

Westholme shrugged; then nodded.

"The communication will be by loud hailer—unless they utilize radio telephones employing the same frequency as yours?"

"Loud hailers," Westholme said.

"Then I would like you to instruct your second officer aboard your tug, to conduct a normal exchange of information with the master of *Blackfish*. The line broke during the night. That is the truth. The tow is now proceeding without difficulty. *Blackfish* need not trouble herself with us further."

"I won't do that," Westholme told him flatly.

"I would be disappointed in you, if you had agreed. However it must be done." Captain Kutskov picked up his own walkie-talkie set and spoke into it. Almost immediately a voice acknowledged him and Kutskov issued his instructions. While he waited he explained to Westholme: "I have asked to talk to your second officer . . . Mr. Fenton, is it? I should inform you as well that your first officer now appears to be in a more satisfactory condition, although he will require surgery at the earliest moment. Dr. Davodov gave me her report earlier today."

Fenton's voice emerged belligerently from the speaker identifying himself. "Is Westholme there?" he demanded. "I want to speak to Captain Westholme."

"In a moment," Kutskov assured him. "Mr. Fenton, we would like you to put the Coast Guard at ease in the event that they should challenge you. Tell them the cable broke, and that there was a delay in rejoining it. Tell them you are now prepared to proceed without difficulty. We will not require their help."

"You're joking!" Fenton said incredulously.

"I am very serious, and there is no time to argue. You must realize by now that I am a determined man."

"I want to talk to Captain Westholme!"

"Very well, but briefly," Kutskov instructed. He handed the walkie-talkie to his first officer who carried it to Westholme and held it in front of him with his fingers on the send-receive control.

"I'm receiving you, Brad," Westholme said. "My orders are absolutely clear. Tell the boys on *Blackfish* we've been pirated. Tell them there are sick and injured aboard both vessels, and that we need all the help we can get . . ."

The set was pulled away from him abruptly and returned to Kutskov. Fenton was talking now:

"I'll try, Christy. The bandage brigade over here is giving us a pretty bad time. I'll put the message across if I don't get slugged first."

"I doubt that you would be injured in full view of the Canadian Coast Guard, Mr. Fenton," Kutskov said sharply, "but we could no longer be responsible for the safety of your captain. Do you understand? Now please co-operate. Send the Coast Guard vessel on its way."

"Let me talk to Captain Westholme . . ."

Kutskov switched off and returned the set to the table. "I am afraid we have posed him a rather difficult problem," he said to Westholme apologetically, "but I had no alternative."

Westholme ignored him. The man's defenses were too thick, his mind too set on the thing he must do. Instead he turned to the others: the somber officers who listened to their captain's directives without comment or question, the two scientists who seemed to be in silent accord with a plan that was totally destructive. "He *had* an alternative," he insisted. "He still has. Get off this ship, all of you. Blow it up! Destroy it! Do whatever the rule book calls for . . . but do it now while you've got a ship out there that can render aid and send for more."

The oceanographer looked at Captain Kutskov in exasperation. "I have already explained to them it is too shallow. Regulations prohibit the scuttling of . . ."

". . . of an intelligence collection ship on any continental shelf where the possibility of the retrieval of classified materials remains." Volkoff recited it as though he had memorized it from an official handbook. "We must buy our rules from the same guy. You don't want to be another *Pueblo*. Right? You don't want Big Brother back home to reprimand you, or cashier you, or stand you up against the wall and shoot you because you wavered from the rule book by one paragraph. I can understand that . . ."

"Thank you, Mr. Volkoff," Captain Kutskov tried to interrupt.

Volkoff pursued his point: "But the facts are that you were forced by natural causes beyond your control to come inside Canada's Twelve Mile limit, and forces beyond your control are keeping you here. There isn't a member of your ship's company who wouldn't testify that you have done everything humanly possible to live by the rule book . . . but it's game over, Captain Kutskov. Quit! Relax. You deserve a medal."

Kutskov waved the argument away with an impatient hand and called to the ship's officer standing watch on the approach of the Coast Guard vessel. The officer reported the position to his captain who reclined below the line of sight. To the others it was apparent that *Haida Noble* and *Blackfish* were about to make contact.

Volkoff turned his argument toward the woman: "Serafima, I think we got to know one another very well in Moscow. The theme of the Oceanographic Congress brought a lot of people together for openers. 'Ocean Research for the good of mankind,' wasn't that it?"

Watching her, Westholme could see that her eyes were begging him to stop. The American was becoming too edgy, pushing too hard, and Kutskov's irritation was beginning to show.

"Be quiet you!" he commanded and then returned his attention inquiringly to the watching officer who had now gone out on the bridge to listen as well as to use the glasses.

"Then what are you doing here in a situation like this?" Volkoff persisted in a violent undertone.

"Research!" she said in a half whisper, goaded out of her silence. "For the good of mankind!"

"For the good of the USSR!"

"What is good for the United States of America is seldom good for the rest of mankind," her fellow scientist said loudly and angrily.

"Fod godssake . . ." Volkoff began in disgust, and was overcome by Kutskov's hand descending palm downward on the surface of the table in a gesture close to rage.

"Stop it! Silence! No sound at all . . . Dr. Baliuk, both of you, we have no further need for scientific opinions. Go now!" To Volkoff, he said: "If we have to restrain you we will—and very effectively too."

Volkoff fell back into silence, watching the two oceanographers leave the room. Serafima's expression was too subtle to analyze; it was more than reproach; mingled with it was regret and the shadow of fear.

Complete silence had now settled over the navigation

bridge. Outside was the muffled rush and sweep of the sea, the soft buffetings of a small wind—and thinly in the distance the tinny sounds of human voices filtered through loud hailers. No words could be distinguished. Inflections were distorted beyond interpretation.

Westholme watched *Haida Noble* and *Blackfish* running a parallel course 1500 feet ahead. A distance of some 40 feet separated the two vessels and he could make out figures standing at both rails as the exchange of conversation went on. One of them would be Fenton, following whose orders, his or Kutskov's? On the *Blackfish* the probability was that Captain Lewis was doing the talking. He knew Jack Lewis from Navy days, a hard-nosed, superlative seaman who had reveled in the hard discipline and order of the Navy and carried much of that attitude into his Coast Guard commission. When *Blackfish* slid down the ways two years ago, Lewis had been the natural choice as master. This would be his last ship before a desk job, Westholme thought. Lewis must be in his fifties. At that moment it never occurred to him that they were contemporaries.

Blackfish began to accelerate, pulling ahead of the crawling tug and swinging in a tight turn to starboard as she came around to approach the Russian ship. Kutskov's walkie-talkie came alive and the Russian captain leaned in to capture the brief message, nodding finally with satisfaction and looking up at Westholme.

"Your second officer is both sensible and loyal to you, Captain. We are being allowed to proceed."

Westholme said nothing. Volkoff struck the chart table in angry frustration and stared at him with unblinking accusation. "You've gone along with him from concession to concession. You've never quite believed that anything or anybody standing in his way is going to be expendable. You don't believe it *now*, by God!"

Westholme watched the approach of *Blackfish*, saw the Russian crew members assembling at the rails to cheer and encourage her, and realized that Lewis would be completely deceived by this display of goodwill. Nothing had gone right, not one break, not the smallest opportunity to gain an advantage.

Blackfish swung in closer, idling down, her crew waving cheerfully at the Russians, catching the packages of cigarettes and chocolate thrown to them. The cutter's spotless decks were soon dappled with oblong and circular packages. Above the general confusion of exchanged greetings and the purr of the cutter's engines a speaker-amplified voice broke through abruptly, every word plainly heard.

"Captain Westholme? Is Captain Westholme aboard? Lewis here."

Kutskov's eyes narrowed for an instant. Then his composure returned. To his first and second officer he said: "Walk out on the bridge. Be friendly. Exchange greetings with them in a genuine way. Take one of the seamen with you and position yourself at intervals along the rail. Take a loud hailer."

"Captain Westholme?" the loud hailer boomed. "Are you there? Lewis."

"Now," Captain Kutskov instructed Westholme, "you know this Lewis?"

Westholme nodded.

"Very well. Go out and join the others. Perform in a natural and friendly manner. Assure him that things go well here."

"I'll need the loud hailer."

"Not necessary, and a dangerous temptation. The fact that you are unharmed, smiling, will be reassurance enough. You are a married man, Captain Westholme?"

"Is that important?"

"At a time like this it is well for a man to think of his loved ones as well as himself."

Westholme swung away from him and walked out to the bridge.

Behind him Volkoff called: "Do you think you'll be able to live with yourself after, Westholme?"

Kutskov had asked, "You are a married man?" It was a threat and Westholme couldn't mistake it . . . but it was also a reminder to him that he was married. He was married to

Lee, a woman who despaired of his ever coming home for good.

At the rail, Westholme looked across and down at Captain Lewis standing solidly on the bridge of the cutter. The look of impatience on his sea-hewn face altered to a broad grin when he spotted Westholme. The distance between them was not more than twenty-five feet. Under other circumstances they could have made themselves heard, but the competition from the two crews eliminated the possibility now.

Lewis held up his loud hailer. "Holed up with some of those nice looking girls, were you?"

Westholme grinned and made an open-palmed gesture of denial. "You know I'm an old married man," he shouted. The cutter was moving slowly past and he walked down the deck to keep abreast of her.

"What was that?" Lewis shouted through his speaker. "Ah, never mind. You sure you don't need some help into port? This ship looks to be in bad shape."

Westholme shook his head, still moving along the deck. "Everything's fine," he shouted. "We've got it under control." Three feet from him, *Irkutsk's* first officer was smiling broadly and waving a big hand at the crew of *Blackfish*. Westholme stepped to the rail beside him, pivoted on his right foot and drove a left hook to the corner of the man's jaw, putting the anger, frustration, and unexpressed grief of the past days into the punch.

The Russian lurched back, the unco-ordinated fingers of his right hand trying to find a grip on the rail, while his left hand dropped the loud hailer and sent it skidding along the deck. Westholme dived for it but never got there. He was tackled from behind by the towering crewmen, and hit immediately after that by the second ship's officer.

Inside the navigation bridge, Volkoff put his shoulder into the side of the third ship's officer and made for the door. Along the deck, between the loud hailer and himself, three men were now struggling with Westholme. From the cutter he could hear Lewis' stern, insistent voice bellowing:

"Hold on there . . . Release Captain Westholme. Take your hands off that man. This is an official order."

Volkoff reached into the breast pocket of his jacket and found the oblong piece of plastic-enclosed pasteboard. He pinched one corner of it between thumb and forefinger, drew it out, and flicked it with a strong wrist and forearm motion toward the cutter. He never knew whether it arrived. The second crewman charged out on deck and hit him behind the right ear with a massive clenched fist, following it up with a blow to the left kidney. Volkoff dropped to the deck without a sound.

Westholme was dragged past his sprawled body and projected violently inside toward Kutskov who wasted no time on him. "Take him and the other to their quarters. Place a guard outside."

As Westholme was hustled away he heard Kutskov begin to issue orders in his own language, precise, unwavering—as much in control as ever.

32 . . .

Politically the *Irkutsk* crisis put Canada's federal government to a test which was to last for the better part of a year. It was not merely the matter of a Canadian vessel and Canadian citizens captured by a foreign power in Canadian waters. There was the bitter running battle that began between the Canadian Department for External Affairs and the United States Department of State over the issue of American nationals innocently involved in the affair. It was strongly suggested by the Canadian Minister for External Affairs, a man usually noted for his meticulous diplomacy, that the U. S. State Department was magnifying out of all proportion the involvement of American citizens in order to force Canada's hand and effect the capture of the Russian ELINT ship.

There is no doubt that the issue was the subject of major

debate both in the United States Senate and House of Representatives with heavy pressure brought to bear on the Department of Defense to take whatever action was required to protect the lives of the Americans involved and to return them safely to United States soil. The doves and the hawks flew at one another in Washington. The State Department insisted, in a strongly worded note to the Canadian Department for External Affairs, that Canada would be held responsible for the safety of the American nationals held captive by a ship flying the flag of the USSR.

Of the three nations involved, the USSR remained most silent, declaring through its official channels that it knew nothing of the incident—that while some or all of the allegations might be true, no word had been received from the master of *Irkutsk* or from the commissar assigned to the vessel, nor had any signals sent to the ship in the period of the crisis been acknowledged.

The immediate course of events was approximately this:

At 1217 on September 29, the Coast Guard Rescue officer, Vancouver, British Columbia, received the following voiced message relayed to him by the master of Coast Guard cutter *Blackfish:* "We have made contact with the salvage tug *Haida Noble* and tow, *Irkutsk.* This is not a put-on. The tug has been taken over by the Russians . . . It's the goddamned truth. I saw Captain Westholme of the *Haida Noble* being manhandled on the Russian's bridge. There's an American on board too. He tossed us his ID card; an employee of British United working on BUTCO 17. Name, Michael M. Volkoff. I'll spell it . . . Les, I wish to hell I was kidding, but this couldn't be more serious . . . Sure I've talked to them. I had words with the first officer not five minutes ago and he gave it to me in plain terms. They want their ship returned to international waters and they're using Westholme and the others as hostages . . . It's hard to tell, Les, the ship has taken heavy damage; collision and fire by the look of it. There's not much doubt about it, she's rigged for intelligence collection. You've got to have some record of her movements. Right . . . right, I'll repeat, and this time use a pencil . . ."

It was clearly not a Department of Transport problem and the Coast Guard Rescue officer immediately made his report by phone to the regional headquarters, Department of National Defense. Coming right on the heels of a natural catastrophe on the Pacific Coast, ruled within hours as a major disaster area, word of the hijacking was in danger of being lost in a flood of incoming emergency reports. Fortunately it went straight to the right man, a colonel with a taste for military rather than civilian crisis. He saw the far-reaching significance of the Coast Guard report and was responsible for setting numerous wheels in action within minutes.

Even before the Minister of National Defense had been apprised of the situation, a Canadian Forces (Air) Albatross, fully armed, had been dispatched from Comox Air Base to fly low-level circuits over *Irkutsk*. One of three Canadian Forces subchasers seconded to the disaster operation was redirected as she departed from Esquimalt and sent at full speed to the scene of the tow. The Government Opposition in the days of post-mortem would complain that there was no need to divert this naval vessel from its vital civilian rescue duties when aerial surveillance had already been laid on. *Irkutsk*, they argued, could be held at bay by a show of strength from the air. The Minister of National Defense was able to destroy the argument effectively by pointing out that the presence of the Canadian Forces plane overhead did not alter the Russian vessel's course or speed in any way. Neither did the appearance of the subchaser at 1745 that afternoon. With the naval vessel flanking her to port and the Coast Guard cutter to starboard, *Irkutsk* moved inexorably ahead at the end of the towing line.

At dusk she was slightly less than six miles from the edge of the Canadian Twelve Mile limit, flames plainly visible on her stern decks, black clouds of smoke billowing and blending into the gray ceiling of cloud. Undoubtedly her master and crew drew encouragement from the appearance in the midafternoon of seven vessels from the scattered Russian fishing flotilla. Their dark silhouettes could be seen in line along the Twelve Mile limit and Aldis lamps began a steady exchange of messages between them and the crippled ship.

It was regrettable in a way that information on the captured Americans was passed to the U.S. authorities at the same time that notice of the incident went forward to Canada's Minister of National Defense. In actual fact the American State Department issued its first note—a combination of inquiry and protest—before Canada had settled on a clear course of action; and when, within the next hour, Canada's Secretary of State for External Affairs had not answered the note through his ambassador in Washington, the U. S. Department of Defense made it known that the Navy Department had dispatched a destroyer from Bremerton. Canada's permission was requested to allow the destroyer entry into Canadian waters for the purpose of lending assistance . . . and the permission was flatly refused in a brisk diplomatic note. Canada recognized her national responsibility and said as much.

Nevertheless, the American destroyer proceeded north along Canada's Twelve Mile limit and took up a post shortly after 2100 hours, one-half mile distant from the remnants of the Russian fleet, establishing her presence with a theatrical display of searchlights and the intermittent launching of parachute flares. The impression created unmistakably was that the United States was watching, waiting, and prepared to pounce.

Canada, in the meantime, had decided on a diplomatic course of action, placing enough importance on the incident to take the ultimate step in the protocol of emergency. In Ottawa the Russian ambassador was summoned to a meeting with Canada's Secretary of State, told of the situation in the plainest terms and asked to take the necessary measures to reduce the growing crisis.

The man professed total ignorance of the event and returned to his embassy with the promise that he would attempt to clarify the situation within the hour. In less time than that the Canadian Secretary of State received his official note. The USSR Academy of Sciences oceanographic vessel *Irkutsk* was indeed reported to be conducting scientific experiments in waters off the Pacific northwest coast of North America. No messages had been received from her, nor had she acknowledged messages since the occurrence of the storm and tsunami reported in that area.

While the Ministry of Foreign Affairs strongly doubted the allegations that the master of *Irkutsk* had engaged in acts of piracy and kidnaping, it was not possible to establish the falsehood since communications with the vessel had broken down.

Canada immediately demanded that a Russian Embassy official be flown from Vancouver and set down on the deck of *Irkutsk* with instructions to examine the situation in company with a Canadian representative. If evidence of piracy or kidnaping were revealed, the Russian official would be empowered to surrender the vessel and return the prisoners.

The Russian ambassador acknowledged that, while this was a logical procedure, it constituted a grave affront to a senior master of an Academy of Sciences scientific vessel. Before proceeding with the radical step demanded by Canada, Russia would require stronger evidence of a serious misdemeanor. With this evidence in hand, Russia would be pleased to co-operate in every way possible.

At the same time, the Russian ambassador let it be known that his country could not tolerate any action that might be construed as punitive directed toward *Irkutsk* until the charges of trespass, piracy, and kidnaping had been proven to the satisfaction of the Russian government.

"It would be regrettable," the smoothly worded note stated, "if Canada were to permit any outside power or influence to interfere with an issue that involves Canada and Russia exclusively."

In the days that followed, Russia's Ministry of Foreign Affairs would deny categorically that it had been in radio contact with the Russian fleet, knew of the presence of the American destroyer in the proximity of the fleet, or by the same token knew of the plight of *Irkutsk*.

The official accusations circled viciously and endlessly, aided and magnified by the international press. Canada accused Russia of deliberately buying the time required to destroy effectively a quasi-military intelligence collection ship masquerading as an oceanographic research vessel—with a callous disregard for human lives. Russia denied this, but in turn accused Canada of conspiring with the United States to deliberately escalate an unfortunate but minor incident into a crisis of international proportions, that Canada, "undisputedly a vassal of the American imperialists, did not hesitate to take refuge behind the United States' gunboat diplomacy."

The American press accused Russia of camouflaging her espionage system and her sea bed militarism behind the skirts of female sailors. The U.S. government deplored what they called "Canada's vacillation and reluctance to counter with appropriate strength, the invasion of Canadian territorial waters, the destruction of Canadian and American property, the theft of Canadian property, the forced confinement and death of Canadian and American nationals."

A hawkish congressman stated it more bluntly, echoing the unofficial attitude of the Department of the Navy. "They pussyfooted, damn it! What the hell's the use of sweetness and light, a 'let's not go off half-cocked' attitude when the goddamned Russians are spying us blind. They should have boarded them and shot the bastards down. Called their bluff. Showed the Commies that they've got some muscle—not just a lot of tongue. It makes one point good and clear, as far as I'm concerned; I don't think Canada has got the muscle we need to defend our northern border . . . and something should damned well be done about it!"

In this manner, while the coastal cities and communities of the Pacific Northwest still lay in the shock of natural disaster and death, the world beyond had learned of another storm developing off the battered coast—a storm involving nations, a storm with a destructive potential overwhelmingly greater than a tidal wave.

33 . . .

The hours after Westholme and Volkoff were returned to the cabin went slowly, but they were not without incident. Volkoff had to be taken care of to begin with. The American had suffered a heavy blow to the back of the head and was only half conscious when they dragged him back to the cabin, mouthing words that were angry but totally incoherent. Westholme did what he could for him, applying a towel soaked in cold water and wrung out, talking him back into consciousness and then trying without too much success to keep him calm.

Volkoff was outraged. The blow to his head was not serious in itself. He had been hit harder and suffered more serious injury in the past. But the punch from the Russian culminated the series of indignities he had suffered to his pride, his emotions, his sense of justice, and the rights to which he had become accustomed in the course of his lifetime.

"The bastards!" he raged. "They can't do this. Who do those bastards think they are . . ."

"Cool it, Mike," Westholme said quietly. "We stuck our necks out and they chopped us. I'm sorry you got hurt."

Volkoff's eyes in the sick light from the lamp were black with anger. "You haven't changed, have you? You're still trying to find excuses for those bastards. They took your boat, killed your deckhand . . . they'll finish you, and you'd still lick their boots if they asked you."

"I don't think so," Westholme said.

"What are you, a Commie? Some kind of half-assed sympathizer? I swear I've never seen anybody to beat you . . . Captain Westholme."

"I may have it figured wrong," Westholme said carefully. "When this is over we can go over the mistakes that were made."

"When this is over! Where do you think we'll be when this is over?"

Westholme ignored the question. "We may discover that we missed an obvious opportunity, or that we should have played a stronger hand. We may have misjudged Kutskov, but I still think he means business. He doesn't bluff."

"He's a Commie machine," Volkoff stated harshly. "The Party wound up his clockwork years ago, extracted his humanity and turned him loose. He's sent thirty or forty of his own people over the side for the sake of his bloody official orders. Do you think he's going to give any thought to us when the chips are down?"

"That's the point," Westholme said. "It looks as though he has considered us all the way along. He put a doctor aboard *Haida Noble* to take care of Lindstrom and your roughneck. He made an effort to treat us with what he calls 'goodwill.' The man's humanity may be his big weakness."

"God almighty!" Volkoff exclaimed disgustedly. He turned his head away in a violent rejection of Westholme's logic.

"That's what got him into trouble in the first place," Westholme insisted, "that plus—what would you call it—a flair for the dramatic? I'm guessing he took the ship into the lee of BUTCO 17 because he wanted to give his company a more comfortable time of it—also because it would make a great story afterward to tell how *Irkutsk* rode out a hurricane in comfort behind a symbol of British and American capitalism . . . and if it hadn't been for the tidal wave, he would have pulled it off."

"He's got his orders to follow," Volkoff said, "and he's going to follow them over our dead bodies, if that's the way it has to be. He's a Commie robot."

"Maybe so," Westholme nodded. "Every move is a chess move planned ahead. When he loses a piece he's ready to play another without a second thought—without wasting a minute."

"God help us if he has to play that last piece," Volkoff said balefully.

Westholme decided to get him onto another subject. "You said you had an idea what this ship was up to. What's your guess?"

"Does it matter?" Volkoff demanded. "What I said up on the bridge still holds. Anything this goddamned ship is doing, an American ship is doing in spades. The next big fight is for control of the sea bed and the international seas. It's no secret."

Westholme pondered it. "I wouldn't know about that, but Kutskov has got to get this ship into international waters for some pretty good reason."

"It's an intelligence ship," Volkoff told him angrily. "I thought that was clear to everybody. In addition to that I'd be willing to bet they're scouting underwater silo sites for the refueling and provisioning of subs and other military vessels, if and when the time comes."

"And Kutskov doesn't want to get caught with the goods."

Volkoff glanced at him impatiently. "That's not the point. It's no great secret that this sort of thing is going on on both sides. Kutskov is playing the game by the book. If his vessel is in danger of capture, it and its records must be destroyed. That's all. The official place for destruction is in deep water —international water. How he goes about it is his own business." Volkoff threw his hands up. "We're being screwed by a Commie book of rules!

"The other thing that burns me," Volkoff said, "is that we were within an inch of laying our hands on a Russian ELINT vessel—one of the best of them too—with a hull crammed with oceanographic gear, electronic stuff that our people are itching to get a look at."

"I thought there wasn't any difference between yours and theirs?"

"In the final analysis there isn't, but the psychological victory would have been great . . . the *Pueblo* vindicated, avenged. However you want to look at it."

"Is it my imagination," Westholme said, "or is the smell of smoke getting stronger in here?"

"The lamp, maybe?" Volkoff suggested. "No . . . I believe

you're right. It's smoke sure enough!" He scrambled off the bunk and crossed to the door, placing his nose against the union of the door and the jamb. "There's something burning out there!" he said in alarm.

Westholme sat on the edge of the bunk considering the possibilities. "Not much chance the fire got itself started again," he said. "They've got enough crew to watch out for that, and to control it if it did happen. More likely they've got a fire going somewhere to warm themselves up." He ran his fingers through the clammy beads of moisture collecting on the metal frame of the bunk. "It's getting damned cold in here."

"Then again they could be getting ready to leave her," Volkoff said uneasily. "It's just about time, isn't it? Chances are they'll leave her burning when they go. I think we'd better check on this."

He pounded loudly on the metal door. "Hello! Is there anybody out there. Hello out there!"

There was a brief pause, and then a heavy object, probably the butt of a rifle, thumped once on the door panel, and a deep voice shouted a few Russian words.

"What did he say?" Westholme asked.

"Roughly translated he wants us to keep our bloody mouths shut. The fire hasn't frightened him off, that's for sure."

Volkoff returned and sat down on the bunk beside Westholme taking a long moment to collect his thoughts. "Look . . . Chris, I know I've been behaving like some kind of a bastard. Before this is through I may make an even bigger idiot of myself, but I want you to know that I haven't intended to be personal. For the life of me I don't know what other action you could have taken—either of us could have taken for that matter."

Westholme took a deep breath. "This has been a hard one to figure. A few years back my mind might have worked faster, or I might have had the kind of ginger it takes to turn the tables in a situation like this." He shook his head dubiously. "I don't know. I don't think I'd have done anything differently. My first responsibility is to my ship and my crew, then to this ship's company and the ship itself. You understand the politics and the international stuff better than I do . . ."

"Not really. The oceanographic bit, yes. I think I know the direction things are heading. That's one of the items that has really shaken me. That very attractive girl—lady—up on the bridge today. Serafima Baliuk. A good oceanographer and a great woman. In 1966 we drank vodka together in Moscow, shared our ideas on the science of oceanography and agreed that it was the coming hope of the world. We were bloody idealists, I guess. Younger than we are now. Enjoying one another's company."

"She's a pleasant-looking woman," Westholme agreed.

"Today she was up there in Kutskov's presence, and in the company of a doctrinaire ocean scientist, endorsing the kind of thing that can turn the sea bed into a final battleground. How do you figure it?" he said dejectedly.

Both of them leaped violently as three short bursts of a siren-like whistle pierced the walls of the cabin, coming from beyond the sealed porthole, beyond the hull of the ship.

"What in Christ's name was that?" Volkoff said.

"Hard to tell," Westholme said. "Without raising anyone's hopes, it sounds like the Navy."

The two men sat and listened to the new sounds, trying without success to gather encouragement from the muffled exchange of loud hailer information that proceeded for the next fifteen minutes, and at intervals later on.

According to Westholme's watch, the naval vessel—if in fact it was a naval vessel—arrived on station at 1740 and held a position close in and to port of the Russian ship.

"It's not the Navy," Volkoff decided abruptly. "We're in international waters. That's a Russian ship out there."

"Does any of that loudspeaker talk sound Russian to you?"

"It sure as hell doesn't sound like any English I ever heard. If it was a Canadian Armed Forces ship we'd be out of here by now."

"I don't think so," Westholme said slowly. "Like Kutskov says 'things haven't changed.' As long as Kutskov has hostages he calls all the shots. . . . unless the Canadian government decided that this ship is more important to the national cause than you, or me, or the *Haida Noble* crew."

He tried to convert the statement into an unsuccessful joke. "If that happens, my dependants would take violent exception."

Volkoff didn't smile.

"You married, Mike?"

"Three days ago I was as ripe for it as I've ever been. Three days! It seems more like three months."

"An American girl?"

"No girl in particular—just a feeling that I was ready to put down the anchor. I was going to take a four-week leave in San Francisco and start some serious girl hunting. It's a good town for that kind of thing . . ."

He stopped and joined Westholme listening to the near sound of jet engines as a plane thundered overhead and was gone.

"That must be the twelfth pass he's made," Westholme observed. "One thing is sure, we've got a lot of witnesses to the crime."

"I'm not optimistic," Volkoff said candidly. "Analyze that Russian bastard's attitude—his frame of mind—and our chances aren't good."

"You mean our personal skins?"

Volkoff nodded.

"With a Canadian Forces plane up top, and the Coast Guard and Navy riding herd, I think we're safe enough. Uncomfortable, but safe. We're just Kutshov's guarantee of delivery to the edge of the Twelve Mile—and then we can go home."

Volkoff shook his head stubbornly. "Alive, we're trouble. I can testify to the destruction of BUTCO 17, and can make some educated guesses on this ship's equipment and assignment. You're in it as deep as I am. If Kutskov sinks this ship, he has to sink us with it. Oh, I think he'll release your crew," he added quickly, "but you and I are star witnesses."

"I hope you're wrong," Westholme said. "We'll just have to sweat it out."

"The guy isn't rational," Volkoff argued. "Those burns are enough to put any man out of his mind. But even if he was as sound as an apple, he has big troubles. Maybe he didn't sink BUTCO 17, but you can bet that British United will do its best to implicate him. He shouldn't have been in Canadian waters under any circumstances—not with an ELINT ship. If he gets back to Russia, he'll be lucky if he rates a life term in Siberia."

Westholme rubbed the heavy stubble beginning to grow through his lacerated face. "I was thinking . . . he might be an interesting guy to know—if none of this had happened. You know what I mean . . ."

Volkoff was no longer angered by Westholme's attitude. His grin was sympathetic. "I'll bet you befriended rattlesnakes when you were a kid because no one else really understood them."

"What I'm saying is that he's got himself backed into a bad corner. Under other circumstances he could be worth knowing."

"We're in the corner," Volkoff reminded him. "Don't feel sorry for the hangman when the rope's around your neck."

Outside, the loud hailers were shouting at one another again. The acrid stench of smoke was becoming more pronounced. Both felt a new intensity of chill in the cabin.

Westholme groped inside his jacket pocket and brought out the tin of chocolate given to him the previous day by the grateful Russian girl. He opened it and offered Volkoff a piece.

Volkoff took two. "We haven't eaten since last night," he recalled. "The hospitality has dropped off around here."

He climbed onto the upper bunk and sat with his legs dangling over the edge, munching on the bittersweet chocolate, his eyes grown distant. "My mother used to buy us stuff like this. It was a special treat when I was growing up. It was amazing what a chunk of hard, dark chocolate could do for the morale on a cold winter day in a Colorado mining town . . . Are you a Canadian born and bred?"

Westholme nodded. "And my folks before me." He stretched himself out on the lower bunk and drew the blankets over his fully clothed frame, to keep out the cold. "My wife's Canadian too—a Nova Scotia girl. She had the Atlantic in her blood and I had the Pacific in mine. Lee used to say it was the ocean that brought us together."

And it was the ocean that had divided them and made them strangers again. How many men and women had the sea alienated, he wondered. How many countless thousands of women in the course of history had waited out their lives for men who seldom—or never—came back from the sea? Thinking back on it he could not recall that his mother had ever complained, even though her husband's ship might be gone for four, even six months at a time. Quite likely it never occurred to her that she was hard done by, nor in those times and circumstances was she deprived. The wife of a seafaring man had to accept loneliness as a way of life. She raised the family and she waited. Christy had never been hungry and he had always worn warm clothes. On the other hand, he had never really known his father.

So much of a stranger was the elder Westholme in his own house, that he had become larger than life in the imaginations of his own family—someone who appeared, huge and ruddy-faced, at infrequent intervals in the course of a year, bringing with him fabulous gifts and marvelous stories. Because of his father, Christy Westholme had willingly chosen to follow the sea, leaving behind another woman—leaving Lee behind, and now regretting it more than anything he had ever done.

"You know," he told Volkoff, and it was a promise more than a statement, "when I get back to port I'm going to put in for a desk job. A man should quit while he's ahead."

"You think you're ahead right now, do you?"

Westholme rolled over and pulled the blankets up around his ears.

"Here it comes again," Volkoff said, staring up at the lamp-lit ceiling. The jet engines could be heard, rushing in from the far distance, approaching at an incredible speed, building to a full roar and fading as quickly.

He swung his legs up on his bunk and pulled up the blankets. "What time have you got now?" he asked.

"A few minutes off 1830."

"We've got to be on top of the Twelve Mile limit," Volkoff insisted.

Westholme didn't answer. He lay in the lamp-streaked darkness, his eyes held open and unblinking by the confusion of thought and conjecture that raced in his mind: thoughts of Lee and her loneliness, and their chances of a future together; thoughts of poor Bibaud lying under tons of twisted cable; thoughts of Lindstrom with the unstemmed flow of blood crowding his brain; thoughts of *Haida Noble*'s crew and of the great tug herself, battered, crippled—as much a captive as any of them. Woven through all these images of distress was the voice, the face, and presence of the Russian captain.

"I apologize, Captain Westholme . . . I mean you and your crew no harm . . . I have tried to extend goodwill . . . I am afraid one of your men has died—and one of mine . . . I have consigned more than thirty of my own company to the sea, including good friends . . . we both have our responsibilities as ship's masters, Captain Westholme . . . another glass of vodka, Captain Westholme?"

He turned on his side, trying to regulate the images, trying to isolate just one of them—Kutskov for instance—trying to isolate Kutskov long enough to solve him . . . and then all the images were erased from his mind as he heard the shots. He raised his head from the pillow as he listened to the sounds appearing to rise from the bowels of the ship: three or four single shots to begin with and then the sustained rattle of an automatic weapon being fired; more isolated shots—and then nothing.

"Did you hear that?" he called up to Volkoff softly.

Volkoff's deep, regular breathing was all the answer he received.

He settled his head back on the pillow to wait and to listen . . . and presently all the conflicting images returned.

34 . . .

How long he lay there he did not know. His condition deteriorated from a keyed-up, hyper-awareness to a torpor close to sleep where reality and dream began to resemble each other. The wavering lamplight created a conflagration on the wall opposite him, a forest fire burning at night, the flames of a distant city reflected against evening clouds. Flickering light and bitter cold; the northern lights hissing and snaking across a black sky above the Bering Sea; the last oil from a sunken tanker burning on a winter ocean halfway to Murmansk. Bibaud was there, dissatisfied with death; and Lee stood hesitantly just outside the light of the fires, hesitating to show herself, preparing to walk away from him into the total darkness.

And yet when the soft tapping began on the door, he was instantly alert to it, knowing that he had heard the footsteps approaching and the preliminary murmur of voices in the corridor. He threw the covers aside and was sitting with his feet firmly planted on the deck when the door opened to admit Dr. Lebedovitch. Behind her he glimpsed the face of the guard and highlights glancing from the blue steel of a gun barrel. Then she closed the door behind her and stood there looking down at him, her eyes shadowed, her strong cheekbones and broadly chiseled nose gleaming in the guttering light of the kerosene flame.

"I had intended to visit you sooner," she said. Her voice was steady and professional—exactly like a doctor explaining the lateness of a house call, "But many people have required my services."

"We're doing fine," Westholme told her.

"This light is very bad," she said disapprovingly.

"I'd put the cold ahead of that," he said. "The temperature must be dropping."

"The entire vessel is cold," she told him. "The injured ones are suffering from it."

"What's that?" Volkoff exclaimed in a loud, slurred voice. "You all right, Westholme?"

"Everything's fine. We've got company, Mike."

Volkoff rolled on his side, his eyes coming level with those of the doctor's.

"The captain said you had taken a blow," she said.

Volkoff sat up and ran his fingers through his thick black hair, trying to sift it back into shape. "I'm all over that," he said. He pulled up the collar of his jacket. "My God, it's cold . . . getting colder."

"Dr. Baliuk wishes me to tell you that she regrets what has happened. The entire—circumstance—is most unfortunate." Her fine contralto voice searched for the appropriate words. "You think you are feeling well? That is good. Do you have local pain in the head—trouble with your vision?"

"Give us a little more light in this place and I can tell you whether or not I can see. I've had worse headaches."

"And you, Captain Westholme . . ." She took a small electric torch from her pocket and played its beam over Westholme's face. "Not too pretty—but you will have no serious scars. There are some places . . ." She placed her voluminous leather bag on Westholme's bunk, opened it and unstoppered several bottles. Deftly she began to swab some of the cuts on Westholme's face.

"I heard gunfire some time ago," he said directly, trying to discount the soothing things she was doing to the individual pains dotting his forehead and jawline.

She applied her medications in silence, seeming not to have heard him, leaning in close to examine what she had done. Finally she said: "These are unfortunate—perhaps tragic circumstances. No one on this ship wishes you any harm, Captain . . . Mr. Volkoff."

Volkoff's voice from the upper bunk was more cynical than

troubled. "I've never understood why they send a doctor to check the health of a condemned man."

"That is not right," she said quickly to both of them. "You are not condemned. You are in grave danger, but not yet condemned." She closed her medical bag with finality. "We are all in danger, of course."

"What were the shots? The smoke?" Westholme asked.

"The shots?" She placed her bag on the deck and studied Westholme's face carefully. "May I sit for a moment?"

Westholme eased himself along the bunk and straightened out the lumped blankets. She sat down beside him without ceremony and extracted a package of cigarettes from her pocket, opened the top and flipped one up, offering it to Westholme. He took it and tried to find a match, finally accepting the flame from her lighter. She lit his and her own, and then passed the lighter up to Volkoff, together with her cigarette package.

"The shots," she said, "were an effort on the part of certain crew members to . . . mutiny." She shook her head violently. "Mutiny is not the right word. Protest?"

"Were they successful?" Westholme asked carefully. He wasn't sure of this woman, any more than he was sure of Kutskov.

"Two are dead, others wounded. This ship has endured great trouble."

"You came here to tell us something," Volkoff said impatiently. "Can you help us?"

She ignored him, directing her words to Westholme. "I am a doctor, not a politician or a statesman," she said. "My training and my inclination is to save lives. It troubles me to see good lives destroyed for principles—even good principles. My father was crushed by German tanks in front of Moscow. He died for good principles. He was also a vital man with a great appreciation for life. I have always resented his death— and the death of so many others."

Volkoff thought he could sense the breakthrough, the first admission of weakness. He put his words together cleverly:

"I can understand that. You'd enjoy meeting my mother.

She has that same female compassion for people—for the importance of life. If she had her way, war, violence, man's inhumanity to man would be an impossibility! Women have an appreciation and a sensitivity for that sort of thing . . . and thank God for it!" Having made this admission, he was prepared to carry it to the next level, to encourage her to ally herself with them in some fashion.

"I don't know what you are saying," she said harshly. "I am telling you that I am a doctor. What has this to do with femaleness? Your mother does not interest me. I am concerned to save lives if I can, and to relieve pain if it is possible. Perhaps that is why I came here." She opened her medical bag again and groped in it, lighting her way with her torch. Finally she found what she was looking for, and passed it up to Volkoff. "Very shortly," she said, "you may be given the single alternative—to die. This will make it more comfortable, almost painless for you. Break off the tip of the vial and swallow the contents."

There was fear in Volkoff's voice. "What the Christ are you talking about?"

"We are, all of us, in a critical situation," she said. "As a physician, I have done what I can." She stood up and lifted her medical bag.

"To you, Captain Westholme, I offer the same release." She extended her hand to him and he received the cold, hard steel of an automatic pistol, identifying it, wrapping his fingers around it and drawing it hastily under the blankets.

She went to the door and rapped on it imperatively turning to Westholme in the failing light. "You should understand," she advised, "that Captain Kutskov is a strong and admirable person . . . in different times, a good person. Circumstances force him to do what he must do."

"Crap!" Volkoff said loudly. He hurled the glass vial toward her. Both men saw the glass shatter, watched the fluid trickle down the steel panel of the door as she opened it and let herself out. In the open doorway, with the guard behind her, she said: "I came here, Captain Westholme, because I believe we share a similar attitude. You have stated that your first responsibility is to the safety and well-being of your crew . . . after that your ship. As a physician I am accustomed to placing people first. I am afraid it is too late to overcome that habit."

She shut the door behind her, and they saw the handle swing upward, sliding the bolt into place.

"Now how do you read that?" Volkoff said softly. "What's she trying to tell us?"

Westholme took the damp cloth he had used for Volkoff's compress, went to the door and swabbed off the pungent smear of liquid. "I don't know what this stuff is, but I wouldn't want us to get it on our hands."

"Potassium cyanide," Volkoff guessed. "They sent her down here to set up a suicide for us! Where's your capsule?"

"She didn't give me one," Westholme said. The heavy bulk of the revolver weighted down his jacket pocket, but he decided not to mention it to the American.

"How do you like that!" Volkoff said agitatedly. "They want me out of the way but not you . . . and it figures. I can hang them with firsthand technical accounts of the drill rig's sinking, and of this ship. Your statement would be an intelligent guess, at best."

"That's true," Westholme said, "but I don't think it's right. I'd say she's done this on her own—as a kind of a favor."

"A comfortable death," Volkoff muttered. "Some favor!" The fight had drained out of him as the full significance of the doctor's capsule established itself. He lay on his bunk, staring vacantly at the ceiling.

"You'd better butt that cigarette or something," Westholme said.

Volkoff knocked the long ash off the Russian cigarette, took one last drag, butted it against the bunk frame and tossed it onto the deck. "What time is it?" he asked.

"2027 . . ."

Above them, through the layers of deck, they heard the low-flying jet approach and pass by. Volkoff slammed an ineffective fist against the side of the bunk, pulled up the blankets and closed his eyes.

Westholme, sitting on the edge of his bunk, feet spread wide on the deck, finished his cigarette in slow, deliberate puffs, examined the half-inch butt narrowly and then ground it out with the heel of his boot. He had stopped guessing and second-guessing. His thinking processes had withdrawn into a place of refuge and were feeding him no impressions at all —neither of fear nor of hope.

In a preoccupied manner, he removed the gun from his pocket and turned it over in his hands, examining it with detached curiosity, becoming familiar with its mechanism, removing and replacing the clip with its neat stack of lead-nosed bullets. What would he do with the gun? He would put it in his pocket and leave it there and perhaps later on . . . something would occur to him.

He stood up, reached for the lantern and pulled it down, staring at the low-burning tooth of flame. Although he knew the trouble was an almost exhausted fuel supply, he experimented meticulously with the wick adjuster, trying to coax more life into the flame. It was a pointless exercise, but it gave him the opportunity to turn his mind to something simple and uncomplicated. In these small, unconscious ways Christy Westholme was conceding defeat.

Cold! His broad hands wrapped themselves around the glass of the lamp, absorbing the small heat, the light filtering redly through the skin and tissues of his fingers.

In the resulting darkness Volkoff's voice rose in alarm. "Westholme? You there?"

Westholme removed his hands and allowed the light of the lamp to escape again. "Still here."

Outside, distantly in the corridor, they heard the scuffling sound of feet approaching, the muffled exchange of conversation outside the door, the restless scraping of a rifle butt on the deck.

Volkoff kicked his legs over the edge of the bunk and sat there in a hunched position, straining to hear. Westholme swung the handle of the lantern up and reached it toward the hook in the ceiling. Huge shadows moved uneasily on the walls as the dangling lantern made lazy arcs.

"This could be the company we've been expecting," he said.

The door handle rattled harshly and the bolt shot back a split second before the door opened to reveal the large figure of *Irkutsk*'s first officer clad in a dark blue, heavy greatcoat and braided hat. Behind him were the two giant crew members who had attended on the navigation bridge earlier that day. Both wore broad leather belts and holstered sidearms.

The first officer wasted no words. "You will come with us to the bridge please."

They emerged from the cabin and fell in behind the rifle-carrying guard who led the way, following the route to the bridge. Taking up the rear in complete silence were the first officer and the two crewmen, their flashlamps casting erratic beams of light ahead of them, carving through blue ropes of smoke that hung in the corridors. The smell was that of burnt or burning paper.

Through an open porthole, as they passed by, Westholme glimpsed the impressive bulk of a vessel, its deck and sides awash with light.

"We were right about the Navy," he said to Volkoff. "There's a Canadian subchaser to port.

"I feel better already," Volkoff retorted.

"Cheer up, for God sake!" Westholme told him in a sudden flash of anger. "You've been burying us for the last twenty-four hours."

Volkoff started to make his own angry reply, but was stopped by the shouted order of the first officer:

"You will not talk!"

Arriving at the jury-rigged catwalk, Westholme was greeted with another spectacle two to three miles ahead of the ship and to port. There were ship's lights out there, scores of them strung out in line, representing at least half a dozen vessels. It was the edge of the Twelve Mile. The Russian flotilla was assembling just as Kutskov had said it would. The Russian was going to achieve his objective.

Beside him he heard Volkoff's strangled explosion of disgust and apprehension. "The bastard's done it!"

Abeam of them, a hundred yards to port, the low-contoured subchaser held its station, several batteries of search-lights painting the hull of *Irkutsk* with dazzling light. Off the starboard beam *Blackfish* held a similar position with fore and aft spotlights playing restlessly along the decks of the Russian ship. The scene was sufficiently arresting to stop Westholme halfway across the catwalk. Behind him the Russian officer's hand pressed into the small of his back and propelled him ahead again, pushing him through the heavy canvas tarpaulin curtain into the shattered remains of the radio room. Volkoff came through after him in the same precipitous manner, and they stopped just short of the guard's flashlit figure, intimidated by the muzzle of the man's automatic weapon held at waist level.

The first officer pushed past them and advanced to the door of the bridge, where he knocked twice and identified himself briefly. The door opened and Westholme and Volkoff were gestured into the familiar, sickeningly stuffy atmosphere of the room.

Captain Kutskov's position and appearance were changed. Fully uniformed, he had walked or been lifted to the navigator's chair. For a moment it appeared to Westholme that the man held his position in the chair unsupported, and then he spotted the black leather strap passing across his waist and fastened to the arms of the chair. How Kutskov could tolerate the weight and friction of shirt and uniform jacket against his raw and blistered flesh, Westholme did not know.

The Russian's face was a yellow-gray in the light of the encircling lanterns, the lines and shadows of pain shockingly apparent. Only the eyes remained unaltered, and the voice with its level, unperturbed inflection.

"Your salvage assignment is nearing its end, Captain Westholme. Many events have occurred in the past several hours. All things considered I am satisfied with our progress. Not ideal, but satisfactory. In two more hours we should be out of your nation's territory."

The first officer and the two crewmen had entered the room, leaving the rifle-carrying guard outside. The only other person attending the captain was Dr. Lebedovitch, and for the first time she was without her familiar black bag.

Ahead of him, through the windows of the bridge, Westholme could see the spread-out lights of the Russian fleet. Somewhere in the center of the line an Aldis lamp blinked a staccato message. Outside on the bridge, *Irkutsk*'s second officer received the signals while a crew member stood by with a lamp to acknowledge or reply.

"Your trawlers?" he asked Kutskov.

"I think you have guessed that. They began to gather at midafternoon. There were seven of them at last count."

"I still say you won't get away with it!" Volkoff blurted. "How do you beat the charge of piracy under international law?"

"In a sense it is an academic question," Kutskov said seriously. "Piracy is an act of theft of shipping and cargo. It may or may not be accompanied by the taking of life for willful gain. In the final analysis we will have taken nothing."

"It's piracy," Volkoff said doggedly, "and you've got plenty to gain—your damaged reputation for starters . . ."

"Cut it, Mike," Westholme ordered sharply. To the Russian captain he said: "You've done what you promised. Neither Volkoff nor I thought you could do it, and neither one of us is happy about it . . ."

"Placing myself in your position, my feelings of resentment would be strong," Kutskov agreed.

"Others resent your success too," Westholme said bluntly. "There were shots this afternoon. My guess is that some of this ship's company don't agree with your decision to return to your fleet instead of the safety of a Canadian port."

"Understandable. My officers and I anticipated a certain reaction from those who do not comprehend the essential nature of our orders. The incident was handled with as little violence as possible. Sit down, gentlemen." His eyes rolled inquiringly toward his first officer. "There is vodka here somewhere?" He repeated the question in impatient Russian and one of the crewmen hurried over with a bottle and racked glasses.

Both Westholme and Volkoff remained standing.

"Where do we go from here," Westholme demanded. "What happens next?"

"I have explained it to you. You will regain possession of your tug. Sit down! Sit down! The least we can do is make you comfortable in the short time we have left. Sit down!" The last invitation was delivered as a ringing command.

Westholme shrugged and settled himself into one of the deck chairs that had been moved into the area. He looked up at Volkoff and indicated another chair with a nod of his head. Volkoff didn't budge.

Westholme thrust his hands deep into his jacket pocket, letting the fingers of his right hand curl around the butt of the revolver. "On some ships," he said, "you would have been ruled incompetent by your officers, on the grounds of illness and behavior endangering your crew and your vessel."

"That is true," Kutskov said. "My officers are not prevented from making that judgment." He glanced at his first officer. "Perhaps they will have to do it yet. Sit down, all of you. Gregori, take off your greatcoat and relax a little."

The first officer hesitated momentarily and then slipped out of his coat and placed it on top of the chart desk, with his hat on top of it.

"Drinks!" Kutskov insisted. "For all of us . . . please. Dr. Lebedovitch, drink with us."

The doctor spoke to him quietly in Russian, and he chuckled halfway through her conversation, silencing her with an upraised hand and beckoning for one of the glasses the crewman was proceeding to fill.

"My doctor has advised me that alcohol is not good for my condition. She is right of course. Dr. Lebedovitch is always right in these matters, but the occasion overcomes all medical logic. We are celebrating."

All of them were seated now—even Volkoff, his hand holding an untasted glass of vodka.

"I believe all of us understand this occasion," the Russian captain said. "The last night at the Naval Academy, with examination successfully passed. Doctor? The evening of the day you saved a patient from certain death. Captain Westholme? The celebration of a sinking ship miraculously towed to port."

He lifted his glass and stared at it speculatively. "I would like to propose a toast . . . to all of us . . . and to better times than these." Perched above them in the high navigator's chair, his gaze traveled the circle of faces. "Drink! Drink up!" He set an example by tossing back the substantial shot of pure vodka and holding his glass out for a refill.

"I don't understand you," Volkoff said hesitantly. "Westholme and I aren't leaving this ship alive, and yet you can sit there . . ."

"You have a diseased imagination," Kutskov told him angrily. "Everything is a bad American motion picture with you."

Volkoff pointed a rigid index finger at the doctor. "You send her to feed us a comfortable dose of potassium cyanide, and now you toast our health. Who the Christ do you think . . ."

Westholme swung his chair toward him and said flatly, "You're out of your mind, Mike."

Volkoff was livid with disbelief. "Are you trying to tell me she didn't give me a capsule?"

"What is he talking about, Doctor?" Kutskov asked pleasantly.

"I visited their cabin this afternoon," she said readily. "Mr. Volkoff showed every sign of needing a sedative. I gave him one to take."

"That's right," Westholme told Volkoff pointedly. "You needed slowing down, Mike."

Kutskov passed swift judgment as he surveyed the three of them. Volkoff's agitated features convinced him, and he lifted his replenished glass. "Here is the only sedative any of us requires at this moment. To you, Mr. Volkoff the ocean scientist—and may we make amends to you one day. Tell us more about your meeting in Moscow with Dr. Serafima Baliuk —nothing scientific, nothing serious. Tell us about the pleasure of it."

"Go to hell," Volkoff muttered. He lifted the glass of vodka to his lips defensively.

"Good!" Kutskov approved. "The best medicine. You will see." He glanced to the side as his second officer hurried in. "Just in time . . . join us." The officer rejected the invitation in hurried monosyllables and handed Kutskov a scribbled message. The captain read it without a change of expression, then handed it to his first officer. He waited until the man had absorbed the contents and then made his announcement:

"In approximately thirty minutes we are going to have a visitor out there . . ." He inclined his head toward international waters. "It is approaching from the south at high speed—exceeding 40 knots—according to the message we have just received from our flotilla." His eyes homed in on Volkoff. "I think we can safely suppose that it is an American destroyer."

Volkoff leaned ahead in his chair and then fell back again, lifting his glass to his lips once again as a subterfuge.

"The right attitude," Kutskov said. "The molehill has grown to a mountain . . . and we should drink to it. What began as a simple arrangement between a crippled ship and a tugboat has now become a *cause célèbre*, complete with planes overhead, submarine chasers and now"—he sipped and savoured his drink—"an American naval vessel of considerable size and speed." He contemplated the situation. "What do we need to complete the scene? Something appropriate, eh, Gregori? Like a nuclear submarine provided by our own country."

He beckoned to the crewman to bring the bottle around. "Fill your glasses everyone. We must place ourselves in a frame of mind to enjoy the spectacle."

232

35 . . .

For thirty-three minutes by Westholme's watch, Captain Kutskov performed the role of host. It was a charade with the quality of nightmare made even more grotesque by the perfection of the man's performance. His ravaged, colorless face managed to convey genial good humor, a conviviality so genuine in contrast to the accumulating tension, that it could only have been the manifestation of an unsettled mind. He was, by turns, a raconteur displaying his command of several languages and their related cultures, an eager and encouraging listener whenever one of the others ventured to start a conversation, and a generous host urging drinks on everyone and seeing to it that his own glass remained filled.

As the minutes passed, the unreality of the scene became intolerable. It triggered reactions in his "guests," ranging from Volkoff's stunned and silent depression, out of which Kutskov's charm could not extract him, to the emergence of Dr. Lebedovitch into the self-imposed role of hostess. It was she who bridged the tight silences when he paused in conversation, or when the first officer's embarrassed attempts to assist the charade heightened the atmosphere of the grotesque. Perhaps her professional experience enabled her to assume this responsibility with a flawless calm. Certainly hers was the rational, stabilizing influence.

Regardless of the bizarre elements of that half-hour, Westholme could not suppress the empathy he felt for the Russian captain. Kutskov might be a natural actor, or a man driven out of his mind by pain and anxiety and now losing himself in the comfort of make-believe. Westholme believed none of it. Kutskov's performance was genuine. The gesture of hospitality was important to him for his own reasons. There had been a consistency in his behavior, from their first moment of meeting. At any given time, Kutskov did what he felt was necessary. He remembered the Russian's words: "I will proceed from crisis to crisis and do whatever is necessary to reach my objective." What was happening now was another critical moment and Kutskov had immersed himself in it, serving it with everything he possessed. Probably everything he said and did in these past minutes was significant, Westholme decided. Captain Kutskov was celebrating—but it was less of a celebration and more of a ritual.

"You talk about the hunting of animals," he said enthusiastically, taking the cue from a hesitating statement made by his first officer. "One must have the instinct to kill, in order to enjoy that sport. I do not deplore the action of the hunter; it is merely that I do not understand it."

"Nor do I," Dr. Lebedovitch admitted. "It is not softness of heart altogether, because I have taken the lives of animals in learning my profession . . ."

"Ah—but that is different," Kutskov said. "Out of that kind of death, life and survival emerge. I am thinking of the other kind of killing—the hardy sport of our old Cossacks in the dead of winter for instance—to find and pursue a wolf for miles in the bitter cold, running it and your horse to the point of exhaustion . . ." His pause, as he took another sip of vodka, was unintentionally dramatic, Westholme thought. "And then, when the wolf is down in the snow, unconquered but incapable of running farther—to whip it to death with rawhide whips. This kind of killing has never interested me, nor do I understand it."

"It was not so much a killing as a ritual," Dr. Lebedovitch suggested. "It was an act of magic perhaps. The wolf was the enemy, and the cruel death the Cossacks gave it was a warning to all wolves to leave the villages alone."

"Perhaps, perhaps," Kutskov said cheerfully. "The subject is a morbid one, and there are some empty glasses. Captain Westholme—yours?"

"I'm doing just fine," Westholme said, but the crewman advanced and tipped the bottle into his glass.

"Your country has many fine animal species," Kutskov encouraged. "The moose; the grizzly bear. You have hunted these?"

"I've done some hunting," Westholme said, "mostly birds. I'd have to want meat pretty badly to drop a deer or a moose. They look good standing on four legs."

"I think perhaps Canadians are good hunters but indifferent killers," the Russian captain said affably. "A hunter is something of a dilettante. He can choose not to pull the trigger. The killer, on the other hand, always pulls the trigger, regardless of the trophy."

"Not unwise in the animal kingdom," Dr. Lebedovitch said. "The grown wolf kills the cub to eliminate a rival."

"Say what you mean, damn it!" Volkoff said, breaking his silence. "It's a cat-and-mouse game."

"Not at all," Kutskov assured him earnestly. "I apologize for the turn the conversation has taken, but . . ." He shaded his eyes at the sudden light piercing the windows of the navigation bridge; the doctor rose and stood beside him, shielding her own eyes as she squinted in the direction of the Russian flotilla.

Westholme's eyeballs throbbed with the sudden attack of the harsh light; one vibrating splash of stark white flame, then another, and then a third descending slowly through the dark night, leaving the zigzag smoke of their burning behind them. Parachute flares!

He raised his left hand to his brow and cut off the intensity of light, focusing at sea level to find the source of the launching. First he saw the lumpy cluster of Russian trawlers spread out to port, an Aldis lamp working busily in its center; and then to the right of the flotilla he made out the staggered decks and protuberances of the destroyer.

Kutskov's voice announced genially: "Our company has arrived. Very impressive! Extremely impressive!"

Volkoff was on his feet, dividing his attention between the Russians and the slowly descending flares. His entire manner had changed.

"Now you'll see some action, you bastards!" he said. "That's a U.S. destroyer."

"We told you it was on its way," the Russian captain reminded him. "I don't think you quite believed us."

"It'll blow you out of the water," Volkoff said, "and your trawlers with you."

Captain Kutskov shook his head reluctantly. "I hope it will not do that." He looked at his drink and then surveyed the others. "One more small glass, and then we must bring this to an end." He nodded briskly to the crewman who began again to top up the glasses. Although Westholme's still contained liquor, he held it out and accepted a few drops more.

Volkoff began to spill his vodka on the deck, thought better of it and set the glass aside, becoming more animated by the minute.

"You couldn't make it," he said. "There was no way you could make it. I'll hand it to you, you had me convinced for a while . . . but how did you think you could get away with it?"

"I am satisfied," Kutskov said. "I am not disappointed with what we have done."

"But you've gained nothing," Volkoff insisted.

"We've gained enough," Kutskov said. "We are now abandoning ship, Mr. Volkoff, and I would like you to be among the first to go."

Neither Volkoff nor Westholme comprehended him.

"I want you to go, Mr. Volkoff. I have no quarrel with you. In fact I regret the action we had to take against you. My first officer will see you to a boat."

"Like hell I'm leaving!" Volkoff told him. "What about Westholme? We're going together."

"You will not leave together," Kutskov said. "I have every hope that you will meet again shortly."

"No deal," Volkoff said, and settled himself heavily into one of the deck chairs.

"I admire your intentions," Kutskov said. He turned to his crewmen abruptly and issued a short command in Russian. Without hesitation they descended on the American and pinned his arms, lifting him bodily out of the chair.

Westholme gripped the hidden revolver and made an involuntary move toward him. He was stopped by the first officer who now held a gun in his hand.

"There is no cause for alarm," Captain Kutskov said in a calm voice. "We are merely playing this game to the finish. Goodbye, Mr. Volkoff . . . and I hope you will not judge us too harshly, when you have had time to think about it." He held out his hand and saw it rejected by the American. "I have no pride left, Mr. Volkoff. It is just a matter of saying goodbye to you."

When Volkoff remained unrelenting, he made a brief gesture and turned away while the American was led from the bridge into the outer darkness. The flares from the destroyer continued to rise and descend, converting a few acres of sea into a harsh semblance of daylight. Westholme saw the light carving the faces of Kutskov, the doctor and the first officer, transforming them to weird masks—cruel and unchanging.

Dr. Lebedovitch turned to him and said: "You mustn't concern yourself like this. He will not be harmed." She placed a hand on his arm and he drew away from it.

"Please believe me," she said in a low, intense voice. Louder she said: "Your face is like stone."

"Yours too," he said.

"The lighting is atrocious!" Kutskov broke in. "None of us look our best. Captain Westholme, I will be honest with you. We need a final hostage, and you are the logical choice."

Westholme settled himself into a chair and reached for the vodka bottle.

"Would you put a little in my glass?" Kutskov asked.

Westholme scanned the bridge defensively, saw the light of the destroyer's pyrotechnics glancing from the three alien faces, glinting on the barrel of the first officer's gun. His eyes moved on to find the vodka bottle. His hand reached for it and lifted it toward Kutskov's waiting glass, tilting it and pouring the crystal clear fluid.

"Let us admit it," Kutskov said sadly. "The evening has not been a good one." He squinted at his drink dejectedly. "It has been abysmal."

"There was no need to try so hard, Mikhail," the doctor said gently.

"You would like to say it was inappropriate," the captain accused her sternly, "and you are right. She is always right," he told Westholme. "Medically and otherwise the doctor possesses admirable judgment."

Westholme sipped his drink without comment.

"So . . ." Captain Kutskov said, "this business is drawing to a close." He slumped back in the navigator's seat, hesitating and controlling himself as his clothing abraded raw flesh, waiting for the pain to subside. "I for one am glad of it. What is our position, Gregori?"

The first officer evaluated the scene: the restless searchlights playing on them from port and starboard, the triumvirate of flares descending above the destroyer and the line of trawlers, the stabs of light from the signal lamps. He gave his report in Russian, and Kutskov halted him.

"In English, so all of us can understand and be part of this."

"We are within fifteen hundred meters," the officer said. "The tugboat will be in international waters shortly."

Captain Kutskov drained his glass and looked toward the doctor. "I am not comfortable," he said testily. "The alcohol doesn't work."

"Not surprising," she told him calmly. "I can give you something better if you wish?"

He waved the suggestion away impatiently. "Not at the moment." Turning to Westholme, he said: "The game is played out, Captain. It is a stalemate of sorts, but I am not entirely dissatisfied. We must stop your tug."

"Go ahead," Westholme said. "Stop it!"

"Some hours ago—a day ago perhaps—you described this incident as 'escalating.' You were right. If we are not very careful, Captain Westholme, we will be the pebble that started the avalanche. The rumbling has begun."

A brilliant, blue-white arc from the destroyer's deck reached toward *Irkutsk* and searched the battered hull.

"It might be better," Westholme said, "to do what you

are doing, and sink your ship here. That destroyer would like to get you into international waters. The trawlers wouldn't be much help to you."

"None at all," Kutskov agreed. "Gregori, what depth of water do we have here?"

"It is difficult to say, Captain. Perhaps a hundred fathoms."

"It will have to do. I am going to turn your tug back to you, Captain Westholme." He pulled his walkie-talkie toward him and switched it on, leaning close to talk in slow-cadenced Russian. Presently a voice replied and the brief exchange of conversation continued. Abruptly Kutskov reverted to English and beckoned to Westholme:

"You are now in command of the tug," he said. "I would be grateful to you if you would accommodate my crew and Dr. Davodov. Your second officer has been sent for. I would like you to stop your tug in Canadian waters, Captain."

Westholme waited to hear Fenton's voice, worrying over the tension in it when finally it came through the speaker:

"Chris? Christy, are you okay?"

"I'm fine, Brad. What's the situation?"

"The buggers have put down their guns. It's all sweetness and light!"

"That's good to hear," Westholme said.

"I don't believe any of it! You sure you're all right?"

"Nothing to worry about, Brad. The tug is ours again. This is the end of the line."

"Then it's the God's truth?"

"That's right. You can start shortening the line. There may be a few of us coming aboard in a few minutes. We're abandoning."

"Is she sinking, Christy?"

Westholme glanced at Captain Kutskov, but could read no message in his face. "That's about it, Brad. How's Lindstrom?"

"Not bad, not good. That Davodov woman is doing everything she can. What's the plan, Chris?"

"Haul in the line. We'll throw the bridle off right away."

He turned to the first officer for confirmation, and the man nodded agreement. "It looks as though we're going home."

"You too?" Fenton asked, his voice heavily suspicious. "What's happening over there?"

"Just start that cable coming in," Westholme told him. "Tell the boys they're going home."

"Okay," Fenton said dubiously.

"The Russian boarding party won't give you any trouble."

"That's for damned sure! We've got them locked up in the wire room."

"Yeah . . . well, go easy on them. The war is over. See you soon, Brad." He turned the set back to Kutskov. "What now?"

"Our people should be ready to disembark. Our sick and injured are on deck, Doctor?"

Dr. Lebedovitch nodded. "They have been moving up for the past half hour. The stretcher cases will be difficult."

"No doubt . . . Gregori, go and see how things are proceeding. I would like to begin the disembarkation."

The first officer departed immediately and silently, leaving the three of them on the bridge. Captain Kutskov's glass was empty; he looked at Dr. Lebedovitch for help and she poured him another drink without a protest or a look of reproach, turning to Westholme with the bottle proffered.

"Pass me," Westholme said. "I've had plenty." He could feel the liquor beginning to pound in his temples.

"If you please," Kutskov insisted. "This will be our last drink together for some time." He nodded imperatively to the doctor, and she poured a short drink into Westholme's glass.

"Yourself as well, Larissa," he insisted.

She did as he told her.

Kutskov lifted his glass to the lantern light. "I think I have always been fortunate," he said speculatively, "fortunate in the people I have known, fortunate in the things I have done—and the things that have been done for me. I would say that my misfortunes have been mainly my own fault.

This trouble we find ourselves in now, Captain Westholme. Largely my own fault."

The doctor spoke to him persuasively in Russian. He shook his head impatiently and turned back to Westholme. "I believe the doctor is afraid I will become maudlin," he chuckled. "All I want is to be honest. It is a time for honesty." He began to reach into his jacket pocket, stopping as pain overcame him. "There are envelopes in there for Captain Westholme."

Dr. Lebedovitch rose quickly and felt inside the jacket, bringing out two long bulky envelopes which she passed to Westholme.

"This is merely a precaution," the Russian captain said. "Naturally I will insist on making my own statement to your authorities . . . but if that is not possible, for one reason or another, my account of this incident has been placed in writing. The responsibility is clearly mine, and I do not hesitate to say so."

Westholme shook his head in protest. "The sea got both of us into trouble."

Kutskov rejected the idea. "The sea is impartial," he said. "I would never blame my mistakes on the sea, she has given me too much. You too, I suspect, Captain?"

Westholme was noncommittal, thinking of Lee: "It gives and it takes," he said.

Kutskov returned to business. "The other envelope contains a rather mixed collection of currency. I am not aware of the most recent rates of exchange, but I believe there is the equivalent of ten thousand dollars. It was the salvage fee agreed to."

Westholme stared into the man's exhausted, rigidly controlled face. The eyes revealed no duplicity. The deep lines of suffering could not possibly mask cunning or a concealed purpose. He admired Kutskov more than he could say:

"Until this minute," he admitted, "I was convinced that, with you, the ends justified the means—that anything and anybody was expendable in order to get the job done."

"You are a good judge of character," Kutskov told him,

"and you are absolutely right." He shrugged his shoulders at the simplicity of the matter. "Now the job is done . . . and you have been paid the agreed amount."

"There is more to it than that," Westholme said almost angrily. "A lot of people are involved in this. Some of them are lined up on your decks now; some are on the bottom."

"No price can be placed on that," Kutskov said. "No price can be placed on the fact that you and I never became friends—in spite of the many things we hold in common. If I regret anything in these later years, it is that I have been cheated out of so many friendships. It is a greed with me that has never been satisfied."

Another salvo of flares burst in the sky and began a slow descent to the restless ocean. The Russian trawlers, caught in the circle of harsh light, rode silently at anchor, their signal lamps darkened and their riding lights dimmed in the destroyer's eye-searing bravura.

"Not an unfamiliar sight," Captain Kutskov said. "As a second officer on a vintage destroyer I can recall meeting the remains of convoys on the approach to Murmansk. Ships low in the water and sinking; corvettes and destroyers hurrying about and turning night into day with their flares and searchlights. Men had died and were dying, but the lights were a celebration for us because they marked the arrival of ships, and food . . . and weapons."

"I was on a Canadian corvette on the Murmansk run," Westholme said: "H.M.C.S. *Dogwood.*"

Kutskov held his glass up. "Then I am sure I drank your health on many occasions." He looked at the doctor. "Larissa, we are not just two sea dogs getting drunk on memories—are we?"

She smiled at him: "Good therapy, Captain."

"I'd like to drink to your health," Westholme said impulsively. "To your health . . . good luck . . ."

Kutskov waved a protesting hand. "Too soon, Captain Westholme. It could be an embarrassment. There are things we require you to do yet. If they go badly we may still have to use you as our last line of defense."

36 . . .

Westholme studied him warily, his whole attitude changing to one of suspicion. "What's your problem?"

"None whatever, if your Coast Guard and naval escorts follow your instructions."

"Mine?"

"You are now giving the orders, Captain. They are logical, I believe, and you cannot object to them."

Behind them the door to the bridge opened to admit the first officer, his face reddened from the cold, salty air. "We can begin the disembarkation," he said.

"Good! What is the tide doing to us?"

"It is ebbing, Captain. We are drifting very slowly toward the fleet."

"How far to go?"

"Perhaps a thousand meters . . . one hour."

"I want us to be off in an hour or less," Captain Kutskov said. "Captain Westholme, we concede defeat and we ask you to intercede on our behalf with the escorting vessels. We are abandoning ship."

"Fair enough," Westholme said. "I'll need a loud hailer."

Kutskov smiled at him: "This time I think you should have one."

Westholme took the loud hailer extended to him by the first officer and walked out to the port rail, holding up his arm against the assault of *Blackfish's* big lights. When the moving beams had passed him, he sent the message across:

"Lewis? Captain Lewis? Christy Westholme here. Jack, can you hear me?"

"I hear you, Captain Westholme. Are you all right?"

"Fine, Jack! Just fine! I've got a request for you."

"Go ahead, Captain Westholme."

Lewis was being formal as hell, Westholme thought in quick anger. Everything was a naval engagement with him.

"This ship is sinking, Jack. We've got to get the crew off in a hurry."

"Is that your opinion as a salvage officer, Captain Westholme?"

"It's my opinion period, goddam it!" Westholme said.

"Can you come aboard to assist?"

"I'm needed here, Jack. Can you start taking them aboard?"

"Are you a prisoner, Captain Westholme?"

"No, but I will be if you don't get cracking! Come on, Jack, for God sake. These people are in the worst possible shape, and this ship is going whether you like it or not."

"Hold off a minute, Christy. I'll check with the Canadian Forces."

"Hurry it up, Jack. It doesn't matter what they say, we've got to get off this hulk."

He stood and waited on the bridge with the cold wind numbing his cheekbones, the fantasy of searchlights and flares streaking ship's hulls and the heaving mounds of the ocean, the sounds of *Irkutsk*'s crew assembled on the decks below him—a hushed cacophony of voices, male and female —signifying apprehension and fear.

Presently the voice came to him from *Blackfish*. "We'll start moving the crew, Christy. All able-bodied and walking-wounded to *Blackfish*; all stretcher cases to the subchaser. Stand by to rig a bo'sun's chair, or some kind of breeches buoy. How much time have we got?"

Westholme looked at his watch. "Forty-five minutes, no more."

"That's pretty rough," Lewis protested. "Let's get started."

"Send over your boats for the able," Westholme instructed. "This ship can lower two or three of its own. Tell the Navy we're standing by for the breeches buoy line."

He lowered the loud hailer and returned to Kutskov, seated imperially in the navigator's chair. "You can start discharging your people. Able-bodied to starboard by ship's boat. Stretcher cases to port. They'll be putting a line aboard any minute."

Kutskov gave his first officer brief instructions and dispatched him to the bridge rail with the loud hailer. He waited and watched until the officer was well into his series of commands, before he turned back to Westholme.

"I would like to think that he will be treated with respect by your authorities. No blame should attach to him for anything I have done. He has followed orders admirably."

"When does a man decide not to take orders?" Westholme said. "I've wondered about that all my life . . . *Blackfish* is worried about our timetable. Do we have to have everyone off in forty-five minutes?"

Captain Kutskov looked at his watch and then back to Westholme. "I am afraid that we must do it in that time. Our rate of drift will take us too close to that"—he nodded his head toward the American destroyer—"rather formidable pyromaniac. I have no desire to create an international crisis."

Without thinking, Westholme picked up the half-finished drink he had rejected minutes before. He took a tentative sip and stared past Kutskov and the doctor, focusing on nothing:

"I've worked hard all my life and enjoyed it. I know my business. I know that tug out there better than I know my own wife . . . but I'll be damned if I know what's going on here. I like you, Kutskov—and you, Dr. Lebedovitch—and all of your people, generally speaking. Now what the hell got us into a mess like this? Who says this ship has to sink, or that certain people must die—either by reputation or in actual fact?"

"I am sympathetic," Kutskov said, "but it is too late to debate the point." He shifted in his chair, trying to find a more comfortable position, grimacing at the pain the movement caused.

"Possibly so," the doctor said swiftly, "but the fact that we are in general agreement is encouraging."

"You are in agreement with us, Doctor?" Kutskov inquired.

"A foolish question," she said in exasperation. "I would suggest that you have a sedative, Captain. You will be more comfortable."

He shook his head impatiently. "Vodka is more appropriate . . . please."

She poured two inches from the bottle into his glass and he raised it to his lips gratefully, sipping a few drops. "I can't think of anything that has not been done. Doctor, you are ready to leave?"

She nodded.

"Obviously my authority and my command of the situation goes when this ship does," Captain Kutskov said, addressing Westholme. "I would like to think you would do whatever you can for Dr. Lebedovitch in particular. She has performed as a doctor . . . and she has performed superbly. I will testify to that."

"I'll support it," Westholme promised. "I have a feeling we'll be seeing one another in court from time-to-time."

Kutskov chuckled grimly. "No doubt. Should we say a stir has been created? Larissa," he said to the doctor, "I think you should go now. Some of the injured will need you during and after the transfer. Even your presence with them will be comforting."

"Yes, Captain."

"It has been a good ship, Doctor; for the most part a happy ship. We should feel fortunate to have been associated with it."

"There will be other ships," she said.

"And I will see to it that you are signed as ship's doctor. It would not be the same without you. Go, now, and don't worry. There will be other good times."

She approached him and encircled his waist lightly with one arm, kissed him gravely on either cheek. "I have never been associated with a finer captain—or a better man. I know there will be other good times." She backed away several steps and turned to Westholme. "I would like to know you better. Perhaps it will be possible . . ."

"I hope so," Westholme said. "I'd put you in a class with my wife as a wonderful person. That's the best compliment I can pay."

246

"I am sure it is. Will you walk to the door with me, Captain Westholme?"

Westholme walked with her as she turned away and proceeded to the door. Before she opened it, out of sight of Captain Kutskov, she said in a low voice: "I would like you to return to me the thing I gave you. You will not need it now."

"Neither will you," Westholme reminded her.

"Please. It was a mistake—a lack of faith in the captain. I believed you were in danger."

"Chances are I was," Westholme told her. He took the gun from his pocket and extended it to her. "What will you do with it?"

"I will see that it goes to the bottom with this ship and all it represents. Goodbye, Captain Westholme." She reached her hand toward him.

He shook it firmly. "For the time being," he said, and watched the door close behind her, before he returned to Kutskov.

The captain's expression was inquiring. "She was troubled about something perhaps?"

Westholme shook his head. "I admire her. I wanted her to know it."

The Russian captain nodded slowly. "For one reason or another I never married; a certain restlessness that has never quite left me; the lack of opportunity; the impossibility of it in wartime . . . but if I did have a wife, she would be the one. You compare her to yours, Captain?"

Westholme nodded. "Female in the best sense of the word, strong—with a sense of the important things. Maybe it's a second sense."

"Possibly a superb sensitivity . . . I know what you are describing. So, we have both been fortunate in our own way."

"I'd say so," Westholme agreed. "How are you making out?" he asked. "Can I do anything for you?"

"Nothing . . . I am remarkably content. It is the kind of satisfaction a man feels when he has accomplished a mission, climbed a mountain—won a battle. It doesn't matter how much he may hurt." He paused and shifted his weight carefully into a more comfortable position. "Perhaps I should tell you what will happen now?"

"I'd appreciate that," Westholme admitted.

"The ship is prepared," Kutskov said. "As soon as the last man is off, she will be ready for destruction. The final documents and logbooks were burned this afternoon . . ."

"We smelled the smoke," Westholme admitted. "Thought the ship was on fire."

"I apologize for what I was obliged to do," Kutskov said earnestly. "Perhaps much of it was uncalled for, but I could leave nothing to chance. I hope you and Mr. Volkoff can understand that I was always concerned for your welfare."

Westholme's smile was dry: "Mike Volkoff said you'd be the saddest one at our funeral."

"And he was right of course," Kutskov agreed. "I think a truly great general must have the capacity to mourn for the enemies and innocent civilians he must annihilate."

"You talk as though we have been at war."

"We have!" Kutskov stated emphatically. "You said it yourself today. 'The war is over,' you said; and it describes perfectly what has happened between us. Beyond the influence or instruction of our countries, we have fought and conspired to save our own domains; my ship and its people; your tug and its crew. Mr. Volkoff's domain was destroyed very early in the battle."

"If there had been a clear winner," Westholme said slowly. "If we could say that something good has come out of all this . . ."

"We both win; we both lose. Of the two of us, you have undoubtedly won the greater victory. Not only that, but the course of action you have been recommending to me for a full day is the action I have finally decided to take." He extended his good hand. "Should we agree that our war is truly over, Captain?"

Westholme's big hand wrapped itself slowly around Kutskov's fingers and squeezed briefly. "What bothers me," he said, "is that something like this can happen again. The precedent has been set . . ."

"Is that the good thing that emerges from our little war? No doubt this will impress our respective countries with the fact that continental shelves and international waters can become formidable battlegrounds." Kutskov shrugged. "In any event it is out of our hands, and I am glad of it." He looked at his watch. "Ten more minutes."

"You'll leave with me?" Westholme questioned.

"Directly after you." He smiled at Westholme. "In my position you would insist on your right to leave your ship last."

"I suppose I would," Westholme agreed. "I don't think there's much doubt that we'll be seeing plenty of one another ashore."

Kutskov nodded and grimaced: "Once our countries and our courts take hold of this incident, we will wish we had stayed at sea."

Both men turned as the door to the bridge opened to admit the first and second officers and one crew member.

"Everyone is off?" Kutskov demanded.

"The last boat is loading now," the first officer informed him. "I think we can begin making our way down."

"Very well," Kutskov said. Once again his hand reached for Westholme's. "There will be better times," he said cheerfully. "I hope to know you under those circumstances."

"See you ashore," Westholme promised. He pulled his jacket collar up and departed the bridge in the company of the second officer, picking his way carefully across the slick surface of the catwalk illuminated by the officer's flashlamp.

37 . . .

The surrounding scene had not altered, except that the formidable lights and pyrotechnics of the American destroyer were considerably closer. The drift and the tide were going to take *Irkutsk* almost to the edge of the Twelve Mile.

"How are you going to get Captain Kutskov off?" he asked the second officer. "The Navy's breeches buoy will be safest for him."

"He will leave by ship's boat in company with the first officer, Captain."

Stumbling through the cold, black bowels of the dead ship, Westholme felt new misgivings growing. Was Kutskov going to make a run for the Russian fleet and leave his ship's company behind to fend for themselves? Had it all been smooth talk after all?

They emerged onto the main deck in the full glare of *Blackfish*'s lights. The deck was empty, but Westholme heard voices and saw a loaded boat on the edge of the searchlight's circle. It was making its way toward the cargo nets draped over *Blackfish*'s port side.

"We have one last request to make of you, Captain," the officer said. "You will ask your Coast Guard vessel and the Canadian Forces ship to stand off five hundred yards immediately upon taking the last person aboard. The demolition of *Irkutsk* will begin within minutes."

"Kutskov? Will he make it off in time?"

"Everything has been carefully planned. Will you go over the side now, please."

Westholme peered over the rail and saw *Haida Noble*'s powered life raft, manned by Russian crew members.

"You will seat yourself in the life raft," the officer instructed. "I will join you."

Westholme went over the side, clambering down the net

until he felt hands below him steadying him for the step-over to the raft. He crab-legged his way to the stern of the raft and watched while the second officer scrambled down and joined the others, making a group of five. The outboard motor sputtered and caught, breaking into a steady roar of power and leveling back as it went into gear and left *Irkutsk's* side.

Halfway between *Blackfish* and the crippled Russian ship, the raft cut its power to idle and sat in the circle of one of the cutter's suspicious lights. The second officer handed a loud hailer across to Westholme.

"You must warn them," he said. "Tell them we will follow at a safe distance."

Westholme lifted the loud hailer: "*Blackfish . . . Blackfish . . .* Captain Westholme here."

"What are you doing out there, Chris? Come aboard." It was Lewis' brittle voice.

"In a few minutes, Jack. No time right now. The Russian ship is going to blow. Advise the subchaser and get some kind of a signal to *Haida Noble.* As soon as the last man is on board stand off at least five hundred yards."

"Come aboard, Chris. We'll wait."

That's not the deal. They'll deliver me when the ship goes."

"Do you believe that, damn it?"

"That's the deal we have to go with. Better hurry, Jack."

He lowered the loud hailer and glanced at the second officer for further directions. The Russian nodded approval.

There was a wait of several minutes while the tension built, while a northwest wind as cold as winter buffeted the raft and its occupants fitfully, while the angry lights and flares of the destroyer continued to demonstrate no more than half a mile away, and while at the same distance the seven Russian trawlers huddled silent as death beneath the magnesium glare of the parachute flares. The coldness in Westholme's marrow was as much apprehension as anything. He was grateful for the cigarette that was handed to him, and for the lighter flame that followed.

Captain Lewis called again from *Blackfish*, "Tell those bastards to travel astern of us by a hundred yards, no tricks. The subchaser will follow."

"We agree to that," the Russian officer told Westholme.

"No argument," Westholme relayed through the loud hailer. "Let's get out of here."

"Is everyone off that hulk?"

"One more boat to come. The captain, first officer, and one of the crew."

Shadowy figures were moving about on *Irkutsk's* boat deck. Bodies eased up and over into the stern of the ship's launch, turned with their backs to the searchlights and busied themselves with the loading and the lowering of the sea boat. The davit mechanism was balky, undoubtedly damaged by the impact of the tidal wave and the collision, but finally the boat was easing downward, hesitating, stopping, descending again toward the chop that rattled against the side of *Irkutsk*. The boat hit the water and the davit lines were cast away.

"That's it," Westholme called to *Blackfish*. "Let's move off."

The Coast Guard cutter began to move almost immediately, swinging away from the Russian ship in a slow turn, its searchlight holding on the life raft which followed in its wake at its maximum of 8 knots. A hundred yards astern again came the Russian ship's launch, its navigation lights burning and a puff of exhaust smoke showing at the stern. Astern of the *Irkutsk*, the raked bow of the subchaser appeared, the entire vessel sliding into view with deck lights picking up the silver curl of a slick bow wave. In a few minutes she had positioned herself to port abeam of the strange procession of vessels, cutting off all possibility of an escape attempt to international waters. Westholme relaxed a little.

One hundred, two hundred, three hundred yards away from *Irkutsk* Westholme watched the pale lanterns burning on her fore and aft decks becoming yellow stars almost eclipsed by the brutal lights from the subchaser and the destroyer. The Russian ship was within minutes of its burial.

Irkutsk had spelled grief for him, death for Ernie Bibaud, and danger for *Haida Noble* and her crew, but it did not prevent him from feeling what every master feels for the death of a good ship. In spirit, Westholme was with Captain Kutskov when the first, barely audible explosion reached his ears.

There was no sign of flame or smoke, nor did the ship react to any visible impact. The following series of explosions however, some of them occurring simultaneously in different parts of the ship's hull, produced ugly gouts of flame along the waterline and subsequently at the various deck levels. The efficiency of the demolition crew had to be admired.

Irkutsk's trim, as she settled into the water, was almost exactly level, with great cauldrons of seawater boiling in the wounds along her sides. The second officer, watching the destruction intently through his night glasses, put them down suddenly and turned away from the scene with a muffled sound. Westholme reached across and took the glasses from him, raised them and focused them hastily. The ship was sinking at an alarming rate, with the entire hull under and geysers of water and steam bursting on the main deck.

The glasses were good ones, bringing the pale angles of the foundering superstructure in so close that they more than filled the field. On the navigation bridge the strings of lanterns burned steadily. He could see the neat rolls of charts slotted in their cubbyholes. He could see the oblong, brass plate attached to a mahogany-paneled stanchion—the plate which spelled out *Irkutsk's* name in Russian characters, the date of her launching, the name of her builder. He could see Kutskov's upper body reclining back in the navigations chair—and was grieved, but not shocked. He had sensed it.

Clearly he saw the arm lifting, the hand holding the glass as it moved toward Kutskov's lips . . . and just before the final series of explosions sent flames and debris up to blot out the bridge, he saw the second figure move past Kutskov and stand behind him, the features grave and tired, but glowing with a tenderness that the distance and the darkness could not conceal. It was a glimpsed thing, but it could not be mistaken, nor would Christy Westholme ever forget it. The captain and Larissa Lebedovitch and the gun went down with *Irkutsk*.

And partly because of that, Westholme elected not to return to *Haida Noble* that night, but to go aboard *Blackfish* where he could use a ship-to-shore telephone to talk with his wife. It didn't mean that he had turned his back on the great tug, or that he ever could . . . but in that final glimpse of the couple in the light of the lamps and the outer flames, he had seen himself and Lee. He saw what they had almost lost—and he wanted to be with her to begin to restore it.

He heard the operator putting the call through, the electronic sounds of the exchange, and then the bell ringing a total of three times—cut off on the fourth as the receiver lifted:

"Hello," Lee said in a low, worried voice.

"Lee, honey . . . It's all over, darling. I'm coming home."

The silence at the other end was as bad as anything he had endured those past five days. "Lee? Are you there?"

"Yes, darling . . . Christy, come home! Now! Please, darling, now—before I lose you again!"

38 . . .

The regularly scheduled meeting of the Sea Bed Committee convened at ten o'clock next morning, New York time. With little more than partially confirmed rumors to go on, the chairman had little hope of conducting a meaningful meeting.

What happened was that the morning's agenda was lost in a barrage of questions, accusations, and counter accusations. The Pakistan delegation began by demanding to know whether or not a Russian intelligence-gathering vessel had been captured by Canadian military vessels in Canadian territorial waters.

Canada denied the capture categorically, subject to official confirmation.

The Russian delegate declared that no so-called spy vessel was operative adjacent to Canadian waters, to his certain knowledge. There were oceanographic vessels in the approximate area, yes—but these were in international waters.

Greece deplored the fact that the meeting was disintegrating into a series of charges and countercharges based on an alleged spy ship incident, when what was needed was more discussion on tidal wave warning systems, and ways to predict tidal wave occurrences well in advance of the events. "Tsunami catastrophes such as the one that has devastated the coasts of North America and Japan in recent days, can be prevented," he declared, "if we agree to apply our full resources."

The scattering of applause he received was cut short by the United States in a sharp attack against Russia. The American held a note in his hand, just received; he referred to it as "strongly supported evidence to indicate that a Russian vessel had entered Canadian waters to attack and sink a drill rig owned and operated by British-American interests." He stated that the USSR must be held accountable for the loss of more than fifty American lives.

"A diversionary tactic," Russia shouted angrily, "designed to draw the energy and the attention of this Committee away from its true objective—the peaceful exploitation of the sea bed for the good of all nations. What are British-American drill rigs doing in Canadian territorial waters if not to stake irrevocable claims for capitalistic imperialists, before international law can prevent it?"

Yugoslavia and East Germany arose simultaneously, and were driven back to their seats by the chairman's sharply rapped gavel.

"We are getting nowhere," he scolded. "An entire morning has been wasted on innuendo, half truth, and no truth at all. We have three meetings left before the conclusion of this year's session. We have many things to resolve—some issues of two and three years' standing—all of them, without exception, of the utmost importance to survival and international welfare. I don't know what the pleasure of this meeting is but . . ."

"Perhaps adjournment until after lunch," Zambia suggested mildly.

"Under the circumstances, probably the best," the chairman said. "Adjournment then until after lunch . . . and please, gentlemen, let us apply ourselves earnestly to the issues at stake."